Ca[illegible] believe this. It had never occurred to her that people would also criticize Myron. She'd been so focused on herself, she hadn't even considered how this might affect him.

These rumors were all her fault. She'd started them by asking for parenting help, and he'd gone out of his way to take care of the boys.

She turned to him. "I'm so sorry."

He looked surprised at her sudden meekness. Then he offered a half-hearted grin. "I guess we're in this together."

That last word echoed in a hollow and lonely place inside Cathy. *Together.* She repeated it silently to herself. *Together.* She'd never heard a more beautiful word. Her whole life, she'd always been outside looking in. Right now, this very minute, Myron had included her on his team.

She blinked her stinging eyes. Her voice raspy, she managed to say, "*Danke.*" Her heart overflowed with gratitude for all he'd done for her, but most of all for making her feel like she belonged. She had no words to express it, and if she didn't get away from here now, she'd break down.

Cathy scrambled into her buggy before any telltale tears slipped out. "Goodbye," she choked out before shutting the door and trotting off. But she couldn't outrun her churning emotions . . .

Books by Rachel J. Good

HIS UNEXPECTED AMISH TWINS

HIS PRETEND AMISH BRIDE

HIS ACCIDENTAL AMISH FAMILY

AN UNEXPECTED AMISH PROPOSAL

AN UNEXPECTED AMISH COURTSHIP

AN UNEXPECTED AMISH CHRISTMAS

AN AMISH MARRIAGE OF CONVENIENCE

HER PRETEND AMISH BOYFRIEND

DATING AN AMISH FLIRT

MISSING HER AMISH BOYFRIEND

AN AMISH SECOND CHANCE ROMANCE

Published by Kensington Publishing Corp.

An Amish Second Chance Romance

RACHEL J. GOOD

ZEBRA BOOKS
Kensington Publishing Corp.
kensingtonbooks.com

ZEBRA BOOKS are published by

Kensington Publishing Corp.
900 Third Avenue
New York, NY 10022

Copyright © 2025 by Rachel J. Good

All rights reserved. No part of this book may be reproduced in any form or by any means without the prior written consent of the Publisher, excepting brief quotes used in reviews.

Without limiting the author's and publisher's exclusive rights, any unauthorized use of this publication to train generative artificial intelligence (AI) technologies is expressly prohibited.

This book is a work of fiction. Names, characters, businesses, organizations, places, events, and incidents either are the product of the author's imagination or are used fictitiously. Any resemblance to actual persons, living or dead, events, or locales is entirely coincidental.

To the extent that the image or images on the cover of this book depict a person or persons, such person or persons are merely models and are not intended to portray any character or characters featured in the book.

If you purchased this book without a cover you should be aware that it is stolen property. It was reported as "unsold and destroyed" to the Publisher, and neither the Author nor the Publisher has received any payment for this "stripped book."

All Kensington titles, imprints, and distributed lines are available at special quantity discounts for bulk purchases for sales promotion, premiums, fund-raising, and educational or institutional use.

Special book excerpts or customized printings can also be created to fit specific needs. For details, write or phone the office of the Kensington Sales Manager: Kensington Publishing Corp., 900 Third Avenue, New York, NY 10022. Attn. Sales Department. Phone: 1-800-221-2647.

ZEBRA BOOKS and the Zebra logo Reg. U.S. Pat. & TM Off.

First Printing: August 2025
ISBN-13: 978-1-4201-5774-1
ISBN-13: 978-1-4201-5775-8 (eBook)

10 9 8 7 6 5 4 3 2 1

Printed in the United States of America

The authorized representative in the EU for product safety and compliance
is eucomply OU, Parnu mnt 139b-14, Apt 123
Tallinn, Berlin 11317, hello@eucompliancepartner.com.

Chapter 1

Myron King awoke with a jolt, his whole body on alert. Something was off. He jumped out of bed. *Tim.* He had to check on Tim.

Every muscle in his body ached. Like most nights, he'd waited up until the wee hours of the morning for his nephew to come in, and he'd fallen asleep on the couch in an awkward position. As he stretched out the kinks in his arms and back after waking, he still didn't know if Tim had made it home.

With a sigh, Myron tiptoed down the hall and opened his nephew's door a crack, hoping it wouldn't squeak. Tim hated his uncle checking up on him, but Myron couldn't go to work without making sure his nephew had returned safely.

That huge lump under the sheet might be Tim. The musky, sickening-sweet odor hanging in the air made Myron's eyes water and his stomach turn. Tim had been out with his *Englisch* friends. The ones who did drugs.

Although the smell provided a clue Tim was sleeping in his bed, Myron waited to be sure his nephew's chest rose and fell. Too many times, Tim had fooled Myron with pillows under his covers. A small snore reassured Myron his nephew lay under the heap of tangled bed-covers. Myron eased the door shut.

No time for coffee or breakfast. He'd overslept, so he had to rush to work. He made it to his shop with only minutes to spare. The leather strap of bells jingled when he flipped the door sign to open. Usually he loved walking around the showroom, inspecting the items for sale, proud of his handiwork. That day, though, his woodworking shop, which had always been his refuge, now seemed like a prison.

He wanted to be home to keep an eye on Tim. Instead of starting on one of his orders, Myron paced back and forth. What was he going to do about his nephew? Now that an electrical fire at the factory had put Tim out of work for weeks, his nephew had gone even more wild than usual.

Myron's two young apprentices, Lloyd and Jed, slipped in the rear employee entrance a few minutes later. The aroma of coffee made Myron's stomach growl. A bag crinkled. His workers must have stopped for fast food on their way in.

Jed popped his head around the doorway of the workshop behind the showroom. He held up a small paper-wrapped English muffin. "Want coffee and a breakfast sandwich? We got extra."

Myron nodded and joined them in the back. When he wrapped his hand around the coffee cup, his whole body filled with gratitude. "You didn't have to get me anything."

"*Jah*, we did. We don't want to deal with a grumpy boss all day." Lloyd flashed Myron a teasing smile.

"So that's what you think of me?" Myron pretended to be annoyed, but his employees were right. If he didn't eat, he acted out of sorts all day. He gave Lloyd and Jed a rueful smile. "Guess you know me too well. *Danke* for this." He unwrapped the bacon and egg sandwich. "Lunch is my treat today."

Jed perked up. "That sounds fair." He eyed Myron with concern. "Not sure if I should tell you this, but my sister Katie was coming home from her late shift last night, and she saw Tim in our neighbor's barn." Jed lowered his gaze. "They were . . ."

At his hesitation, Myron finished the sentence. "Doing drugs?"

"*Jah.*" Jed squirmed. "I thought maybe you'd waited up for him and wouldn't get much sleep, so you probably didn't have time to eat this morning."

How had Myron ended up with such kind and thoughtful employees when he was a grouch most days? He tried not to bring his family problems to work, but he must not have succeeded.

"I'm sorry if I take things out on you."

Lloyd's lips curved into an understanding smile. "We understand. All of us are worried about Tim too."

"We're praying for him. And you." Jed stood and crumpled his wrapper. "Guess we'd better get to work, huh?"

"That's what I'm paying you for." Myron tried to sound stern, but his grin gave him away.

If only Tim had agreed to work here, maybe Myron

would be bantering with his nephew like this. He shook his head. He was dreaming. Tim had made it clear he wanted nothing to do with the business or with Myron. Everything Myron asked of Tim, every rule Myron set, Tim broke it on purpose. And he made sure Myron knew of his defiance.

Shoving those painful thoughts aside, Myron threw himself into sanding the chest he had to finish by tomorrow. The rhythmic movements across the maple surface brought peace to his troubled mind. The comforting wood scent and the dainty curving lines filled him with satisfaction. He excelled in craftmanship. God had given him a talent, and he used it for the Lord's glory. If only that competency extended to his parenting skills.

Time after time, Myron vowed to be a better father figure, but Tim's misbehavior fueled Myron's anger and propelled arguments and hurtful words. Deep inside, Myron blamed himself for Tim's rebelliousness. Myron had been young, single, and inexperienced when he'd taken on the care of his orphaned nephew and niece. *It's all my fault. I didn't know how to raise children.*

He threw himself into his work to forget, but when they stopped for lunch, all the pain and guilt flooded back. Myron couldn't take it anymore. He had to do something.

After his apprentices finished the pizza Myron ordered for lunch, he retreated to his office with two cold leftover slices. He set a hand on his business phone. Two o'clock. His brother would have a few hours before the afternoon milking on his dairy farm. Myron wished they lived closer so he could stop by and talk to Hank in person.

He dialed his brother's business phone and prayed someone would answer. Relief flooded through him when Abe picked up.

"*Guten tag*, Myron."

His nephew's cheerful greeting lifted Myron's spirits. Why couldn't Tim be more like Abe? Obedient, thoughtful, hardworking, kind? Abe was only a few years older than Tim, but he acted much more mature.

"Could I talk to your *daed*?"

"Sure. I'll go get him. Be right back." The receiver clunked onto a counter.

Soon, Hank's confident voice vibrated through the phone line. "Myron? What's going on?"

When he was young, Myron had always counted on his older brother to help when he got into trouble. That hadn't changed since they'd become adults. Whenever Myron had a problem, he appreciated talking it over and hearing Hank's wise advice.

"I hate to ask for another favor since Abe only left here three weeks ago, but the factory where Tim works burned down, so he has too much free time. He's getting into trouble."

"Drugs again?"

How did Hank always seem to know the problem before Myron told him? "*Jah.* And staying out most of the night. Now that he doesn't have to report to a job, he's gotten even more wild and disobedient."

Hank exhaled a long sigh. "Abe and I'll be praying."

"*Danke.* I'm doing the same, but I hoped—" Myron

swallowed hard. It was a lot to expect, but whenever Abe came to visit, Tim calmed down and semi-followed the rules. Myron desperately needed to rein in Tim's rebelliousness.

Again, Hank sensed the request before Myron managed to put it into words. "I wish I could send Abe, but all my other children as well as my neighbors are busy in the fields. I have nobody to take Abe's place."

Myron had known it was too much to ask. "I understand." He sighed heavily.

"You think we could talk Tim into coming up here?" Hank asked. "We could use an extra hand."

"I don't know." Myron doubted Tim would leave his friends and illegal activities to go to New York State to milk cows.

"Tell you what—why don't I have Abe call Tim and talk him into it? Abe has Tim's cell number."

Myron grimaced. Despite his objections, one of Tim's first purchases after he started his factory job had been that phone. He carried it everywhere.

"You there?" Hank asked with concern.

"*Jah.* Maybe Abe can convince Tim to visit. It's worth a try."

"Meanwhile, we'll all be praying."

Hank's words echoed in Myron's ears after he hung up. He'd been begging God for years to work in Tim's heart, but lately Myron despaired of ever receiving an answer.

Myron still couldn't believe Tim had agreed, but Abe must have said something to convince his cousin. Tim had gone willingly, if not cheerfully. Or maybe he had been happy about visiting Fort Plain, but refused to let Myron know. Even Tim's last comments before leaving had been cutting and sarcastic.

A few days later, Myron rolled out of bed feeling edgy and headed to check on Tim out of habit. Halfway down the hall, the truth kicked in. Tim wasn't here. He'd gone to Fort Plain, New York. Myron sagged in relief. If his brother Hank wasn't kidding, Tim was getting up at four every morning to milk cows.

Myron shook his head in disbelief. After all the trouble he'd had with Tim, he couldn't believe his rebellious nephew would willingly rise early and do physical work. Here in Lancaster, Tim complained if Myron asked him to take out the trash.

It still didn't seem real that the daily clashes and heartache had ended—at least temporarily. Myron had no idea when Tim would return, but he'd be in New York for a while longer. Still, Myron couldn't shake off the past. He and Tim had butted heads for so long, Myron woke every day expecting to fight and scold and lecture. It might be a long time before he could accept Tim was gone and relax.

Despite his relief over Tim being in New York, Myron discovered that life without his nephew could be lonely.

Loud knocking on the front door jerked Cathy Zehr from a deep sleep. She rolled over and squinted at her alarm clock. Nine thirty? She'd gotten into bed and fallen asleep an hour ago so she could get up at four to make donuts for her market stand.

The pounding continued. Cathy dragged herself out of bed. "I'm coming," she yelled.

Grumbling, she pulled on a robe and hurried downstairs. Who'd be here at this time of night? This better not be a prank. If it was, she'd give those teens a piece of her mind.

Everyone in the neighborhood knew she went to sleep early. Some of the *Englisch* kids took advantage of that to egg or toilet paper her house. Whenever she caught the culprits, she gave them a tongue-lashing and reported them to their parents, hoping they'd get a fitting punishment. Now they all glared at her sullenly whenever they saw her. *Hmph.* Served them right.

Annoyed, she yanked the door open a crack, but she peeked warily from behind it to hide her nightclothes and to be sure her face wasn't a target for a rotten tomato or an egg. You couldn't trust those kids any farther than you could throw them.

"Cathy?" Barb Smucker from next door held out a cell phone. "Your nephew's on the phone."

Frowning, Cathy stared at the offending device, reluctant to touch it. She'd never understood why other Amish families used such worldly things.

"Can't you take a message?" Her clipped words expressed her annoyance at being woken and her disapproval of *Englisch* tools.

"He wants to talk to you."

Barb never lost her perpetual smile. An *I-love-everyone-in-the-world* smile that grated on Cathy's nerves. Her neighbor acted like nothing ever went wrong. Maybe for her, nothing ever did.

Cathy ground her teeth. *Changing places with me might wipe that cheery expression off your face.*

"It's an emergency." Barb stuck her hand through the thin gap between the door and the jamb.

"Why didn't you say so?" Cathy snatched the phone from Barb's hand. "Wayne?" She didn't have to wonder which nephew. None of her other nieces or nephews kept in touch with her.

"*Aenti?*"

His somber tone scared Cathy. The last time he had sounded like this, his wife had died. She gripped the phone tighter, praying she didn't accidentally push one of those buttons and cut him off. "Is one of the boys hurt?" *Or, heaven forbid, dead?*

She didn't want to put that awful thought into words. Her nephew and his two sons were the only kin who visited her, sent her holiday cards, and seemed to care about her.

Through his ragged breathing, Wayne choked out, "Not the boys. Me. I have cancer."

Cancer? Cathy squeezed the plastic so hard every ridge pressed into her palm.

"It's stage four. I'm going to Mexico for treatment."

"Oh, Wayne, no." Many Amish people chose Mexico. Prices were cheaper, and they could get treatments not approved in the United States. But Cathy didn't agree with going out of the country. Another thought struck her. "What about the boys?"

"That's why I'm calling. W-would you watch them while I'm gone?"

"Me?" Her voice squeaked. She knew nothing about raising children.

"I don't have anyone else."

Wayne's admission tore at Cathy's heart. Like her, he'd been estranged from the rest of the family for years. Of all her relatives, he was the only one who'd supported her when she broke from her family and fled from New Wilmington to Lancaster to live on her own. He'd been much younger than she was, but he had a wisdom beyond his years. Now he needed her help. How could she deny him?

"Are you there?" Wayne asked, his voice thick with tears.

"I'm here." She'd always be here for him. "I'll do whatever you need."

"*Danke, danke.* I'm leaving in two weeks. I'll send the boys with a driver I trust. I can't tell you how much—" His voice broke.

Two weeks? She had only two weeks to prepare? How would she ever get ready? She was terrible with kids. All the little ones in the community avoided her. Her gruff tone scared them off. Cathy preferred that. She was not fond of sticky fingers, runny noses, whiny pleas. The thought of that curdled her stomach.

These were her grandnephews, though. She didn't want them to go to strangers. But couldn't someone in his *g'may* care for them?

Before she could voice her question, Wayne said a

shaky goodbye. "I know you need your sleep. Sorry for waking you." And he hung up.

Cathy stared at the phone in her hand. She still had so many questions, so much she wanted to say.

"Is everything all right?" Concern in her soft, caring eyes, Barb studied Cathy.

"No." Cathy thrust the phone at Barb.

She didn't want to share Wayne's news with anyone. Especially not someone like Barb, who would try to find the silver lining. As far as Cathy could see, this situation had no positive side. It was a tragedy.

Barb took the phone. "I'm sorry. I'll be praying."

Cathy grunted something she hoped sounded like *danke* before she shut the door. Her sleep totally disrupted, she sank onto the living room couch, fretting over all the things that could go wrong.

CHAPTER 2

Standing in the back of her Dough-Re-Mi donut stand at the Green Valley Farmer's Market, Cathy flipped over a batch of donuts in the fryer. Normally, she ran out of glazed donuts first, but this morning, she'd had a run on lemon and blueberry cake donuts. She hadn't made enough of either of those flavors. Most customers didn't buy as many donuts on hot summer days. Today had been an exception.

It didn't help that she'd overcooked two batches. She'd been struggling to keep her mind on her work. She hadn't even had enough energy to warn other people about trouble. Some people called it gossip, but Cathy had made it her mission to tell people things she'd seen that might affect their lives or relationships. At the moment, though, she'd been too consumed by her own problems.

Ever since her nephew's phone call, she'd been gripped by fear. She had no idea how to care for children. David and John would be five and six by now.

What did she know about boys that age? Only that they were noisy, dirty, and unruly. At least the ones she saw after church on Sundays seemed to be. And smelly, once they'd been running around and playing in the yard after church.

The last time they'd visited her, David and John had been three and four. They'd been with both their parents, who'd made sure they behaved. Still, her main memories included a few tantrums, crying at bedtime, spilled food, and toys strewn everywhere. Oh, and sticky faces, sticky hands, and—*ACH!*—sticky kisses.

She drained the donuts and set them on the cooling rack. When she turned around, she spied a face she hadn't expected to see. What was Abe King doing here at the market? Odd that his cousin Tim wasn't with him.

Actually, she hadn't seen Tim around for a while now. He often came to bother Caroline at Hartzler's Chicken Barbecue. He was sweet on her, but anyone could tell she had eyes only for that handsome auctioneer. Cathy had spent a lot of time trying to dig up dirt on Noah because she didn't want Caroline to get burned.

But where was Tim today? He couldn't be at work, because the factory had burned. Cathy hoped he wasn't out doing drugs with his troublemaking *Englisch* friends.

Usually, when Abe visited, the two cousins went everywhere together. It was unusual for Abe to be back here so soon. He'd left for his home in Fort Plain about three weeks ago. If Cathy weren't so upset about her own worries, she'd be able to pinpoint the exact date he'd left. He must be here to see Anna Mary Zook. That meant the two of them were getting serious.

With no customers lined up at her stand, Cathy slipped into the aisle to follow Abe. She couldn't wait to see his meeting with Anna Mary. That would tell her a lot about the state of their relationship. But Cathy ended up as disappointed as Abe.

Although he stared longingly in Anna Mary's direction, his girlfriend was too busy to notice him. He couldn't even get close enough to attract her attention.

Why was Hartzler's Chicken Barbecue doing so well when business at Cathy's stand had slowed just now?

She'd had her usual crowds when she first opened. Perhaps some of these Hartzler customers would head to her stand for dessert. She had to get back so she wouldn't miss them.

But Abe looked dejected. She should talk to him and find out why he was here in Lancaster. Then a brilliant idea popped into her head.

She scurried over and gripped Abe's arm. He tried to jerk away, but she held firm. "Come with me," she commanded. "I have something for you."

Despite his reluctance, she pulled him past the quilt stand and into the small niche beyond it, where her tiny donut stand was tucked.

Abe studied her wooden sign decorated with musical notes, *Dough-Re-Mi*, that hung above her small glass case filled with donuts.

Because he seemed puzzled, she explained, "I love to sing, so . . ."

He nodded, and his smile indicated he thought the sign was clever. But from the way his eyes darted around, he obviously couldn't wait to escape.

"Could you take something to your *onkel* for me?" Cathy tried to keep the pleading tone from her voice, but she wasn't quite successful. She didn't want him to think she was needy. Even if she was.

"Myron?" He appeared confused.

What a foolish question. "Do you have any others?" she asked tartly. She knew for a fact Myron and Tim were his only relatives around here. He surely didn't think she'd be giving him something for any *onkels* in Fort Plain she'd never met.

She motioned for him to wait while she filled a box with a dozen donuts. Then she jotted a quick note, slid it into an envelope, and taped on the box top.

Maybe she didn't need to give Abe an explanation for giving his uncle an unexpected treat, but she didn't want anyone getting the wrong idea. "I need him to do something for me. I hope this might sweeten him up."

Lord, please help Myron to say jah.

Abe glanced at her askance when he thought she wasn't looking, and he appeared reluctant to take the box. She thrust it into his hands. Sometimes you had to push other people to do what you wanted.

He turned and rushed from the stand as if he couldn't wait to put a huge distance between them. A lot of people scurried away from her like that. Cathy sighed. Not everyone appreciated her helpful information or her avid interest in their lives.

"*Danke,*" she called after Abe as he wove his way through the crowd. He'd probably head back to Hartzler's, but for once, she didn't have the urge to follow him and spy on him and Anna Mary. She had more pressing concerns on her mind.

Scorching July sunshine rose in shimmers from the asphalt as Myron King drove the last few miles home and pulled into his gravel driveway. He mopped his brow with a rag while he unhitched his buggy. Then he rubbed down his horse and fed both horses. After a busy day at his woodworking shop, Myron dragged himself into the house.

With one hand on the doorknob, he hesitated to enter the empty house. He hadn't realized how lonely he'd be now that Tim had gone to New York State to help Hank in the dairy business. As much as Tim frustrated Myron, his nephew's absence ached like the emptiness of the gap from a missing tooth. You were grateful to be rid of the painful tooth, but the hole left behind felt deeper than a canyon.

Hank had surprised Myron by asking to send Abe to Pennsylvania shortly after Tim arrived. Evidently, Tim had taken to milking right away. His nephew remembered his early childhood visits to Fort Plain every summer before his *daed* had died and he'd moved in with Myron. Hank assured Myron that Tim set right to work each day. Myron could hardly believe they were talking about the same teen.

Abe was supposed to arrive today, but most likely, he'd spend all his time with his girlfriend. Not that Myron blamed him. But it'd still leave him with an empty house except when Abe came back here to sleep. By that time, Myron would be in bed.

With a sigh, Myron opened the kitchen door and did a double take. Abe stood by the stove, and two bowls sat on the table. "You're eating here?"

At his obvious pleasure, Abe looked guilty. "I'm sorry I wasn't around much last time I was here."

"Didn't expect you to be. You're here for a reason, and that reason's over there." Myron waved a hand in the direction of Anna Mary's house.

"I shouldn't have ignored you. I'm sorry."

"Nothing to be sorry about. That *maedel* should have all your attention. It's only right and fair."

Myron stepped closer to the pot Abe was stirring. Bits of celery and carrot floated to the surface of the broth, scenting the air with chicken. Egg noodles swirled around the spoon, along with chunks of meat. A lump blocked Myron's throat, and his eyes stung. He turned quickly and pulled out a chair before Abe noticed.

"I want to be with you too," Abe said as he turned off the flame under the chicken corn soup.

"I'm honored." His throat tight, Myron's voice came out husky.

Abe ladled the soup into the bowls and set sandwiches on their plates. Then he sank into his usual chair, and they bowed their heads.

Myron took a moment to compose himself before he prayed. Being so sentimental over a pot of soup and friendly company seemed ridiculous. Shaking off the emotion, he prayed fervently and added a petition that God would touch Tim's heart.

When Myron lifted his head, he was surprised by Abe's defeated expression. "What's the matter? You look so glum." He hoped his nephew and Anna Mary hadn't had an argument. Myron knew the pain of that firsthand. And for Abe to break up when he was so far from home would be even more agonizing.

Abe swallowed hard. "Daed fell for Anna Mary's *mamm*, Esther, when the family came to visit us in Fort Plain. They spent so much time together and seemed to enjoy each other's company. Daed proposed to Esther before they left."

Myron nodded. "Your *daed* told me he planned to do that. He didn't mention a word about it afterward, so I figured it must not have gone well."

"You're right. While Esther visited, Daed was happier than I've ever seen him since Mamm passed. But Esther has cold feet. She's lost two husbands. Anna Mary says her mother fears marrying again and losing a third."

Rubbing his chin, Myron stared at the table. "I understand how she feels." He cleared his throat. "Guess I'm not the best person to give advice on this, because I've done the same. Shut myself off from pain. When you do that, you wall yourself off from all love."

If anyone would know about that, it'd be him. After

his fiancée had died, he'd never dated anyone. Not for the past twenty-five years. Once your heart has been broken, it's hard to love again. And in his case, he'd also had to live with guilt. He'd never told anyone she'd jilted him right before she died in a buggy accident.

Abe broke into Myron's musings. "Do you have any idea how to help her?"

Myron gazed off into the distance. "Only thing I can suggest is give her time."

He could see the question in Abe's eyes. *How much time?*

Myron squirmed. How could he answer his nephew when he himself had shut down for decades after his loss? Hank couldn't wait that long. Nor could Abe and Anna Mary.

"You know . . ." Myron's voice came out hoarse and rusty. He cleared his throat and tried again. "I've been thinking. I made a mistake. God didn't mean for a man to be alone. If I'd had a wife, maybe Tim woulda turned out better."

Abe started to protest, but Myron held up a hand. "If I'd married, Tim would've had regular meals, someone to read him bedtime stories, someone to tuck him in bed at night, someone to—" His voice broke. There was so much he wished he'd done differently. So much he would have changed if he had it to do over again.

Abe glanced at Myron with pity. "You did what you could."

Myron shook his head. "*Neh*, I failed him in so many ways. I was too wrapped up in my sorrow to help him deal with his. I hope Esther doesn't make the same mistake." He fell silent, lost in thought.

If only he'd let go of his heartbreak years ago, he wouldn't be lonely, coming home to an empty house, dealing with a rebellious *youngie*. If he had moved on, he'd have someone to share his frustrations with, someone to pray with, someone to love. Maybe he could prevent Esther from experiencing the years of loneliness and unhappiness he'd suffered.

He came out of his reverie. "Regretting the past won't change the future. Only doing things differently in the present can do that."

Abe nodded, but he fidgeted as if eager to get back to Anna Mary.

As much as Myron wanted company, he shouldn't be keeping Abe from his girlfriend. Myron finished the last of his chicken corn soup, pushed back his chair, and stood. "What's that big box on the counter? Snacks from your trip? Anything we can have for dessert?"

Abe started. "*Ach*, I was supposed to give you that." He hopped up and brought the box to the table. "Cathy Zehr from the farmer's market asked me to give this to you."

At her name, Myron's lip curled. He smoothed it out, sorry he'd made his distaste for the woman obvious.

Abe glanced at him in surprise. "You know her?"

"*Neh.* But I know of her. Tim had some run-ins with her. I understand she's an awful gossip." He picked up the envelope. "A note too?"

As he read it, shock coursed through him. His hands

shook. How could anyone be so cruel? "What is this? A prank Tim cooked up?"

"*Neh*, it's really from Cathy."

"Please don't tell Tim this because it might encourage him to do more, but I think this is one of his cruelest jokes." Myron struggled to regain his composure. "I can't believe you agreed to take part in this."

"Myron, I don't know anything about it. What does the note say?"

"Read it for yourself." He tossed the paper toward Abe, still unsure if he'd helped Tim carry this out.

But when Abe sucked in a breath and stared down at the words as if stunned, it proved his innocence. His lips tightened, showing he was deeply upset. Myron appreciated how much Abe cared.

It couldn't erase Myron's searing agony. Nobody could have picked something that would hurt him more. He'd heard about Cathy's bluntness. Her rudeness. How her gossip hurt people or broke up couples. But nothing compared to this cruelty.

He scanned the words over Abe's shoulder one more time to be sure he hadn't misread them, but the spiky handwriting said exactly what he thought it had the first time.

Myron,

Our church has an off-Sunday tomorrow. I know you don't, but could I meet you after church to ask your advice? Around three o'clock? My nephew, a single father, needs me to watch his two unruly boys, ages five and six. I'd like to talk to you about how you parented Tim after you adopted him at age seven.

Until then,
Cathy Zehr

This woman had a lot of nerve. First of all, writing something this nasty. Second, signing it *Until then*. She gave him no chance to say *neh*. What nerve!

Everyone in the area knew the struggles he'd had to raise Tim. With Cathy's reputation as a rumormonger, Myron was positive she'd passed on plenty of stories about Tim's rebelliousness, refusal to join the church, and brushes with the law. She'd probably dug up more bad information on Tim than Myron had ever learned.

Cathy would never show up here tomorrow for advice. But he couldn't understand why she'd write a message like this in the first place. The thought that Tim had put her up to it seemed the only explanation.

Abe shifted from foot to foot as if he wanted to head to Anna Mary's but felt guilty about leaving when Myron was so upset. Much as he'd like to, Myron couldn't keep his nephew here.

"I'm sorry." Abe crumpled the note and threw it away. "I never would have brought this home from the market if I'd known."

That box of donuts made Myron sick to his stomach. He wasn't sure if he'd ever want to eat another donut.

"Take the box to your girlfriend's family." He waved toward the counter. "I can't bear to throw away food, but I'll never touch one of those woman's donuts. The little girls don't need to know the poison that came with the sweets."

Then he headed for the sink with his plate and glass, trying to throw off the unsettled feeling inside. "Best get these cleared away so's you can get back to your girlfriend."

Abe grabbed his dishes and crossed the room, but Myron blocked his path.

"I'll take those. You go on. Spend as much time as you can with your girl."

"*Danke.*" Abe shot him an appreciative smile.

As he reached the door, Myron said, "If you think it would help, I could talk to Esther."

Abe beamed at him. "That'd be great if you want to try."

Myron wasn't sure he could do much more than Abe and Anna Mary had. If they hadn't been successful in convincing Esther to give up her fears, would he be any better? He did have one small advantage. For years, similar fears had kept him from opening his heart to another relationship. That might help him understand her, and maybe she'd be willing to take advice from someone who'd gone through the same suffering. But he had a better way to assist.

"Don't forget to pray," Myron called before the door swung shut.

The same advice everyone had been giving him

about Tim. Myron bowed his head and prayed for everyone in the family. Then he turned his petition toward Cathy. He had no idea what her needs were, but the Lord did.

Heavenly Father, please, please, please help this Cathy Zehr find the perfect solution to her problem.

Although he desperately wanted to, Myron couldn't quite bring himself to add, *Just don't let it be me*. But he could hope that. And he did.

CHAPTER 3

Thick vines wrapped around Cathy, yanking her backward to a dark, scary place. Terrified, she screamed and twisted, struggling to escape, but her bonds only tightened. She thrashed. Hit out at her captor. Whimpered. Cried. Begged for freedom. But she was going down, down, down. She'd never get away.

As she collapsed, trapped and helpless, light and heat burned her face. Sunshine. Daylight. Her bedroom window. Sunbeams blinded her after the darkness of the captivity. She squeezed her burning eyes shut.

Something still held her in its grip. She squirmed to loosen the restraints that held her. But the more she wriggled, the tighter they closed around her.

Please, God, help me.

A still, small voice whispered, *Let go, Cathy. Let Me deal with it.*

I can't, Lord, she gasped to herself. *I can't.*

I have You, my child, but you must trust Me.

Cathy wrestled her way to consciousness, still caught in the terror of the unknown, still tussling against her captor. Her heart battered against her ribs. She eased her eyes open to find she'd been battling her bedcovers.

How foolish. Her sheets bound her like a cocoon.

As she unwound them and stepped out of bed, she couldn't shake the dread of the nightmare. Panic clung to her as she made the bed and ate her breakfast. Even feeding the horse didn't help.

Off-Sundays always left her feeling at loose ends. Not having chores or other people to distract her, she had to focus on her own troubles—something she avoided during the week by staying busy.

Even worse, off-Sundays left her lonely. Nobody ever invited her over for a visit. During the week or at church, she bustled around, filling her days with work or with investigating other people's lives. But on quiet off-Sundays, she faced her own shortcomings.

And today, another huge problem loomed over her. Her lack of childcare skills. She had such a short time to become a competent parent.

Myron arrived home from church and couldn't settle his nerves. He was pacing up and down the living room when Abe and Anna Mary arrived.

Although he appreciated their support, it did little to settle his anxiety. "Do you think she'll come? I hope Tim set all this up as a joke." Yet, something inside Myron warned him the message was real.

Abe shrugged. "I saw her write the note and pack up the donuts."

Myron groaned. As the clock inched closer to three,

he wrung his hands. "I should have told her *neh*. Why didn't I?" He could have dropped a letter in her mailbox. Or asked one of her neighbors to give her a message. Or knocked on her front door himself.

Abe whispered something to Anna Mary, and she glanced at Myron with pity. They must see him as a foolish old man. If forty-two could be considered old.

At the crunch of buggy wheels outside the window, he winced. No escaping her now. He'd have to endure this visit. His stomach cratered. What would they talk about? How would he endure Cathy bringing up all his mistakes in parenting? Even if they were true, he hated facing them. Worse would be admitting them in front of not only family, but a stranger too.

Why had God tasked him with the job of raising his dead brother's son when he knew nothing about raising children? And why was He letting Cathy come here to expose his failures?

Cathy slowed her horse as she neared Myron's house. Anxiety pooled in her stomach. Had she made an error in setting this appointment? Her earlier nightmare returned in full force. Terror washed over her in waves.

This was ridiculous. She was never indecisive. Every day, she walked right up and confronted people. It never mattered to her what they thought of her. At least, that's what she wanted everyone to think. Most people would never believe anything could scare her, but she dreaded being exposed. If she kept the focus on others' problems, nobody could shine that spotlight back at her.

Don't be silly. There's nothing to be afraid of. He's not going to question your competence or expose your deep, dark secrets. You're here to ask him about parenting.

Despite her inner pep talk, she drove past his house. Once. Twice.

What if he saw me? Suppose his neighbors are watching?

She was tempted to keep going and take a different route home. If only she could take back that note and forget the whole thing. She'd given him a free box of donuts. Was that a fair exchange for the time he'd lose waiting for her? Most likely he'd be too busy to fret over her not showing up. Talking to her had to be at the bottom of his list. He'd probably found more important things to do.

Cathy's conscience nagged at her. She'd set up an appointment. If you made a commitment, you had to keep it, and you had to be on time. Those were two of her *onkel*'s many ironclad rules. She still followed every single one.

A glance at her wristwatch showed she had two minutes. Reluctantly, she turned her buggy around and headed to Myron's house and up his driveway. Her watch ticked to 3:01 as she tied her horse to the hitching post. For the first time in her life, she'd be late.

Myron's heart sank as Cathy marched to his front door, purpose in every stride, bearing a bakery box.

Ach. Not another one. He'd sworn off donuts after her cruel message. He certainly wouldn't be eating these.

Cathy's stiff, no-nonsense posture indicated she had little sympathy for people's faults. And the grim slash of her mouth revealed she found this visit as distasteful as he did.

Her loud and insistent knock came across as a demand to open the door at once. Something inside Myron rebelled at her insistence. As soon as he'd seen her through the window, he'd headed for the door. Though he stood only three steps away, he paused. Let her wait. He wouldn't be bossed around by this gossip who'd barged her way into his life and his privacy.

"*Onkel?*" Abe's soft, conciliatory tone made Myron ashamed.

What was he doing? Playing childish games? He'd always been determined to win, to be number one whatever the cost. He'd kept that desire hidden because the Amish community valued humility. Growing up, he'd tried to outdo his older brothers and never quite succeeded. He'd always come in last in games, sports, and life—even as an adult. His brothers had both married and had children, but Myron had lost the woman he'd planned to marry. And then when he did end up with a makeshift family, he lost his two-year-old daughter and alienated his son. In everything in life, he'd failed miserably.

An impatient *rat-a-tat* shook the front door. He jumped at the noise. It jerked him out of his memories and back to the present.

The banging started again.

Hmph. Cathy Zehr sure didn't follow the Bible's advice to be patient.

Forcing his lips into a semblance of a smile, Myron opened the door.

She didn't bother with the usual pleasantries. Instead, she thrust the box at him. "They're day-olds, of course, but I thought I should give you something for the help you'll be giving me."

Her shrill tone grated on Myron's nerves like a rasp against metal. If he were honest, everything about her rubbed him the wrong way.

Without waiting to be invited, she strode past him into the living room and plopped onto a chair. Her eyebrows rose a little when she noticed Anna Mary and Abe. "You two coming for some parenting advice too?"

Anna Mary gasped. Abe hurried over and took the bakery box from Myron, whose nerveless fingers were about to drop it. Abe carried it into the kitchen and returned to take a seat on the couch near Anna Mary, but not within touching distance.

Myron nodded his approval. A wise choice. No need to give Cathy anything more to gossip about. She'd already found plenty.

"I'm Cathy Zehr."

"I know."

She thrust out her hand to Myron. He recoiled as if she'd asked him to pet a poisonous snake. He tamped down his distaste and crossed the room. After giving her a limp handshake, he hurried across the room to the spot farthest from her and dropped into the rocker.

Cathy cleared her throat. "I wasn't sure you knew me. You've never stopped at my market stand." She almost seemed hurt. "I guess you got my message?" Without waiting for a response, she plowed on. "As I said in my note, my nephew needs me to watch his boys." She swallowed hard, and her eyes misted.

Her sudden rush of emotion caught Myron by surprise. She obviously cared about her nephew. That caused him to squirm. When Tim had left for New York, Myron felt nothing but relief from a heavy load of guilt. Even in his loneliness since, he hadn't felt that rush of caring.

"He—he . . ." Cathy took a breath that did little to calm the underlying trembling in her voice. "He'll be going to Mexico for several months for cancer treatment. I've never spent much time around children, so I need some advice."

Take-charge, bossy Cathy asking for advice seemed so out of character. Myron's jaw dropped, but he snapped it shut. Why in the world had she come to him?

He shook his head. "I'm the last person who can help. I knew nothing about parenting when Tim and his sister came to live with me, and I still don't."

"That's exactly why I chose you."

All three of them stared at her.

"Tim was unruly just like my two grandnephews. And he was around seven, right? My nephew's boys are five and six. Almost the same situation."

"*Jah*, he was seven and quite a handful." Actually, that wasn't quite true. When Tim first arrived, he was shy and docile. He spent most of his time comforting his little sister, Ivy. An ache blossomed in Myron's chest. She'd only been two.

After she'd disappeared, Tim had taken his fury and grief out on Myron. Tim's tantrums escalated into kicking and screaming fits so violent that he hurt Myron. When Myron forbade any talk of Ivy, hoping it would help Tim forget, the boy no longer hit out. Instead, he'd grown sullen and resentful.

Myron snapped back to the room. Everyone was staring at him—Abe and Anna Mary with concern, Cathy with irritation. She sure disliked not being in control. Myron could see she wanted to steer the conversation back to her request. He had to make it clear he had no advice.

"Like I already told you, I didn't know what to do, how to handle Tim. And besides—"

Cathy cut him off. "Perfect. So we're in the same situation. I don't have any idea how to handle these boys either."

"I don't see how I can help you." Myron hung his head. "I failed with Tim. He rebelled and ran wild. I—"

"That's exactly what I need."

Myron's eyes practically bugged out. "That doesn't make sense. I'm the last—"

Again, she cut him off. "You made mistakes—bad mistakes—while raising Tim. I want you to tell me everything you did. Then I won't make the same errors."

Myron sat in shocked silence. Had she just said that? Abe and Anna Mary appeared just as stunned.

His low groan ended on a snicker. Then a rusty chuckle came from deep within his chest and grew to a full-blown belly laugh. Finally, he wiped his eyes and spoke. "First time I've ever been asked that. Might be the smartest way to go about it. If that's the kind of advice you're after, I have plenty of it."

"*Gut.*" Cathy stood. "When do you want to meet for our first lesson?"

He gulped. She'd trapped him. "Um . . ." He longed to say *Never*.

As usual, Cathy took charge. "Tuesday after we both get off work?" Without waiting for a response, she galloped on. "I'll bring supper since I assume they"—she waved toward Anna Mary and Abe—"will be too busy. I hope you like spaghetti and meatballs and garlic bread."

Myron gurgled something that might have been a *jah*, but sounded more like a hairball stuck in his throat.

Cathy sailed to the door. "See you at six." A few seconds later, the door slammed behind her.

Myron rocked back in his chair and groaned. "She sure don't give you time to answer her questions."

Abe studied Myron. "You're really going to do this?"

"Seems like I don't have much choice."

"You could tell her *neh*," Anna Mary suggested.

Myron laughed. "She don't seem like a woman to take *neh* for an answer." Then he sobered. "Might make up for the many errors I made with Tim. Perhaps God's giving me a second chance to get things right."

"Second chances can be a good thing," Abe said.

"Definitely," Anna Mary agreed. "Sometimes it takes a mistake to make things much better the next time."

Myron could only hope they were right.

CHAPTER 4

The last thing Myron wanted to do was sit around the house thinking about Cathy Zehr and her request. He had to keep busy. He needed something to push all these worries and memories from his mind. Weren't they supposed to talk to Anna Mary's *mamm*?

"Speaking of second chances, don't we have someone else who needs one?"

At his question, Abe bowed his head.

Leave it to his nephew to do the one thing that hadn't occurred to Myron since Cathy had walked—no, barged—into his house.

Lord, please show me the way out of this tangled mess.

Myron saw no way to escape, but he had to trust the Lord for answers.

After Abe raised his head, Myron smiled. "*Gut* idea. We can use all the heavenly help we can get." That was for sure and certain.

He picked up the box of donuts in the kitchen and

handed them to Anna Mary. "If your sisters don't mind day-old donuts?"

Anna Mary flashed him a grateful smile. "They'll love them. *Danke.*"

"Don't thank me. Thank Cathy Zehr."

Abe chuckled, and Myron's spirits lifted a little. He doubted he'd be much help to the community gossip, and recalling old memories would be painful, but maybe he could help his brother marry the woman he loved.

As they exited the house, Anna Mary leaned close to Abe. "I wonder what Cathy would think if she knew my sisters were eating all her donuts."

Abe laughed. "We won't tell her."

Myron chuckled to himself as he hitched his horse. He suspected Cathy wouldn't appreciate him passing off her gifts. That woman seemed determined to control every detail of her life as well as everyone else's. If she insisted on trying to bully him, she'd soon discover her mistake. A small worry niggled its way into his mind. She'd already forced her will on him. Showing up today? Meeting him Tuesday night? Eating supper together?

He groaned. By not saying *neh* to her plans, he'd agreed to all of it. Even her choice of menu. Although he had to admit, he did love spaghetti.

Myron's mood drooped a bit at that realization. She'd managed to get her way, and he'd been a pushover. Tuesday night, he'd have to be on guard. Unless he came up with a way to get out of it.

While he mused on ways to foil Cathy, his horse plodded along behind Tim's. Myron was glad he'd suggested that Abe use Tim's horse and buggy. For once, Tim's horse wasn't galloping through town, the buggy swerving wildly and screeching to abrupt halts. Unlike Tim, Abe treated the horse with care.

Dealing with Tim had many similarities to handling Cathy. They both tended to ride roughshod over everyone and ignore other people's advice.

Myron's conscience jabbed at him. *And you don't do the same?*

He shook off the prodding. He didn't want to examine the answer to that question. Luckily, he didn't have to. They'd arrived at Anna Mary's house.

As Abe got out holding the bakery box, Anna Mary's little sisters crowded around him. Jealousy prickled at Myron as the girls hugged Abe, asked questions, and seemed overjoyed to see him. Myron had never held that kind of attraction for children.

Would Ivy have loved him and hugged him if she'd grown up in his house? Or would she have turned as angry and rebellious as Tim? Maybe the Lord had taken her from him because he'd have been an even worse parent for a little girl than he'd been for Tim. Myron blinked back moisture in his eyes.

Not a day went by that he didn't think of Ivy or wonder where she was. He'd hired various detectives over the years, but they all came to the same conclusion.

Ivy had disappeared without a trace. And he blamed himself.

"Myron, you coming in?" Anna Mary's sweet voice carried across the backyard.

He'd been standing in the same place, fiddling with his horse's reins. "Be right there."

Keeping his back turned, he looped the reins over the rail and waited until he'd regained enough composure to head toward the house. As he approached, he focused on Hank and Esther. Myron longed to help his brother win the woman he loved.

Lord, if it's Your will for them to be together, please give me the wisdom and words to say to convince Esther.

Anna Mary held the door open for Myron. Still surrounded by the small girls, Abe lifted the lid of the donut box to hushed *achs*. They each pointed out their favorites.

A woman stood in the shadows, her face beautiful, but wan. Myron preferred women with sturdier farm-girl builds, like Anna Mary's. And like his ex-fiancée's. Yet, he could see how Anna Mary's fragile and delicate mother might appeal to his brother.

Abe introduced Myron to Esther and added, "He's my *daed*'s brother."

"I could tell." Tiny creases formed between her eyes. After a quick handshake and hello, she looked away.

Maybe his resemblance to Hank bothered her. Myron had always been a rougher-cut version of his brother, but they had many of the same mannerisms. Myron shifted from foot to foot, unsure what to say next. He'd never been one for social conversations or idle chitchat.

"I can see why my *bruder* fell in love with you," he blurted out.

From Abe's shocked expression, the comment had been tactless and inappropriate. Since Myron didn't socialize with anyone except a few male friends, he hadn't spent time talking to women about anything except furniture orders or occasional church plans. He must have sounded as blunt and rude as Cathy Zehr. The thought galled him. So did the way she kept popping into his thoughts.

To his surprise, Esther colored and seemed pleased by the compliment. "He's a *wunderbar* man."

"Why don't we go into the living room?" Anna Mary suggested. She settled her sisters in the kitchen with the box of donuts before carrying a small selection of them with her to the living room for the adults.

Once they'd taken seats, Myron worried over how to start the talk, so he bulldozed right into the conversation. "It's been painful hearing my *bruder*'s heartache over losing you."

Esther drew in a ragged breath, and her face contorted. "I can't . . ."

"Do you love him?" Although he regretted his bluntness, if she didn't love Hank, there was no point in continuing.

At his probing question, Esther hunched into herself. "I don't think that's your business."

Her response nettled Myron. "It is if my *bruder*'s suffering."

She flinched, but didn't respond.

He plunged on. "If the answer's *neh*, I'll tell him to stop torturing himself and move on."

Esther paled and twisted her hands in her lap. That comment seemed to have hit her like a dart.

But he didn't let up. "So, what's the answer? *Jah* or *neh*?"

Head down, words barely audible, Esther admitted, "*Jah.*" Then she murmured, "With all my heart."

At least that's what Myron thought she'd said. If so, she'd never told his *bruder*. Myron couldn't believe Hank would have let her go. Not if he'd known she loved him back.

Although Myron was pretty sure he knew the answer, he asked anyway. "Have you ever told Hank?"

Esther's fingers pinched ridges in her apron. "*Neh,*" she mumbled.

"Don't you think he deserves to know? He's broken-hearted over you rejecting him, convinced he'll never be *gut* enough for you."

She gasped. "That's not true. I'm the one who's not *gut* enough for him. I—"

He waved a hand to cut her off. "If you've never told him that or that you love him, what else would he think?"

"I never wanted him to think this is his fault," Esther cried. Distress carved lines in her face. She held out an imploring hand.

Despite Esther's anguished expression, Myron plowed on. "What else is he supposed to think?"

"I—I don't know."

At her plaintive answer, Anna Mary leaned over to take her *mamm*'s hands in hers.

"Don't coddle her." Myron believed in tough love. Sometimes you have to keep the pressure on to get results.

Abe's brow furrowed. The criticism in his eyes made Myron pause for a moment. He could almost read the message in his nephew's eyes. *No wonder Tim turned out rebellious.*

Anna Mary ignored Myron's barked order, and Abe smiled at her to offer his support.

Abe turned to Myron. "A little love and caring can sometimes encourage people to change."

But Myron had discovered something earlier that he hadn't appreciated until now. "Cathy Zehr taught me a lesson today about confronting people."

Esther's head jerked up, and she mouthed, *Cathy Zehr?*

At her puzzled look, Abe smiled and nodded.

Myron grinned. "*Jah.* She showed me pointing out the error of people's ways can be freeing for them."

"Not always," Abe said dryly.

"Well, if somebody had forced me to face up to things years ago, my life might have been different. And I'm not going to stand by and let this couple ruin their lives."

Before Abe could get a word in edgewise, Myron

pinned Esther with a question. "You love him, and he loves you. What's holding you back?"

Esther went mute. Once again, she bowed her head and twisted her fingers together.

This time Myron spoke from the depth of his heart and from past errors. He'd never have a second chance, but Esther could. "Sometimes fear causes you to make foolish mistakes. It can make you deny yourself new opportunities and happiness."

Anna Mary bit her lip and examined her *mamm* anxiously. Myron disliked upsetting Anna Mary. The poor girl had spent years coddling and protecting her mother. Though he could see Anna Mary wanted to interfere, he hoped she wouldn't. From Esther's expression, his words were getting through to her. Perhaps someone should have given her this kind of straight talk years ago. She was nowhere near as weak and fragile as she appeared.

Myron waited for a response, but when none came, he confessed, "I should know. I've spent twenty-five years walling myself off from hurt. It doesn't protect you. In the end, it only leaves you lonely."

A tear trickled down Esther's cheek. "I know."

"Hank feels that loneliness now. Maybe he always will. Does it make sense for two people to hurt each other like this when they could be spending their days loving and supporting each other?"

"I didn't mean"—Esther gulped—"to hurt him."

"But you did. And you're hurting yourself too. And

your children. Wouldn't they be better off with a loving, caring father?"

Esther covered her face with her hands, and her shoulders shook with sobs. "But . . ." Her words came out in a wail. "I've lost two husbands. I can't bear to lose another."

"I understand that pain." Myron gentled his voice. He totally understood and sympathized with her fears. He'd had the same ones. Not only that, he'd given in to them, refusing to even consider loving someone again. "I lost my fiancée."

"I'm sorry," Esther said. "The hurting never stops."

"What's worse is when you let it keep you from experiencing life, from trying again with someone new. Instead, you hide it inside and let it shrivel you up until you're nothing more than an empty shell." He knew all this firsthand. It's how he'd been living his life. And it might be partly why he'd been such an incompetent parent.

Esther cried harder. "I'm sorry." She stood and stumbled toward her bedroom.

"Don't run away from it, Esther. You can never run far enough to escape."

Anna Mary jumped up and put an arm around her *mamm*.

Myron shook his head. "Anna Mary, I think you've overprotected her too much. She needs to face up to things."

"I'm just going to walk her to her bedroom." In the

doorway, Anna Mary hugged her mother. “I love you, Mamm.”

Myron’s heart went out to both of them. Lucky Esther to have a daughter who loved her like that. He’d never know the love of a child.

“Esther,” Myron called after her, “God gives second chances.”

“What about third chances?” Esther’s snappy reply boded well for her bouncing back. She shut the door behind her with a loud *click*.

Myron smiled. “I think she took it to heart.” He stood. “Now I need to go home and do what Esther’s doing. Wrestle with God.” He muttered as he walked to the door, “This old fool”—he bounced a finger off his chest—“was lecturing himself more than speaking to Esther.”

But a huge gap existed between his situation and hers. Esther had a man who loved her with all his heart. Hank would be a giving, caring husband as well as a good father to her children.

But even if Myron released all the fears that bound him, he’d never get a second chance at love. Who would want him after all these years?

Cathy woke with a jolt in the wee hours of Tuesday morning. *Ach!* As she stumbled through the dark to her kitchen to mix dough for the day, Sunday’s visit to Myron’s filled her thoughts. She couldn’t believe she had to head to the house of that crusty old bachelor again. He’d been less than welcoming, but he had indicated he'd answer her questions. And she needed answers. Lots of answers.

Raising two boys for the months Wayne had treatments would be a challenge. Learning things to avoid might help.

Cathy only hoped her previous visit to Myron's house hadn't been noticed. Why had she suggested supper today? Anyone heading home from work might see her, and gossip would spread like wildfire.

Not that she'd mind having her name connected to romantic rumors, but she could hear the comments now. *Cathy Zehr went to Myron King's house to bring him supper. She must be sweet on him. Pretty desperate chasing him, because he's never even looked at a woman since his fiancée died years ago. But that's the best she can do. Nobody else would even consider her. And neither will he.*

Not that she'd be interested in Myron, but it pained her when people laughed and talked about her behind her back. She'd been the punch line of many nasty jokes over the years. As much as she pretended not to care, every single one knifed through her.

The imagined comment about nobody wanting her ripped her apart inside, because it was true. Not only would Myron not want her, but nobody else would either. She was destined to be an *alt maedel*. *Ach*, who was she fooling? At thirty-six, she'd already become one years ago. And though she never wanted to marry, it still hurt that nobody had asked her.

Because men had passed her by for years, all those people gossiping about her would never believe the truth that she had no interest in a relationship. Besides, Myron King was the last person on earth she'd be interested in. The lines etched on his face drooped, giving him a permanent hangdog look. And his nephew, Tim, was the worst *youngie* in the area among all the *g'mays*. Not easy, considering he had some strong contenders for top troublemaker. All she wanted from Myron was information. Not anything else.

Then why had she gone to so much trouble to make her best recipe for supper?

Chapter 5

A feeling of dread hung over Myron as he opened his woodworking shop on Tuesday morning. He still couldn't believe he'd let Cathy push him into agreeing to dinner tonight. Without Abe and Anna Mary around, he'd be alone with the town's worst gossip and pain in the neck.

What would they talk about? With Cathy, it might not be a problem. She'd probably prattle on, not giving him a chance to get a word in edgewise. Just the thought of enduring an evening with that chatterbox gave Myron a headache.

Maybe he could call a few church friends for a hasty meeting tonight. They needed to plan a fundraiser for the Miller baby's operation. If they met at someone else's house, he could put a note of apology on his front door for Cathy. That seemed a cowardly way to avoid her, but he had no way to get in touch with her. She'd probably counted on that when she set this up for today.

The shop phone rang, and Myron hurried to answer it.

"Myron? This is Liesl Vandenberg. I drove by your

shop this weekend and fell in love with that blue hand-painted cupboard. The one with the hummingbirds and flowers on the doors."

Wunderbar! He'd love to sell that. It was one of the most time-consuming and expensive pieces he'd ever made, but this wealthy *Englischer* could afford it.

"Is it still available?"

"*Jah*, it is." And likely would be for a long time unless Mrs. Vandenberg bought it.

"Great. But I'd need to have it delivered as soon as possible this morning."

"My apprentices should be here in twenty minutes. I'll have them take it out to your house right away."

"Actually, it's not for my house. And I was hoping to talk to you in person. Could you bring it to my office at the market?"

"Me? I never leave the store during the day. The young men who work here are apprentices, so I—"

"You don't trust them?"

Although she might not have meant it as a dig, it brought Myron up short. Did she mean to imply he had a problem trusting people? Mrs. Vandenberg might be right, but business was business. And this business was his responsibility. Instead of pondering her underlying meaning, he should answer the question she'd asked.

"Both my apprentices are dependable."

"Excellent. Then I'm sure you can leave one of them in the store while you do the delivery. You won't be gone long."

With that, she hung up without even giving him a chance to protest. He was debating about calling her back to ask if he could bring the cupboard after work when Jed and Lloyd strolled in. They might as well get this done now. After all, he always stressed putting customers first and doing your best to please them.

"Lloyd, I'd like you to watch the shop for an hour this morning while Jed and I do a delivery."

Lloyd stared at Myron, taken aback. "You sure?"

Jed's eyes bugged out when Myron nodded. "Will I get a turn too?"

Myron understood that so well. His old childhood desire of doing everything his older brothers did flooded back. He had to treat both employees equally. Though it pained him a bit to say it, he'd give them an equal chance. "Next time it'll be your turn, Jed."

As Jed's face lit up, Myron squirmed with guilt. He had no intention of ever leaving his shop again during working hours. "Come on, Jed. I promised this delivery right away." Myron motioned to the blue cupboard. "Let's get it out to the delivery wagon."

An idea struck him while they settled the cupboard atop thick padding and blankets. Since they were going to the farmer's market, he could stop at Cathy's stand to get a few donuts as a thank-you for his apprentices and cancel tonight's appointment with her. His mood brightened as he and Jed wrapped up the cupboard and tied it down with bungee cords. Myron intended to return from this trip a free man.

Cathy had a long line of customers when Myron King entered, carrying the blue cupboard from his showroom window. The furniture caught her attention first because she'd often admired that piece when the store was closed. She loved the swooping wood curlicues on top. The swirls of leaves on the doors echoed those curves. Multicolored blossoms adorned vines and leaf clusters. All around, ruby-throated hummingbirds sipped nectar or took flight. Every detail made her long to burst into song.

Customers turned to see what she was gaping at. Only then did Cathy realize Myron held up the opposite end.

Heat rushed to her face. *Ach!* Did everyone think she'd been staring longingly at him?

She couldn't believe she'd made a laughingstock of herself. She'd always loved having a market stall with a perfect view of the main doors as well as the staircase. Now she longed for a place to hide. The crowd that had backed up behind the cupboard delivery flowed through those doors, and they'd all been peeking in while she gawked. Many of them wore mocking smiles as if they'd caught her doing something they yearned to pass on as juicy gossip.

She wanted to shout to all of them that she'd been concentrating on the cupboard, but who'd believe her? Clues less obvious than her intense focus had given her fodder for lots of stories. Stories that other people had eagerly shared. Cathy groaned inside.

Despite wishing she could study the cabinet in greater detail, she forced herself to turn back to her work. But at the thought of people snickering behind her back, her hand trembled. She fumbled as she dropped three donuts into a bag. One squirted from her fingers, shot across the counter, and plopped onto her shoe.

She froze in embarrassment and shame. How many more ways could she make a fool of herself this morning?

If she moved, the donut would slither off her shoe onto the floor, where she'd squish it if she turned toward the counter. Or she'd slide across the linoleum mat she'd laid down to cover the cement. Or, worse yet, she'd slip in the icing and fall on her backside.

But if she picked it up, people might wonder how often she dropped donuts and worry she that she would put dirty donuts back into the display case. At least, that's what she'd have suspected if it happened in another market stand. She'd probably have told others about it too.

"Hey, I don't got all day," a man yelled.

He jerked Cathy back to her duties. With a flick of her foot, she tossed the donut into a far corner and prayed the health inspector wouldn't arrive before she could clean it up.

She added one more donut to the bag, stepped carefully to the counter, and returned to waiting on people. But she couldn't help wondering where Myron had been taking that cupboard.

Although she could never afford it and wouldn't spend that much money on one piece of furniture even if she could, her heart craved that beauty. Everything in her house came from yard sales or the Salvation Army Thrift Store. She chuckled to herself as she imagined that fancy cupboard sitting in a room filled with other people's cast-off goods.

Seeing Myron again reminded her of her earlier worries. Maybe she could wave him over when he came downstairs and ask to change their meeting time. But what time would work to keep their meeting secret? Five in the morning while she fried donuts? She couldn't ask him to do that, could she?

Mrs. Vandenberg greeted Myron and exclaimed over the cabinet with such joy it made him apprehensive. Because of her reputation as a matchmaker, he'd overheard warnings to be cautious when she made unusual requests. Bringing this cupboard into her market office counted as an odd request.

Then she beamed at Jed in the same way, and Myron relaxed. Perhaps she had plans for his apprentice. But she couldn't have known which helper would accompany him.

"Let me pay you for that." She wrote a check and handed it to him.

"This isn't the right amount," he protested.

"Oh, no, did the price go up?" Mrs. Vandenberg reached for her checkbook.

Myron shook his head. "*Neh*, this is way too much."

She stood and brushed at her skirt. "The extra's for delivery."

"We don't charge for delivery."

"You should." She waved toward Jed. "Some can be

a bonus for Jed's help and for Lloyd taking over at the shop."

How did she know his employees' names? Did she keep tabs on everyone in town this way? If Myron split the extra money three ways, his apprentices would get the equivalent of two weeks' salary.

"Oh, and I told the hospital I'd cover the Miller baby's operation, so no need for a fundraiser."

"*Danke,*" he stuttered. As much as he appreciated her generosity, part of him recoiled, afraid she'd found a way to read his mind. And now she'd taken away his excuse to back out of meeting Cathy tonight. Yet, he still needed to express gratitude for her kindness. "The family and our church community will be grateful."

Mrs. Vandenberg nodded. "Happy to help. While you're here, could you do me two favors?"

Myron stiffened. Maybe this was when she'd try to fix him up with a woman.

Without waiting for an answer, she pointed to the far wall. "I'd like a bookcase along there. Eight feet long, two feet deep, and six feet high. Could you do that?"

"No problem." Myron took the sketch she held out. The detailed drawing and instructions made everything clear, from the shelf heights to the materials, finish, and a deadline several months away.

"Now for my other favor."

This time Myron's teeth clenched, but she surprised him.

"I accidentally left my cane on the first floor. Would you help me downstairs to get it?"

Before Myron could suggest Jed as a stronger support,

Mrs. Vandenberg clamped on to his arm with a grip that seemed strong enough to whack a home run in a *youngies*' baseball game. She could have clung to the railing to make her own trip downstairs, but he liked the old lady. Plus, she'd given him his largest sale ever in his fifteen years in business.

When they reached the first floor, Mrs. Vandenberg tipped her head to the left. Myron gulped. They'd pass Cathy's Dough-Re-Mi stand. Except they didn't go by. Instead, Mrs. Vandenberg signaled for him to turn in.

Neh, neh, not Cathy's stand.

No customers waited in line. Better yet, there was no sign of Cathy. Myron's tight shoulders sagged in relief.

Mrs. Vandenberg waved to the far corner back near the empty fry baskets. Myron glanced around. He didn't like walking into someone else's stall without their permission, but Mrs. Vandenberg let go of his arm and braced herself against a nearby pole. With a *get-a-move-on* nod, she directed him toward her cane.

After one more uncomfortable scan behind him to be sure Cathy wasn't heading their way, he stepped gingerly inside, almost expecting her to come up behind him, grab him by the collar, and haul him out. But when that didn't happen, he regained his confidence.

After two brisk steps, a loud screech stopped him.

"Get out of here," Cathy screamed. She popped up from a crouched position on the floor, clutching a rag. She rushed toward him, waving it in shooing motions. Suddenly, she slid on the linoleum and crashed into his chest.

Stunned by the impact, he stumbled back into the

wall. He grabbed at her for support. The second his arms went around her, he realized he'd made a terrible mistake.

Passersby gasped or pointed. Those who hadn't seen the accident appeared scandalized. Nobody had ever seen an Amish couple—even a married couple—in an embrace. Even those, like Jed, who'd watched the skid happen, looked shocked.

Whispers flew around the air outside the stand. "Do you believe they're hugging in public?" "Thought the Amish didn't believe in PDA." "That's the owner of King's Woodworking Shop in town." "What does he see in that gossip?" "I never pictured those two together."

Cathy battered his chest with one fist and a stinky wet rag, flinging blobs of icing and cream filling all over his shirt and face. "Let me go," she snarled.

He dropped his hands so quickly she almost tumbled to the floor. *I'm sorry*, he mouthed.

She wobbled a few steps back and glared up at him. "You have a lot of nerve coming into my stand to steal donuts."

"I wasn't stealing donuts. Why were you hiding on the floor?"

"I was cleaning up a donut. Now it's even more of a mess because of you." She gestured to the corner. "If you weren't stealing, why'd you sneak in here?"

"I didn't sneak—" Myron supposed he probably had appeared to be a thief, with the tentative steps he had taken and the way he kept glancing over his shoulder. "I came to get Mrs. Vandenberg's cane." He pointed to the fryers.

"What?" Her eyes widened. "How did that get back there?"

"I must have left it there this morning when you showed me how to turn donuts." Mrs. Vandenberg grinned at them. "But it worked out well. You both need to talk to each other."

Myron gaped at her. How did she know?

"Would you bring me the cane, Myron? And perhaps Jed can see me upstairs to the office?"

With a nod, Myron rushed for the cane, keeping an eye on the floor for slippery spots. He didn't want to end up skidding like Cathy.

When he returned and presented the cane to Mrs. Vandenberg, she leaned close and whispered, "I hope you'll meet with her. She really does need help, and you're just the one to give it to her."

Myron decided to be blunt. "I don't want to be matched up, so you can just forget about that."

"Don't worry. Cathy's not interested in you. Besides, neither of you is ready for romance."

Ouch! Even though Myron wouldn't want to have anything to do with Cathy, it hurt to hear Mrs. Vandenberg's honest assessment of Cathy's opinion.

Mrs. Vandenberg seared him with a look that reached deep into his soul. "God gives me nudges from time to time, and He's assured me your wisdom and understanding will help her out of a dark situation. Promise me you'll follow God's lead."

"Of course I will." He always wanted to do God's will, but he sure hoped it didn't mean spending a lot of time with Cathy.

"Good. That's all you need to do." Mrs. Vandenberg tottered over to Jed, who escorted her to the stairs.

Most of the gawking mob got in line for donuts, perhaps hoping to see more interactions between the two of them to gossip about.

Myron had caused that curious crowd and damaged both their reputations. He couldn't help Cathy handle all those customers, but he had to do something to ease his guilt. In a quiet voice, he asked, "Can I help by cleaning up that mess?"

Through gritted teeth, she grumped, "You've caused enough problems around here. I have half a mind not to show up tonight."

Hallelujah!! He bit back a grin. "That's all right. You don't have to come." He hadn't even had to ask.

Her expression became even glummer. "Too bad. I never break my promises." She turned away to wait on people.

What did that mean? Was she coming or not? Declaring she'd bring supper wasn't a promise, was it? To him, it felt more like a threat.

Chapter 6

What a ghastly day! Cathy couldn't believe everything that had happened. First, people thought she'd been eyeing Myron. It had made her so nervous she'd dropped a donut. To make matters worse, she'd kicked it away, creating a safety hazard. Then she'd slipped on it and landed in Myron's arms. *Ach!* That had only reinforced the rumors.

Everyone she waited on made sly comments or asked intrusive questions. If she heard *So when's the wedding?* one more time, she'd scream. Not only wasn't it funny, it cut her to the core. They knew she had no chance of marrying anyone, so their teasing was spiteful.

She'd run out of donuts before closing time, so she had to turn people away. They'd grumbled and complained, but she had no energy left to make more. Plus, she still had to clean up the squished donut. She'd thrown dish towels over the slippery spots, which left her with no towels to clean up. She'd have to come in tomorrow to clean. And twice now, she'd broken her *onkel*'s rule—*Before you leave a place, make sure it's spotless.*

He would have punished her for kicking the donut into the corner and for leaving tonight before cleaning everything. Even though he'd passed several years ago, his furious face loomed over her as she shut the half door and hurried out of her stall. But the market would soon close, and she had an appointment tonight. *I won't be late again.*

The small girl deep inside her still cowered as her *onkel*'s critical words echoed over and over inside her head. She not only had to listen to her memory reprimand her for all her faults and failures, she also had to face Myron after sliding into his arms this afternoon. She wasn't sure she could look him in the eye. It would be humiliating if he thought she'd done it on purpose. Perhaps they could pretend it never happened, but with all the gossip they'd stirred up, it would be hard to forget.

Cathy's brain still whirled with all the day's worries as she baked the spaghetti casserole and prepared garlic bread to broil later. After everything that had happened, she shouldn't go to his house. It would only add to the rumors. Why hadn't she canceled when he'd given her the opportunity?

Too late now. She'd committed to it. And she'd show up on time.

Forty minutes later, she climbed into her buggy and set a hand on the hot casserole dish wrapped in towels beside her. To cut through some of the negative thoughts and criticism, she concentrated on one thing she did right—cooking. Everyone raved about her baked spaghetti and meatballs when they shared potluck meals at church events. Myron had never tasted it. She hoped he'd like it.

She really needed his advice, but he seemed reluctant to talk to her. Maybe after a good meal, he'd be more helpful.

This time, instead of dillydallying, she drove right up his driveway fifteen minutes early and strode to the door before she had any more misgivings. She cradled the towel-wrapped casserole in one arm and balanced the foil-wrapped garlic bread on top. In the other hand, she juggled a cake carrier holding a strawberry short-cake covered in whipped cream. He might be tired of donuts by now. She definitely was.

While she stood on his doorstep, puzzling over how she'd manage to knock with no free hand, the door opened. Cathy's worries kicked into full gear.

Had Myron been watching her out the window? That thought set her nerves zinging. She hated being ob-served. It made her worry about being judged. Even worse, it gave her a creepy feeling. And after what had happened today . . .

Myron had paced for the past half hour, wishing he could find a way to call this off. Ever since he'd agreed to the meeting, he'd had heartburn and stomach pains. Maybe he could use sickness as an excuse. But he wasn't a coward. He'd do his duty.

Mrs. Vandenberg had been clear that Myron needed

to help Cathy. The more he thought about it, the more it seemed God had given him a chance to right some of the mistakes he'd made while raising Tim. Cathy seemed as stubborn and headstrong as Myron, so learning about his failures might prevent her from making the same ones.

Not that he had many insights into how to be a better parent. If he did, he'd have applied them to his relationship with Tim. Myron only hoped Cathy could gain some wisdom from his errors.

As soon as he opened the door, Cathy barreled through. "This cake needs to go in the refrigerator."

He'd been right about *headstrong*. And he could also add *rude*, *bossy*, *inconsiderate*, and . . .

Garlic and onion scented the air as she passed, and Myron lost his train of thought. Whatever she carried smelled delicious. It had been ages since he'd had a home-cooked meal. Years, even. Except for Abe's chicken corn soup yesterday and the few weeks Abe had visited earlier this summer, the only time Myron had real cooking was at church potluck dinners.

Cathy set a bundle of towels on the counter, pulled open the refrigerator, and frowned at his almost bare shelves. She should have seen them before Abe arrived. Most of the time, Myron kept it empty except for pickles, condiments, and a jug of milk.

When she slid a white fluffy cake onto the top shelf, Myron's mouth watered. He'd sworn off donuts, but he couldn't wait to taste that delicious dessert.

The refrigerator door slammed shut, and Cathy unwrapped the towels to reveal a lidded glass casserole dish and two pot holders. A tangy tomato aroma floated toward him. He inhaled its spiciness, and his stomach gurgled.

She turned and sailed past him to the stove. "I'll put this on the stovetop to keep warm while I broil the garlic bread. You could set the table."

Definitely bossy.

What would she do if he refused to do her bidding? The childish part of him yearned to fold his arms across his chest and say, *Do it yourself.* The hungry part of him opened the cupboard and clattered plates, silverware, and glasses onto the kitchen table. No point in arguing until he'd had a meal.

Hmm. That might make a good parenting tip. He and Tim never had regular meals. Most days, they ate sugary cereals, canned soup, and fast food. And with Tim's irregular factory schedule before the fire, his nephew had been left to fend for himself as far as meals went.

"You gonna stand there staring into space? What about filling the glasses? If you take much longer, the food'll get cold."

Myron's jaw tightened. *Strong-willed. Controlling. Critical.* The list of Cathy's annoying traits kept growing. By the time they finished dinner, Myron might have a page full.

"Water or milk?" His tone had a sharp edge.

"Milk with spaghetti? That would compete with the blend of cheeses. And milk and tomato don't go well together."

Huh? Myron often drank milk with his SpaghettiOs. He'd never noticed it spoiling the flavor.

Know-it-all. The list got longer each time Cathy opened her mouth.

He filled her cup with water and considered defying her to have his usual glass of milk. With a sigh, he decided to follow her advice. He didn't want to ruin a delicious meal. Plus, he wouldn't put it past Cathy to take her casserole and stomp off. Myron couldn't take that chance.

Bad-tempered went on his list even though Cathy had only stomped out in his imagination. He could tell she'd probably do it.

Sitting at the table across from another socially awkward person made for an uncomfortable silence where the only sounds included chewing, slurping, and swallowing. After one quick glance at his face, she'd bowed for prayer, then kept her gaze glued to her plate.

Perhaps she was as embarrassed as he was about their collision in the market. All afternoon, he'd debated—should he apologize for grabbing her or act like he'd forgotten all about it? Ignoring it seemed the better choice. An apology might lead to a tongue-lashing. So far, she hadn't said a word about it. Better to keep it that way.

Once he'd taken the first bite of hot pasta, ground beef, mozzarella, and perfectly blended spices, Myron didn't want to waste any time talking. And he'd be even happier if Cathy never spoke either. His tastebuds danced in rapture, and he only wanted to savor each mouthful.

At his loud *Mmm*, Cathy flicked her attention to his face, and her lips quivered upward for a second before she lowered her head to hide a hesitant grin. He hadn't meant to allow that noise to escape. But he couldn't help it. Every bite was more delicious than the last.

She waited until he'd finished his plateful and crunched through three helpings of garlic bread before she asked, "Do you want more?" She pushed the casserole dish closer to him.

Since she'd eaten less than half of her portion, he heaped more on his plate and gobbled it while she finished hers. He debated about taking one more serving, but as usual, her domineering voice interrupted his intentions.

"Save room for dessert," she ordered.

Why did her demands make him want to do the opposite?

For a brief moment, Myron flipped places with Tim. Is this how his nephew reacted to being told what to do? Myron definitely wasn't as irritating as Cathy. Or was he? He'd be afraid to ask Tim that question.

About Cathy, though. Had he put *irritating* on the list?

Cathy could barely believe the change in Myron's expression as he set down his fork. Except for the flicker of annoyance when she reminded him about dessert, most of the tension lines had smoothed out. He appeared . . . Cathy fished for a word to describe him. *Contented? Neh*, more than that. *Blissful.* That was it.

When he wasn't scowling, he might even be considered good-looking, in a rugged sort of way. It seemed odd for a man of his age to be beardless. He'd be even more attractive with one. She yanked her gaze away from his features. Thank heavens, he'd been too busy staring at the remainder of the casserole to notice her studying him.

"I'll leave the rest for you," she said. "I can pick up my dish the next time we meet."

His eyes popped wide open at the words *next time.* Did he honestly think she could learn about parenting in a few hours? She had even less desire than he did to spend that much time together. But it was necessary.

She stood and carried the cake to the table. "Don't worry. I'll bring the meals. I don't expect you to feed me."

Tension, fear, and distaste flashed across his face one after the other, but as she lifted the cake from the carrier, his expression settled into pure joy. Not that he'd been focusing on her. *Neh*, his sole focus stayed on the slices of cake she was cutting.

After his first bite, he closed his eyes and leaned back in his chair. At the delight on his face, pain shot through her. Ever since she was a teen, she'd longed to have a man look at her that way. But this was for her baking, not for her. She'd never bring that expression to any man's face.

Although she insisted she had no interest in dating, the truth was much more complicated. Blinking back the moisture gathering in her eyes, she concentrated on spearing a strawberry and swirling it through the whipped cream. She let it linger on her tongue. The sweetness filled a little of the deep longing in her heart. It was why she'd chosen to make donuts. Although sweet treats helped soothe some of her yearnings, no amount of sugar could make up for the lack of love in her life.

Cathy had been quiet for so long, Myron got concerned. He'd dived into the cake and enjoyed each bite, but her fork hadn't even scraped her plate.

Across from him, she had her head down while she toyed with her whipped cream, dragging the tines of the fork through the creamy mounds, but never once lifting it to her lips.

"Too full?"

Her hand jerked and flipped a blob onto her lap. She scrambled to scoop it up. She hopped up from her chair, holding her apron away from her dress, and rushed over to the sink. Using the edge of one of her towels, she scrubbed at the stain with hard, rapid motions.

He regretted startling her. After she'd made such a lovely supper, it didn't seem fair he'd ended the meal by upsetting her.

More words flooded his mind. *Nervous. Frantic. Frightened.* This time, he had no desire to add them to the list. The defeated lines of her shoulders brought to mind two more. *Sad. Heartbroken.*

He knew that pain. Had she lost someone she'd loved?

Something inside him wanted to reach out, to comfort her. But he didn't know how.

"I'm sorry about your apron. I shouldn't have—"

She waved an impatient hand to dismiss his apology. "Not your fault. I shouldn't be careless." Her words came out gruff, but carried a note of deep sorrow that confirmed his suspicions.

The most he could do was change the subject. He stood and picked up his dishes. "Everything was delicious." Ordinarily, he would have stopped there, but something in her called out for more. "You're an excellent cook. I don't think I've ever tasted anything that good."

The slight lift of her lips at *excellent cook* soured into a scoffing expression. "Really?" Her distrustful tone implied he'd lied.

Myron bristled. He'd only been trying to make her feel better. And here she was, challenging his honesty. For a second, he almost got into a grade-school spat.

I'm not a liar. Jah, *you are.* Neh, *I'm not.*

Good sense took over before he blasted out the words to start that argument. "I can honestly say I haven't had a meal this good in years."

That seemed to mollify her. A little.

"I doubt it." The defiant edge had been replaced by insecurity.

This woman was a bundle of contradictions. Prickly, but sensitive. Pushy, but insecure. Self-assured, but needy. He'd hate to be the man who'd have to deal with all those opposites. Maybe that's why she had never been married.

Cathy rubbed at the stain as she tried to get her emotions under control. If she scoured any harder, she'd end up with a hole in her apron. She wished she hadn't done something so embarrassing the first time—well, the third, actually—she'd been with Myron. What would he think of her?

She must have unnerved him, because he'd paid her over-the-top compliments. She didn't appreciate liars. That's why she'd never liked social niceties like people asking *how are you?* when they didn't really care and you answering *fine* when you ached inside.

Although it had been kind of him to lessen her embarrassment, he shouldn't have fibbed. That lowered her opinion of him. Not that she'd had a high one in the first place.

She rinsed the spot on her apron one last time as he carried over the dirty dishes. Now she had a huge wet patch on the front of her. She grabbed her other towel and tucked the edge into her apron band. It probably looked ridiculous, but the spot made her even more uncomfortable.

Myron brushed her arm as he reached past her to turn on the water faucet, and she jumped. Feeling his touch twice in one day was too overwhelming. All she wanted to do was flee. He must think her a total fool.

While she'd been worrying, he'd filled the sink with sudsy water and dropped in all the dishes, including hers. He'd left only her cake plate.

"Why don't you finish that while I do the dishes?" He waved toward the table.

The idea of sitting down to eat the cake after she'd made a mess curdled her stomach. She pictured her childhood dinner table. If she'd played with her dessert or slopped her food, she'd have been sent to her room hungry. One of her siblings would have cleaned her plate. Even now as an adult, that old guilt overwhelmed her. *I don't have to punish myself for every mistake anymore.* But part of her refused to believe it.

Cornered by Myron's concerned gaze, she sat at the table. He watched until she began eating, then returned to washing dishes. She forced herself to clean her plate. This visit had gotten off to a terrible start.

CHAPTER 7

Myron wished he could put Cathy at ease, but even finishing her cake had seemed to be a trial. He sensed she wanted to leave. He'd be happy if she did, but he didn't want to be the one who said it. If he did, she'd probably start a rumor about him being unfriendly and throwing people out of his house.

Still, he'd dislike spending the rest of the evening with them both awkward and reluctant to be here. It might be rude, but he turned to her. "Do you even want to stay?"

"Not really."

For the first time since he'd met her, he appreciated her bluntness. He'd be equally honest. "The meal was great, but I don't think this was a good idea."

Cathy nodded. Then her expression changed. "If I leave, how will I learn about your mistakes?"

"You can make your own." After all, he had.

"I don't want to do that." She appeared almost

humble. "Would you tell me a few of the worst things you did?"

How could he resist such a heartfelt plea?

After washing and drying her dessert plate, he motioned her to the living room. He dreaded baring his soul.

God, help me to give advice she can use. And give me the courage to be honest.

He sank into the chair opposite the one she'd chosen. "My most important piece of advice is never leave little ones alone." Myron squeezed his eyes shut. An ache expanded in his chest and crushed his lungs until it choked off his breath.

He croaked out, "I know that's not the Amish way. We're supposed to trust God's will." He forced himself to explain. "Tim was seven and Ivy was two. I let them play in the backyard together alone. He came in the house to ask for a snack. By the time I fixed one and he took it outside, Ivy was gone."

Cathy sucked in a breath. "I remember that. I'm sorry."

Surprised, he opened his eyes. She appeared close to tears. He hadn't expected her to be that compassionate.

"It happened about ten years ago. We never found her. I haven't stopped looking."

"I didn't mean to make you relive such painful memories."

"If you want to hear mistakes, they'll be painful." None of his other stories would be that gut-wrenching, though.

"I'm sorry."

"The rest won't be as bad." He flapped a hand as if to make light of them. At least not the ones he'd be telling her. But he'd made some terrible decisions that had destroyed other lives.

As Myron mulled over what he'd share with Cathy, incidents blazed before his eyes. Times when he'd made light of things. Times when he'd criticized instead of empathizing, scolded instead of apologizing, punished instead of listening. Times when he'd squashed dreams . . .

Rather than pushing him to continue, Cathy stared at him with sympathy. Her understanding expression encouraged him to continue.

"Before that . . ." Myron swallowed hard. "Tim had been quiet, withdrawn, and sad. He missed his *daed*, so he poured all his love into Ivy. Afterward, he raged at me, blamed me for his sister's disappearance."

Cathy whispered something Myron didn't quite catch. It sounded like *Poor boy*. He wasn't sure he'd heard right.

"That's when I made the next biggest mistake of my life. I wanted to shut down the accusations, the temper tantrums, the uncontrollable sobbing. I—I forbade Tim to say Ivy's name. After that we never talked about her."

Myron kept his head lowered. He didn't want to see the judgment on Cathy's face.

"I hoped it would help him forget. I kept searching for her but never let him know. His resentment built and turned into rebellion. I suspect everything he's done since then is to get back at me, to make me pay."

Cathy's eyes brimmed with tears. "I wish I'd never asked you to do this. Relieving the past can be agonizing."

That was for sure. Recounting all this ripped Myron to shreds inside. He tried not to let it show, but Cathy seemed to pick up on his distress.

"I think I've bothered you enough. Guess I'll just follow my nephew's advice. Give them lots of love and prayers plus good meals."

If only someone had given Myron that advice when Tim was little. "I wish I'd prayed more, especially when the kids were younger. Most of the time I was too overwhelmed to remember to take problems to the Lord. As for love, I had plenty bottled up inside. Not sure it showed on the outside."

Cathy bit her lip. "I'm like that too. I'm no good at expressing love."

"You can learn." Despite her abrasive manner, he could tell she had a caring heart. The things she'd done tonight—making him a special meal, listening to him without judgment, even wanting to be a good caretaker for the boys—all showed she could give love.

She shook her head. "I'm not so sure I can."

"Pray about it, then try." He hung his head. "It's too late for me to show Tim love and affection. He'd think it was fake. Also, all through his childhood, I never did well with food or regular meals." Perhaps they could work on that when Tim returned. It might be a step in the right direction.

"I'm sure it's hard for a single *daed* to make meals."

No harder than for a widowed *mamm* like Esther. Myron wanted to lighten the mood. "Your grandnephews will have plenty of delicious meals. And all the donuts they can eat."

Cathy grimaced. "I guess." She stood. "I should be going. I didn't mean to make you dig up so many sad memories."

"It's been difficult, but confession's good for the soul." And dredging up the past helped him see events in a different light. After so many years had passed, his glaring errors stood out more clearly.

She stood and headed for the door. "I appreciate your honesty. Not many people would have shared their failings the way you did tonight."

Her eyes revealed she meant every word. Someone as blunt and forthright as Cathy valued the truth. A man would always know where he stood with her. Myron had to admire her for that.

He opened the door, and she stepped onto the porch.

"*Danke* for coming and for the meal." To his surprise, he didn't just say it to be polite. He meant both.

"And *danke* for your help. I promise not to trouble you again."

That final comment bothered Myron, but he couldn't explain why.

On the drive home, small squiggles of guilt curled through Cathy's conscience. Hearing the story from

Myron's point of view poked holes in tales she had been telling everyone for years. The facts—Ivy's disappearance and Tim's misbehavior—were true, but she'd been mistaken about Myron's carelessness and indifference. She'd painted him as a self-absorbed grouch who paid no attention to his nephew's terrible deeds. A man who'd made no effort to correct his adopted child because he'd given up on his responsibilities. From the pain in his eyes as he recounted the incidents, she had to admit her assumptions had been wrong. Totally wrong.

She owed Myron an apology. Cathy prided herself on her honesty, but what if she based the information she shared on flawed conclusions? What if she'd also gotten her stories about his breakup with his fiancée incorrect? Perhaps she should ask him about that and do what she could to fix the damage she'd done to his reputation.

The incident today at the market revealed how people could misinterpret something innocent. All the snide comments and nasty jabs she'd endured had proved how hurtful errors like that could be. And once the news began to circulate, it grew as others added juicy tidbits to it. She could only imagine what everyone would be saying when she returned to the market.

Cathy went to bed that night carrying an unbearable weight of guilt, and when she woke the next morning, it lay even heavier on her heart. She slogged through her morning chores and headed to the closed market with fresh towels and rags. While she was on hands and knees scrubbing, her mind kept replaying yesterday's collision with Myron.

Her *onkel* would have accused her of planning it. She could have thrown down towels earlier to prevent slipping. *Neh*, she defended herself to her irritated *onkel*. She'd been cleaning it all up. And she couldn't possibly have known Myron would sneak into her stall. *So there.*

Why did she keep trying to prove herself to her *onkel* when he was no longer here on earth? She carried him everywhere she went. Ever since yesterday, he'd been nagging at her to apologize to Myron for the false information she'd spread about his character.

"All right, all right. I'll do it," she yelled, and her words echoed back in the empty market. She longed to add, *Now leave me alone*, but she couldn't be disrespectful even to an imaginary relative.

When her stand was spotless, she gathered up the bag filled with dirty towels and headed home to wash them. With them on the line, she had to fulfill her promise about Myron. Since she'd broken with her parents and moved away from home, Cathy had never apologized to anyone. Every fiber of her being fought against doing it now.

Perhaps a meal could say *I'm sorry* for her. Myron had liked the strawberry shortcake, so he might enjoy her apple crumble. She could top it with extra whipped cream. Ice cream was tastier, but that would melt. Meatloaf and scalloped potatoes went well with an apple dessert. Most people complimented both of those dishes. With her green bean casserole, it made a well-rounded dinner.

Cathy started baking a little early and timed her cooking so she could reach Myron's house as he arrived home from work. Collecting information about everyone in the area meant she kept track of each person's regular departure and arrival times. That way, she noticed anything out of the ordinary. Those telling details often led to interesting stories—secret relationships, children defying house rules, new jobs, unusual friendships, doctor appointments, and so much more. She was always the first with the latest scoop.

When everything had finished baking, she wrapped it in towels and headed to Myron's. She reached his house before he did and pulled her buggy around back so nobody could see it from the street. No point in setting tongues wagging. They'd be totally wrong. She had one quick mission—force out an apology, hand over the food, and escape.

Sweat rolled down Myron's face as he guided his horse onto his street. Today had been an exhausting race to finish two last-minute jobs while coping with a barrage of customers, some of whom only stopped in to question him about Cathy. News traveled fast in the community and picked up plenty of sensational, but untrue, details.

People slyly hinted at courtships and weddings. Old friends called him a dark horse. Well-meaning ladies warned him of Cathy's fondness for gossip. Several heartbroken individuals recounted tales of how Cathy's rumors had broken up their relationships. If he heard Cathy's name one more time this week, he'd explode.

All he wanted to do was take a cool shower, turn on the battery-powered fan, and relax in his recliner with a book. He always preferred solitude, but today, even more than usual, he craved peace and quiet. With the farmer's market closed today, Abe had plans with Anna Mary all day. Myron couldn't help being grateful Tim wouldn't be around to disturb the serenity.

With a deep sense of relief, Myron turned his horse into the driveway. Before he reached the barn, movement behind the house drew him to a swift halt. He had company. The last thing he wanted.

He didn't recognize the buggy, but when he caught sight of the figure sitting on the back porch, his heart sank. *Ach, neh!*

His already low spirits plunged to the depths. How would he get rid of her? Had she come for more parenting advice? Or had she mistaken his holding her as a sign of interest? Even worse, did she believe he had to save her reputation by marrying her?

Neh, please God, *neh*.

She didn't approach him as he cared for his horse and moved the buggy into the barn. For that, he was grateful. It gave him time to mull over what to say, but when he emerged from the barn to find her placing food on the wicker table on his back porch, he lost his temper.

"What are you doing here? I didn't agree to meet again. I hoped by us staying apart the rumors would die down. You'll stir up more gossip."

He'd planned to storm past her and slam into the house, but her quivering lips stopped him. He'd only ever seen and heard of her defiance.

She bowed her head, and the humility of the gesture hit him hard.

"I'm sorry," he managed to say. "I had a bad day, but I shouldn't have taken it out on you." He pinched his mouth shut before adding, *Even though you have no business being here.*

"*Neh*, I'm the one who should apologize. I'm not good at it, so I brought this." She gestured to the assortment of delicious-looking dishes on the table. "But I didn't mean to be a burden." She scurried toward her buggy.

"Wait," he called after her. "Aren't you going to stay to eat?" If he ate her food after chasing her away, he'd be filled with guilt.

"I didn't plan to. That's to show I'm sorry. I can tell you why some other time."

"I'm not eating this alone." He might be making a mistake. But he couldn't let her leave. "It would be a shame for it all to go to waste."

"You can give it to someone, then. It's yours to do with as you please."

"That's not what I meant."

Some of her usual spunk returned. She spun around

and planted her hands on her hips. "Then what did you mean?"

Why was it so hard to say the simple words? Reluctantly, he pushed out an invitation. "Why don't you, um, stay and have some too?"

No doubt he'd end up regretting it, but he couldn't let his temper and cruel words send another woman away upset. Upset enough to have an accident. He already had one blot on his conscience.

CHAPTER 8

Cathy hesitated. Myron didn't sound as if he meant his invitation. Besides, if she confessed her guilt, she didn't want to stay around. Plus, with the way her insides were heaving, she'd never be able to eat.

"It's too much food for one person," he pointed out.

Was he criticizing her again? That's what you got for trying to do something nice for someone. She stuck her nose in the air. "You can eat the leftovers another day."

He must have sensed her annoyance because he changed his tone. "Please?" The word itself wasn't exactly gracious. But since she wasn't known for her gentleness or tact, she had no call to criticize.

"All right." Her agreement sounded a bit surly. She'd come to apologize but instead seemed to be fixing for an argument. "You don't have to share, you know."

"I know." When he didn't add *I want to*, her opinion of him rose. She liked that he didn't add the polite nothing. Yesterday, she'd also noted his honesty.

He waited while she scooted a rocker closer to the

table. She despised men who coddled women. Perhaps he'd sensed it and was letting her keep her independence. Or, more likely, it had never occurred to him to be chivalrous.

She plopped down across from him. Once they'd prayed, he served himself, but waited until she'd taken a small portion of everything to begin eating.

The enjoyment on his face as he savored the meal warmed Cathy inside. She decided to wait to give her apology. No point in spoiling his appetite. They ate in appreciative silence, both watching the birds swoop and dip in the backyard with a freedom Cathy envied.

After Myron finished his second helping of apple crisp, it was now or never.

Cathy cleared her throat. "The meal was meant as an apology."

Myron smiled and patted his stomach. "Apology accepted." His brows scrunched. "But for what?"

She focused on her hands clenched in her lap. "After you told me about what happened when Tim first came here, I realized that I lied when I told people those stories."

Across from her, Myron shifted uncomfortably in his chair. "It's so long ago, it doesn't matter anymore."

"But things I said about your character weren't true."

"They might be closer to the truth than you know."

"I-I'm sorry for everything I said that damaged your reputation. I want to find a way to make it right."

"Don't bother. Most likely, it'll just stir up different rumors. Best to leave it alone."

"But I made so many wrong assumptions about you and about the situation. I pride myself on telling people facts, but I colored them and added my own interpretations."

"Look, Cathy . . ." Myron leaned across the small table, forcing her to look up. "I said drop it, and I mean that."

"But . . ."

"Talking to you last night was painful. I don't want to relive it. Not even a cleaned-up version. It'll rip open all the old wounds."

When she started to answer, he held up his hand. "Do me a favor. Use it as a lesson for the future. Before you share people's private information, even if it's true, think about how it might hurt them and others."

His request brought her up short. "I see now that adding my interpretation is wrong," she said with a humbleness that surprised Myron. "But how can knowing the truth possibly hurt anyone? It'll help them be prepared. It may prevent something bad from happening."

"Sounds like you wish someone had told the truth about something in your life." Myron pinned her with a searching gaze.

Bile rose in her throat and choked her. She lowered her head to avoid Myron's scrutiny. He'd never know how desperately she'd wanted the truth to come out. Since then, she'd made it her mission to expose facts, especially those that were being concealed, to prevent others from being hurt or blindsided.

His voice softened. "Was there a time when the truth would have prevented something bad in your life?"

Cathy jumped to her feet, setting the chair rocking violently. Then, slapping a hand over her mouth to prevent herself from losing the food she'd just eaten, she raced to her buggy.

"What's wrong?" Myron leapt up to follow her.

She threw out a hand, urging him to let her be. Before he could reach her, she unlooped her reins, climbed into the buggy, and hightailed it down the driveway.

Distressed, Myron stared after her. What had he said to cause such an unexpected reaction? Should he go after her to be sure she made it home safely?

Once before, he'd made the mistake of letting someone take off in a state like that. Myron rose from his chair and hurried toward the barn. As he opened the door, Tim's horse clomped up the driveway.

"Abe?" Myron waved for him to stop. "I need to use this buggy now. If you have to go out, you can take mine. Also, eat whatever you want on the table there." He waved toward the porch. "Please put the leftovers away. I'm in a hurry."

"Is it an emergency?" Abe stared at him in alarm. "Can I drive you somewhere?"

"It's not that kind of emergency. And I need to go alone."

Abe hopped to the ground. "Drive carefully."

"I will. *Danke.*" Abe jumped out of the way as Myron turned the buggy and flicked the lines to encourage the horse into a trot.

With an ironic laugh, Myron wondered if people seeing the buggy racing down the road would assume Tim had returned. He hoped they wouldn't look closely enough to recognize him speeding through town. He'd start even more rumors if they discovered he was chasing Cathy.

Maybe he was an old fool, but she'd been distraught. He had to be sure she made it home.

He made it almost to her house before he spotted her. She'd slowed to a safe speed, so he followed her at that pace. When she pulled into her driveway, he did too.

"What are you doing?" she yelled as she eased out of the buggy, her face creased in lines of distress.

"I wanted to be sure you're all right. What's the matter?"

"None of your business." Looking sick, she tied her horse to a post.

"Was it something I said?"

"It's not your fault. You didn't do anything wrong." She stalked to the house, bent over, clutching her middle.

"Do you need a doctor?"

"*Neh.* Just leave me alone." She went inside and slammed the door behind her.

Myron stood, uncertain, torn between knocking on the door or leaving. She didn't want him to bother her, but he didn't feel right taking off when she appeared so troubled or ill. With the way she'd looked, he doubted she'd be going out again tonight. Before he left, he unhitched her horse, cared for it, and pulled her buggy inside. Then he drove home slowly, wondering what he'd said to set her off like that.

The shooting pains in her head and stomach had become unbearable, so Cathy kicked off her shoes and curled up on the couch. If only she hadn't taken supper to Myron. She'd made a mess of things. First, her apology had gone wrong. Then, he'd pointed out how she'd hurt other people by telling the truth.

Over the years, she'd heard whispers and received nasty glares, but no one had ever confronted her directly the way Myron had. After his comment tonight about considering how her truthtelling might hurt people and the false gossip following her collision with Myron this afternoon, she'd been smacked in the face twice with her *hochmut*. She'd always prided herself on doing her duty, keeping people informed. She'd never thought about how passing along stories could hurt or destroy others. Now that she'd been the victim of a runaway rumor and realized the damage she'd done to Myron's reputation by misrepresenting his past actions, her insides flipped over.

All along, she'd convinced herself exposing everyone else's faults or telling them devastating truths was for their good, but had she been selfish? Had she been sharing that information to help them or to distract from her own failings? If she focused on other people's wrongs, nobody could shine a light on the darkness in her own life.

Even worse, his final question had ripped open a festering wound, exposing her own hidden suffering. She'd never be able to tell Myron, but he'd been right—*jah*, there had been a time in her life when the truth would have prevented something bad, something cruel, something evil. Instead, the deceit had destroyed her.

From that time on, she believed so strongly in her need to reveal liars and cheats because she wished someone had done that years ago to protect her from a lifetime of agony.

Cathy forced herself up from the couch. Lying around wallowing in self-pity and dwelling on long-ago miseries wouldn't get the work done. Though her head ached with years' worth of unshed tears and her stomach churned with the ugliness of the past, she had to take care of her horse.

When she reached the door, she panicked. Her horse and buggy were gone. Had she forgotten to tie— *Neh*, she'd used the post right there. Her stable door was shut. Hadn't she left it open? She sprinted over and yanked on it. Her horse had water and was nibbling on the last of his feed.

Then the dam broke, and tears she'd been holding in forever poured down her cheeks. That one small kindness released oceans of pain.

Cathy had no idea how long she'd been bawling, but at the sound of her neighbor's car growling into their driveway, she came to an abrupt stop. Sniffling and rubbing her eyes, she tried to regain her composure.

Barb bounced out of the car and waved to her. "Hey, Cathy, how's everything going?"

As she waved back, Cathy hoped the distance between them would prevent her neighbor from seeing her swollen eyes. Then she turned and busied herself with her horse, hoping Barb wouldn't come over for a chat. To Cathy's relief, Barb picked up her grocery bags and went into the house.

Inhaling in relief, Cathy shut the stable door and hurried into her own house. She couldn't get over Myron's thoughtfulness, especially after she'd rushed away from his house and then been so rude when he'd checked on her. It made her ashamed of all the critical stories she'd told about him over the years. How many other people's reputations had she damaged?

She'd started getting ready for bed when someone knocked on the front door. Cathy debated ignoring it. She continued splashing cold water on her face and eyes, but the rapping came again, louder and more insistent.

With a sigh, she dried her face and headed downstairs. Barb stood on the porch.

"I left my phone at home when I ran out for groceries earlier and didn't check it right away when I returned, so I just got this message from your nephew." She pushed play, and Wayne's voice filled the room.

"Barb, can you let my *aenti* know I'll be leaving sooner than expected? A passenger canceled for Friday on Melard's Mexico Connections bus. They gave me the spot. I'll be bringing the boys with me to Ephrata, and I've arranged for the driver to bring them to her place after he drops me off at five a.m. They should get there around six."

Anxiety overshadowed the joy at hearing her nephew's voice "*Ach!* They weren't supposed to be here for another week. I'm not ready yet. What am I going to do?"

Tucking her phone in her pocket, Barb gave Cathy a *calm-down* smile. "I can come over tomorrow to help you clean and prepare."

"But Thursdays and Fridays are our busiest days at the market."

"Can't you close your stand or find someone to take your place?"

"I've never closed in the twelve years I've worked there." The thought of not showing up horrified Cathy.

Barb studied her with compassion. "You work harder than anyone I know. People will understand if you take off for a family emergency. I've seen signs posted on stands with messages like that."

Once again, Cathy's *onkel* glared at her from the deep recesses of her mind. *Shirking your duties again?*

She shook her head. "I can't miss work."

"Cathy, people aren't going to die if they don't get donuts with their coffee. They'll understand."

If she could quiet her *onkel*'s voice, she might be able to make a better decision. One without his input.

Lord, please show me what to do.

Barb's infectious grin grew wider. "What about going in for half a day? Most people buy donuts in the morning, right? Then you can come back here, and we'll tackle the work together. I doubt there's much to do. After all, your house is always spotless."

Was that God's answer to her prayers? But Cathy couldn't let someone else do jobs she was supposed to do.

"How will I ever pay you back?" She'd have her nephews for two months. She wouldn't have time to do chores at Barb's.

"Haven't you learned yet, you don't have to pay back every kindness?" Barb laughed, but not in a snarky way. "Besides, you've given my children plenty of donuts over the years. We all appreciate that."

"This will take a lot more of your time than a few leftover donuts."

"Tell you what. How about you bake one of your delicious cakes for Annie's fifth birthday next month?" Barb reached out and squeezed Cathy's arm.

Cathy tried not to recoil. She disliked people touching her. "I'd be happy to do that, but it won't be enough."

"Then pass on the favor to someone else." Barb laughed. "Actually, you already are. You're taking care of your nephew's children. See how kindness goes full circle?"

Although Cathy struggled to view it the same way, she understood Barb's point. Part of her would feel guilty until she'd repaid Barb. And Myron. *Ach*, how would she ever repay him? Another meal?

Barb broke into Cathy's worries. "Relax—you don't have to repay everyone who does something for you. Don't you get joy from helping others? You don't expect them to give you something in return."

That was true. If only she could let go of her *onkel*'s directives and relax like Barb said. Taking a deep breath, she decided to try it for once in her life. "I'll close the stand tomorrow afternoon. And I'd appreciate the help."

So there, Onkel. Cathy might not get out from under the load of guilt he'd pile on when she skipped a half day of work tomorrow, but Barb's plan made *gut* sense.

Chapter 9

Myron hadn't anticipated putting Jed in charge of the woodworking shop so soon, but all morning long, he'd worried about Cathy. Her abrupt departure last night and the sick look on her face had haunted his dreams. Maybe he should have stayed around to be sure she was all right. He couldn't tell if her reaction had been physical or emotional, but either way, she'd needed help. Help she was reluctant to accept.

He had to reassure himself she'd recovered. "Listen, Jed, I'm going to run an errand at lunchtime today, so you can have your turn to be the boss."

Both apprentices gaped at him.

"You need me for a delivery?" Lloyd asked.

"Not this time. It's a different type of errand."

Lloyd and Jed exchanged concerned glances.

"Don't worry. Nothing's wrong. I just need to check on something." *Someone* would be more accurate, but if he said that, he'd let himself in for all kinds of questions and wild guesses. Jed had been with him when

Cathy slid into him at the market. Better not to start rumors.

After his employees finished their lunch, Myron helped with a sudden rush of customers. Once things slowed down, he smiled at Jed. "Your turn to handle things. If anything comes up you don't have an answer for, tell people I'll be back in an hour."

Jed beamed as Myron headed off. Myron should have done this before. His apprentices should learn how to deal with the shop in case he ever needed to take time off. Not that he planned to, but it was good practice.

He pulled into the busy market. He'd run in and grab a quick lunch at Hartzler's Chicken Barbecue. On his way inside, he'd just peek over to be sure Cathy looked all right. No need to let her know he'd come.

But as soon as he pushed open the doors to enter, he froze. The *Dough-Re-Mi* sign swung forlornly over empty bakery shelves. A huge *CLOSED* banner plastered the glass cases.

She must have been sick last night, and she was still under the weather. As far as he knew, she had no family in the area, and she had no Amish neighbors, so nobody in the community would know she'd gotten ill. Who would look in on her?

He stood there, shifting from foot to foot. Running to her house would take too long. He couldn't leave Jed and Lloyd alone for more than an hour.

The jaunty *tap-tap* of a cane alerted Myron to Mrs. Vandenberg's approach before she touched his arm.

"You're worried about her, aren't you? No need to

be. Someone's with her today, but she'll really need your help tomorrow."

"I have to work." He couldn't take a full day off. "I'm sure someone from her *g'may* would be happy to take care of her."

"It's *your* help she needs." Mrs. Vandenberg's bright smile made Myron feel trapped. "You may not know it, but you did a lot for her last night."

"What did I do last ni—?" He broke off and stared at the elderly woman. How did she know about it? Had rumors been floating around the market today?

He ran a finger around his too-tight collar while his neck burned. Who else knew? What would people think about him being at her place last night after their compromising position in this stand on Tuesday?

Mrs. Vandenberg patted his arm. "Don't worry. Nobody else knows. Your secret is safe with me."

Could she read his mind? He gulped. What did she mean by *your secret*?

This was the second time she'd tried to throw him and Cathy together. Had she gotten the wrong idea? Some of that was his fault for stopping here in the middle of the day. She'd assured him she didn't think he and Cathy were meant to be a couple, hadn't she? What if she'd changed her mind?

"Will you stop by to check on her tomorrow?"

"Only because you asked." That wasn't entirely true. He'd been planning to as soon as he saw the *CLOSED* sign.

She patted his arm. "I'm so glad I can count on you.

And you might be surprised how much it'll help you. Thank the Lord for second chances."

She hobbled off, and Myron scrambled for the door without getting lunch. The fewer people who saw him staring at Cathy's stand, the better, especially with Mrs. Vandenberg at his side.

Guilt had nagged at Cathy as she'd hung a closed sign on her stand before lunch. With the boys arriving in the morning, she'd have to keep her stand closed tomorrow too. Although she tried to ignore it, her *onkel*'s voice tormented her the whole way home. *Lazy. Selfish. Shirking your duties. Ignoring your customers. Not taking responsibility.* All his criticisms replayed on a loop in the back of her mind.

"Stop it," she yelled to her nonexistent tormentor. "I am doing my duty. I need to take care of two children."

The driver of a car passing her stared at her in shock. Could he hear what she was saying? Or did he think she was *narrish* for shouting at nobody?

As soon as Cathy pulled into the driveway, Barb darted across the lawn, carrying a bucket of cleaning supplies and a small cooler. Her cheery expression had to be fake. Cathy distrusted people who always appeared upbeat. She couldn't believe anyone would be this overjoyed to help someone else clean.

"Need help taking care of the horse?" Barb asked.

"I can do it myself." Cathy cringed inside. She sounded like her five-year-old self. The little girl who tried to assert her independence, but messed it all up, which had ended with punishment.

Barb only laughed. "I know you can. You're so competent at everything. I admire that about you."

It bugged Cathy when people tried to flatter others. *Competent at everything?* That was ridiculous. Cathy couldn't think of one thing she did well. Perhaps cooking? Most of the time.

Irritated, Cathy rushed through her barn chores and put away the buggy. Deep inside, though, she had to admit she wasn't annoyed at Barb, but at herself. A needy part of her liked Barb's compliments and longed for more. But that was *hochmut*.

They walked to the house together in companionable silence. Normally, Cathy would fill any gaps in conversation with tidbits about the neighbors, but Myron's words about hurting people kept coming back to her. She'd been mistaken about him. Suppose she spilled the information about that pretty young woman going into Mr. Garvey's house down the street while his wife was gone, and it turned out to be a relative or a home health aide?

Cathy gritted her teeth. If she examined everything before she shared it, she'd have nothing to say to people. It might give others a chance to pry into her life. And that would be dangerous.

Her prediction proved to be true as soon as she and Barb settled at the kitchen table with the lunch her neighbor had brought. Cathy had protested she should make the meal because Barb was doing her a favor, but Barb only laughed.

"I already have it made, and tuna sandwiches won't keep long. They'll get too soggy."

But the lovely lunch came with a price.

"So," Barb said as soon as they'd eaten a few bites, "what's this I hear about you having a suitor?"

Cathy almost choked on her sandwich. "What gave you that idea?"

"I ran into Irene from the farmer's market, and she mentioned you were the hottest topic on Tuesday. Something about a man pulling you into his arms."

"Don't believe everything you hear."

"Well, I might have discounted it because I couldn't see you accepting a man's advances, but then as I was backing out of my driveway to get groceries yesterday, I saw your buggy rushing in, with him following."

How would Cathy explain an Amish man chasing her home? "He saw me feeling sick yesterday, and he was worried."

"So worried he followed you home? And tended to your horse?"

Cathy had never considered Barb a snoopy neighbor. "Have you been keeping an eye on me?" she snapped crossly.

"Couldn't help seeing you coming in with another buggy right on your tail. I checked to be sure you weren't being chased by a bad guy."

"In a buggy?"

Barb shrugged. "You never know nowadays." Her

eyes twinkled. "But when I saw the handsome gentleman get out to speak to you, I minded my own business."

Handsome gentleman? Myron? Grudgingly, Cathy had to admit she'd thought so herself when he smiled or leaned back with an expression of bliss after eating her cooking.

"But I must say, when I got back home and saw him tending your horse and putting away your buggy, well . . ." Barb nudged Cathy. "That man's a keeper."

Cathy should be grateful for her caring neighbor, but the talk of Myron irked her. And the fact that Barb had seen him coming and going made Cathy even more uncomfortable. Plus, Barb had heard the rumors from the market. How many people had passed that embarrassing falsehood around?

The whole conversation left Cathy anxious and edgy. It replayed in her mind after she and Barb had divided up the cleaning and each of them had started working in different areas of the house. Cathy regretted not sharing the news about Mr. Garvey. If she had, they'd have discussed him at lunch instead of Cathy and Myron's alleged relationship.

Despite her snoopiness, Barb was a big help. They cleaned the house from top to bottom and set up the bedroom across the hall from Cathy's with two twin beds so the boys could be together. After Barb went home, Cathy baked cookies and granola bars, sliced fruit and vegetables, popped popcorn, and made trail mix. Everything was ready. Everything except her. She was totally unprepared.

Talking with Myron had made her see her own faults more clearly. She'd never be a fit parent. As much as she'd loved the boys when they'd visited, she'd been grateful to leave their care to their parents. Now she'd be responsible for every decision. How would she do it?

Lord, help me, she begged over and over throughout her sleepless night. And she rose at her usual time with dread sloshing in her stomach. This was going to be a disaster.

Before he left for work, Myron gave himself a pep talk. All he had to do was stop in after closing to see how she was. He didn't have to stay. She was probably fine by now.

But what excuse could he make for stopping at her house? *Her casserole dishes*. He could return them. That would work. Just hand them over and go. If she had a cold or something, he could offer to stop at Glick's Natural Products for an herbal remedy. With any luck, she wouldn't need anything.

He smiled to himself. Last night, Abe had brought some soups and other home-canned goods from Anna Mary as a thank-you for the donuts and for talking to her *mamm*. Perhaps Myron could take a jar of chicken corn soup along. That would be a nice way to pay her back for the two meals she'd made.

Quickly, he wrapped the remaining meatloaf in foil

and put the leftover potatoes and green beans into small baking pans so he could warm them after he got home. He also wrapped up the last few slices of the strawberry shortcake and apple crumble. As he scrubbed out the empty dishes, an idea came to him. He had some of Tim's old toys in the attic. Maybe Cathy's grandnephews would enjoy playing with them.

A short while later, he staggered down the stairs with two large cartons. He'd found a train set, trucks and cars, blocks, a tin of crayons, sidewalk chalk, puzzles, a few stuffed animals, and an assortment of balls for every sport imaginable. He loaded them into the buggy with Cathy's dishes and the soup.

All day long, he was antsy, wishing for the day to be over so he could get this obligation to Cathy out of the way. Yet, as soon as he sat in his buggy at the end of the day, the last place he wanted to head was her house.

Lord, please help me to get into the spirit of giving.

Praying strengthened his resolve, and he flicked the reins. He arrived at Cathy's much sooner than he'd expected. As he reached the porch with his arms full, pounding and yowling came from inside. Cathy? *Neh*, it sounded more like a temper tantrum.

Fighting the urge to flee, he set down the boxes and knocked loudly enough to be heard over the din. The noise stopped. Cathy opened the door, her *kapp* askew, her apron covered in flour, and her eyes desperate. Behind her, two boys stared out excitedly.

"Daed," one yelled joyfully. Then his face fell. "It's not Daed."

As his face screwed up into a howl, Myron pointed

to the boxes. "Here's a present for each of you." With his toe, he nudged a box closer to the almost-crying boy.

"What about me?" The other one charged over.

"You can open this one." Myron pushed it in his direction. "But you have to share."

While the boys dug into the boxes, Myron handed over Cathy's dishes and the soup.

"What's this?" she asked suspiciously as she took the jar.

"Chicken corn soup. You probably make it better, but I thought you might be sick and . . ." Embarrassed, he trailed off. Other than the stress on her face and her disheveled clothes, she looked the picture of health.

"Sick?" Her cheeks flushed a pretty rosy shade. "You mean the other night? That wasn't—" She looked away.

So she'd been upset, not ill. *Gut.* Relieved he'd done his duty, Myron backed up, ready to take his leave. He'd checked on her, the toys had quieted the boys, and all was well. He could breathe easier until . . .

She glanced up at him with pleading eyes. "Would you like to come in? I have chicken with gravy in the oven and cinnamon rolls for dessert. It's just about done. I thought the boys might like to make something, but even kneading and rolling out dough didn't help much." She sounded close to tears. "This is the first time they've been quiet since they got here this morning."

Myron longed to escape, but Cathy appeared so distraught, he didn't have the heart to refuse. "They must be missing their *daed*."

"How did you guess?" Her words held a touch of sarcasm.

He ignored her snarky tone. It hadn't been hard to figure out, even by someone as unskilled in parenting as he was. The boys had been excited to answer the door and disappointed not to see their father.

She led him into the kitchen and nodded toward a chair. "*Danke* for the peace. I thought they'd never stop crying."

"I know what it's like." He'd endured endless days and nights while Tim had sobbed for his *daed*. Myron's helplessness during those times flooded back. Forbidding Tim to cry hadn't worked. Distracting him did little to stop his bawling. Myron had been frantic to find anything to comfort his nephew. Cathy must be experiencing the same thing.

"Why don't I take the boys into the yard to play ball? Maybe it will take their minds off their *daed*."

"Oh, would you?" She sounded like a drowning woman being thrown a life preserver.

Myron headed into the living room to find the boys engrossed in hooking train cars together and assembling the tracks. Might be best to leave them to their play. He slipped out without them noticing him.

"They're having fun, so I didn't want to disturb them."

She nodded. "You'll stay for supper?"

He had meatloaf waiting for him at home, but the tantalizing aromas of cinnamon rolls and crisping chicken skin made it hard to resist her offer. "For a short while. Can I help with anything?"

Cathy shook her head. "I work better alone." She motioned for him to sit again, then she bustled around the kitchen preparing noodles and peas.

Myron debated whether or not to bring up work, but the closed sign at the market made him curious. "Will you keep your stand closed while they're here?"

Her head shot up. "I hadn't even thought about that. My stand is too small for all three of us, and crying boys will drive away customers." She set both pans on the stove and adjusted the burners.

"True. People will miss your donuts, but family comes first."

"What am I going to do?" She pressed a hand to her forehead and sank into a chair. "I can't afford to close. How will I pay my stand rent and all my other bills?"

This must be the help Mrs. Vandenberg meant for him to give. An idea occurred to him. "I could take them to my shop tomorrow so you can work. I set up a playroom in the back for Tim and"—Myron swallowed down the lump blocking his throat—"Ivy."

A sharp pain shot through him at the memories. Tim cuddling Ivy close as tears ran down their faces. Both of them with forlorn eyes clinging to ratty teddy bears. Tim sounding out words to read stories to Ivy. He'd always struggled with reading.

Cathy brushed her hands together and stood. "I couldn't do that. Taking care of the boys is my responsibility." She set a pan of butter on the stove to brown.

"It's not a problem. It's a safe area, and they won't interfere with the work."

Unlike Tim, these boys might even be interested in

learning woodworking. Myron didn't mention that to Cathy, because it might worry her.

"I also have a fenced-in yard behind the shop where Tim played ball. It even has a basketball hoop." It had been years since Tim used it. Myron might need to replace the hoop, but that wouldn't take long.

She looked hesitant. "*Nehhh.*"

"It would be nice to hear children's voices in that room again."

With a quick head shake, she snapped off the burners and drained the noodles.

What was he thinking? His parenting had been a major failure.

"Never mind. I shouldn't have offered. I can see why you wouldn't trust me. I made so many mistakes raising Tim." His next words came out strangled. "And . . . losing . . . Ivy . . ." He couldn't go on.

Cathy sucked in a breath. "It's not that. I can't let other people do my job."

Myron recalled Mrs. Vandenberg's words. Maybe God had given him this opportunity to make amends. "It might be a chance to correct my past wrongs."

"If only it was that easy."

He winced, unsure if Cathy's tart remark was a jab at him or referred to her own life.

"Supper," she called as she ladled food into bowls.

When the boys didn't respond, Myron went after them. They each clutched a stuffed animal. The oldest, with red-rimmed eyes, hugged Tim's teddy bear. His younger brother sucked on the matted ear of Ivy's rabbit. Tim had slept with that bunny and his bear until he turned ten.

Myron started to herd the boys into the kitchen, but Cathy stood in the doorway.

"No filthy toys at the table." She pointed to the boxes he'd brought. "Leave them in there."

Her sharp command echoed the orders he used to snap at Tim. Myron cringed inside as the boys' lower lips wobbled. They looked ready to burst into tears.

"Could they put them on the chairs next to them while they eat?" Myron sent her a placating glance over the boys' heads. "It might make it a little easier for them."

Her lips thinned into a tight line. She obviously didn't like being told what to do. After a moment, she said in a clipped voice, "Fine." Then she whirled around and marched back into the kitchen. "But they'll be washed before bed."

Their eyes bright with unshed tears, the boys hugged the stuffed animals tight and gave Myron tentative smiles. He put an arm around each of their shoulders and ushered them to the table. He made sure the animals stayed hidden from Cathy's view but remained close enough for the boys to touch. It seemed to comfort them a little.

Cathy's delicious meal helped as well. The boys shoveled in forkfuls of brown butter noodles, chicken with gravy, and peas. But as Cathy got up to serve dessert, a downcast look crossed the older boy's face.

"Why can't we go with Daed? The bus has bunk beds."

"*Jah*, it does, but only twelve of them." Several of

Myron's friends had gone on that bus for dental or medical treatments.

"That's lots of beds."

"Not for twenty-four people," he explained. "They take turns sleeping."

"We know how to take turns."

"That's enough, David." Cathy's no-nonsense tone signaled an end to that conversation. "Your *daed* is going to a clinic. It's no place for children. Now eat your dessert."

David's eyes brimmed with tears. So did his brother's.

Myron couldn't blame Cathy. He'd done the same with Tim, and he'd even told Anna Mary not to coddle her *mamm* just a few days ago. But for some reason, cutting off the boys' questions seemed like it would lead to greater problems than talking it out. Or maybe he was growing too soft.

After weighing whether or not to rouse Cathy's wrath, he stayed silent.

Chapter 10

Cathy rose an hour earlier than usual, exhausted. Last night, the boys had refused to go to bed, and when she'd insisted, they'd cried for hours and begged for their *daed*. Finally, long after her usual bedtime, John fell asleep mid-cry. David continued *brutzing* for another forty minutes before he, too, tired himself out. By that time, her whole body ached as if she'd been battered around on a storm-tossed boat. The few hours of restless sleep she'd gotten hadn't helped. If anything, she was more tired this morning than she had been last night.

She dragged herself downstairs to prepare the dough. Usually, she did the batches of yeast dough and let them rise on the way to the market, where she'd start a batch frying while she prepped the cake donuts. But she couldn't wake the boys at five and drop them at Myron's. That wouldn't be fair to him—or to them.

She was uneasy about letting him watch the boys. They were her responsibility, and it bothered her to let someone else take care of them. After today, she'd figure out a better schedule. Near the end of the month,

John would start school here for six weeks. Then both boys would go back home as soon as Wayne was ready for them.

A calendar hung on her wall. Cathy went over and crossed off yesterday. One day down. Sixty more to go. Thinking about that number overwhelmed her, so she pushed it from her mind and set to work.

She fried some donuts on her stove but could only do small batches. At this rate, she'd have to get up at two in the morning. This plan wasn't working. She needed her fryers at the market. As much as she dreaded doing it, she'd have to wake the boys. Otherwise, she'd never be ready to open her stand.

First, though, she hitched up her horse and loaded everything into the buggy, leaving two donuts each for the boys. Maybe some sugar would sweeten their dispositions. Last night, before bed, she'd made overnight oatmeal along with lunch and dinner for Myron and the boys. She slid those into a cooler and carried it outside. Then, much as she wished she didn't have to, she had no excuse not to get the boys out of bed.

When she opened their door, her heart expanded. Two little angels lay in their beds, each cuddling a freshly washed stuffed animal. Despite the chorus of howls, Cathy had insisted on sterilizing the toys and laundering all the stuffed animals yesterday after Myron left. The boys' shrieks had pierced her eardrums when she'd hung the stuffed bear and rabbit on the clothesline by their ears. You'd have thought the animals were real from the way David and John had carried on. Wincing at the memory, Cathy steeled herself to face the inevitable bawling.

Putting on her best imitation of a cheerful voice, she entered the room. "Time to get up. We have donuts down in the kitchen."

David groaned and batted her hand away when she shook him. John only whimpered and huddled deeper into his covers.

Cathy had to drop them off at Myron's and head to the market. Usually, she'd already have the display case partially filled by now. She was so far behind. They had no time to waste.

She picked up David to set him on his feet. He squealed.

John shot out of his bed. "You leave my brother alone. Stop hurting him." He pulled on Cathy's arms to free his brother.

"Stop it," she shouted, lifting David higher into the air, where John couldn't reach him.

David wailed louder, kicking and flailing. One kick landed on Cathy's stomach. She doubled over and almost dropped the wriggling boy. She managed to lower him to the floor and back away from both boys.

With as much dignity as she could muster, she barked out an ultimatum. "Enough of this nonsense. Get your clothes on and get downstairs to the table now."

She sailed to the door, but cast a quick backward look to see if they obeyed.

They were both staring after her with fearful eyes. At least they'd stopped crying. John went over and put an arm around David.

"Maybe if we get dressed, she'll take us back to Daed."

David brightened and hurried over to the chair where Cathy had laid out their clothes last night. "I can't do this up."

She almost turned around and offered, but John went over to help his brother.

They'd be sorely disappointed when they found out they weren't going to see their *daed*, but temporary peace reigned. With a sigh of relief for a brief lull in the bawling, Cathy headed downstairs.

The boys padded into the kitchen a short while later. To save time, she handed them their donuts to eat in the buggy. They both followed her outside, meek and cooperative, but exchanging secretive smiles.

Cathy's usual honesty demanded she tell them the truth about this trip, but her wearied spirit couldn't face the tantrums. They both crawled into the back seat, and John slipped an arm around David. For one of the first times since they'd come, both boys stayed quiet as they munched on their donuts.

They frowned when Cathy pulled into Myron's driveway. In the yard next door, an Amish teen hung laundry on the line while a younger girl fed the chickens and another picked beans in the garden. A boy carried produce out to a small roadside stand. Like most Amish children, they went about their chores without fussing. If only her nephews would act like that.

"Why are we stopping here?" John's voice held irritation.

Myron stepped out of the house and waved.

"That's Myron. You'll be spending the day with him."

"What?" David shrieked. "I thought we were going to the bus."

Cathy had no time or patience to deal with drama. "You thought wrong. Myron will take you to his woodworking shop for the day." She hopped out, tied the horse to a post, opened the passenger door, and pulled the seat forward so they could get out.

Both of them dissolved into tears.

"I want Daed," John screamed as he kicked at Cathy's outstretched hands.

She jerked back out of range. "I have never seen Amish children behave this way."

"Let me," Myron said, stepping close to the door.

When she moved away, he swooped in, avoiding the kicking feet, and picked John up around the waist. Holding him out in the air far from his body, he deposited the small boy on the grass beside the driveway. John collapsed into a sobbing heap as Myron bent to get David, who'd plastered himself against the side wall. But the buggy was small enough Myron had an easy reach.

Rather than kicking, David turned pale and went rigid. Fear and uncertainty swam in his eyes along with his tears. Cathy's heart went out to him. She'd experienced those sensations many times as a child. As Myron set David down beside his weeping brother, tears trickled down both their cheeks.

The teen girl next door came running over. "*Ach*, are they all right? I'm Abby. Can I help?"

Before Cathy could tell the girl nothing would help with these two, Abby sank onto the grass beside the boys. She lifted David onto her lap and stroked his hair. He leaned into her.

"What's wrong?" she whispered. Then she reached out an arm and pulled John close. "Are you hurt?"

John shook his head. "Our *daed*'s going to Mexico, and we want to go with him."

"I miss him." David sniffled.

Abby hugged them. "That must be so hard. Is he going for treatments?"

John blinked and fought back tears. "*Jah*, he has cancer."

"So, you're worried about him?"

Both boys nodded vigorously.

"We want our *daed*." David's voice wavered. He sniffed and wiped his nose on his short sleeve.

"You don't like to be away from him, do you? And it's scary not knowing what's happening to him."

They stared up at her with wet eyes. "*Jah*."

"You want to be with him."

John nodded. "And we miss our house and our *mamm*."

"Your *mamm*'s not with you?"

"She died." Although David stated it flatly, his lower lip trembled.

Abby's eyes filled with sympathy. "So, you're missing your *mamm* and your *daed* and your house? I see why you've been crying." She pulled them both closer. "That's a lot to deal with all at once."

David reached up and twined his arms around her neck. “You’re nice.”

“You know,” Abby said, giving them both serious looks, “there’s one thing you can do to help your *daed*.”

“There is?” Eagerness shone in John’s eyes. “What?”

“Pray for him.”

John’s face fell a little. “I thought you meant go visit him.”

“I know you’d like to do that, but your *daed* needs to rest and do what the doctors say. You can help him by being good, listening to the people who are caring for you, and praying for your *daed* every time you think about him.”

Although John frowned, he nodded. David stared adoringly up at Abby.

“Why don’t we pray for him now?”

“*Jah*, that’s a good idea.” John glanced at Abby. “Will you pray too?”

“Of course.” She bowed her head and prayed first.

The boys followed with brief petitions for their *daed* to get well and come back soon.

When they lifted their heads, Abby said, “Would you like to play a game with my sisters and brothers?”

John and David both jumped to their feet.

Abby brushed off her skirt, then looked over at Cathy and Myron, who both stood there staring at her in surprise. “Would it be all right if they played with us for a while?”

“I have to get to work.” Cathy’s words came out sharper and more critical than she’d intended. This teen girl had put Cathy to shame. Abby had stopped the boys' crying in less than five minutes by listening and empathizing, while all Cathy's ultimatums and scolding last night had only escalated it. She felt like a failure.

Abby stood waiting for an answer, the boys' hands tucked in hers.

"It's up to Myron." Cathy gestured in his direction. "He's taking care of them today."

Myron just gazed at Abby in awe. "Um, *jah*, I guess that would be all right. We'll need to leave in an hour, but they could play until then."

Abby beamed. "Great. I'm sure Mamm'll let us take that much time from our chores to help—" She looked down at the boys. "I don't know your names."

They introduced themselves and trotted off happily with Abby.

"I can't believe this." Cathy shook her head. "If you'd seen how much trouble I had trying to get them to sleep last night."

"I can imagine. I tried to make Tim stop crying by ordering him to be quiet and to stop being such a baby. If only Abby had been around back then. She's amazing."

Cathy sniffed. "I don't believe in coddling children that way."

"Neither did I, but it worked, ain't so?" Myron tapped a knuckle against his lip. "You know, when our friends are grieving, we sit and listen without saying much. We just let them talk and murmur *mm-hmm*s or *I'm sorry*s."

"I don't," Cathy said.

"Maybe you should."

"*Humph.*" Cathy turned and headed for her buggy in a huff. *He should talk. Look how his nephew turned out.*

She'd headed partway down the driveway before she remembered the cooler. "Myron," she called after him, "I have something in the back for you and the boys."

Already, Cathy regretted being so bad-tempered with him. Even though he'd hurt her feelings, he'd been right. She should be kinder and more caring. Besides, nobody told her their sob stories. They pretty much avoided her.

Myron reached the buggy. "Look, I'm sorry. I shouldn't have said that."

"You were right, though."

He appeared surprised at her admission. That hurt her almost more than his comment. Did he think she couldn't admit her faults?

"There's a cooler in the back." She tried to use a conciliatory tone. "I made breakfast, lunch, and dinner for the three of you."

"You didn't have to do that."

Cathy couldn't meet his eyes. "I wanted to. Besides, I couldn't expect you to feed the boys. That's my responsibility." A responsibility she was shirking.

Chapter 11

Myron went behind the buggy and lifted out the cooler. Cathy's mood changes gave him whiplash. She went from nice to *grexy* and back again faster than he blinked. "Thanks for this."

Because his hands were full, he flicked his head in a goodbye nod. He hoped she didn't interpret it as good riddance—although part of him did lean in that direction. But with a cooler full of her delicious cooking, he couldn't be that dismissive.

Shrieks of joy came from the yard next door. Some of the tension in Myron's shoulders relaxed. He'd been expecting to deal with crying children most of the morning, but Abby had taught him a technique he could use. If only he'd known it when Tim had arrived years ago. Would they have had a better relationship?

Maybe if he'd been understanding of Tim's loss and pain from the start, Tim wouldn't have turned out so angry and rebellious. Then again, he'd still have been furious about Ivy's disappearance. Talking about it, letting Tim say her name and spill out his sorrow, and listening like Abby had might have lessened some of his agony.

Myron regretted all the lost years, but he couldn't change the past. All he could do was move forward and act differently now. Maybe he should call Tim and apologize. Not today, though. He had two boys to watch.

While they played with the neighbors, Myron moved that night's dinner to the refrigerator. He lifted covers and foil to peek inside. Brownies. The chocolaty aroma made him want to try one now, but he forced himself to set the container on the counter. The ground beef and noodle casserole smelled of garlic and Worcestershire sauce. Myron couldn't wait to try it. Cathy had taped instructions on the lid. A green bean casserole with a cheesy cracker crust joined the main dish on a refrigerator shelf. For the first time in a long while, Myron was eager to come home for supper.

If Abe came back this evening, he'd be surprised. But his nephew had been eating most of his meals with Anna Mary. Usually, Myron missed Abe, but tonight, with two small boys joining him, there'd be no time for loneliness.

Myron pulled out a jar labeled "Overnight Oats." Underneath, it explained to stir it well and serve cold. He mixed in the raisins and chopped almonds Cathy had layered on top. A light scent of vanilla rose as he stirred. Delicious. She always added a little extra touch that made her food special.

Myron peeked out the window. He didn't want to disturb the boys at play. Seeing them giggling with the neighbors lifted his spirits. He sent up a prayer of thanksgiving for Abby. Myron had prayed last night to do a better job caring for these boys than he had with Tim. God had certainly answered his prayers.

Not only had he learned an effective technique to deal with crying, but he had three healthy meals to feed them. He'd been trying to figure out what to pack for lunch when Cathy had arrived with this bounty. Her lunch consisted of thick ham and cheese sandwiches, red beet eggs, pickles, and chips. He could hardly wait for noontime. Meals like this might have made a big difference in his and Tim's dispositions.

Twenty minutes before he had to leave, Myron went outside and called the boys. Their faces fell, but Abby walked them over.

"We have to leave soon," he explained. "We have overnight oats for breakfast."

"Yum," Abby exclaimed, her face animated. "I love those."

"You do?" David asked. When she nodded, he smiled. "I do too."

Myron appreciated Abby's enthusiasm. "Would you like to join us?" They had plenty.

"*Danke*, but I need to get back to my chores. Will the boys be back to play anytime soon?"

"They'll be here for supper. Cathy works at the market until eight tonight."

"Oh, could they come over after they eat? Mamm promised we'd make ice cream tonight. The boys might like to help churn."

"*Jah*, and eat it," David added. "Can we go?" He and John both looked up at Myron with pleading eyes.

"That sounds good. I can bring brownies." Cathy's huge panful should be enough to feed everyone.

"Perfect." A lovely smile spread across Abby's face.

David and John jumped up and down. "Ice cream. Ice cream," they chanted in unison.

"Brownies too." David's face lit up. "And we can play again."

"You sure can," Abby assured him. "I'll see all of you tonight. Mamm'll be happy to have guests."

Myron smiled after her as she bounced across the lawn. Why couldn't Tim have dated a girl like that? Not that Abby could or would agree to go out with his nephew even if Tim asked. He hadn't joined the church and had no intention of doing so.

That broke Myron's heart. Of all the mistakes he'd made in raising Tim, the one that pained the most was knowing he'd been responsible for Tim turning his back on God.

"Come on." Myron pushed away the guilt and herded the boys into the kitchen, where they chattered excitedly about their new friends and tonight's dessert.

They finished breakfast and took off for Myron's woodworking shop, waving wildly at their new friends, who were working in the garden and tending the roadside stand. Once the boys arrived at the shop, they explored all the furniture on display, opening cupboards and drawers, lifting lids, and peeking inside.

When Myron ushered them into the play area, their eyes grew wide.

David dashed over to a box with a handle. "What's this?" He cranked the handle, and his eyes widened as music came out.

John rushed over, but before he could take his turn, the lid flew up and a monkey popped out, almost bopping David in the nose. His face scrunched as if he were about to cry. John leapt back, his eyes wide with fear.

Myron laughed. "It's only a jack-in-the-box." He'd said the same thing to Tim when the monkey had startled his nephew. But Myron didn't want to repeat the same mistakes. Abby came to mind. How would she handle this?

He hurried over, knelt next to the boys, and put an arm around each of them. He'd never been a hugger, but he gave them awkward squeezes. "That was scary, wasn't it?"

They both nodded.

He reached for the box. "See, you can push it back inside." Then he latched the lid.

Holding it far from both boys, he wound the crank. Just before the monkey popped up, he warned, "Now watch this."

The lid flew up. Both boys jumped.

Myron pulled it closer. "It's just fabric with some metal springs under it. Here, feel this." He directed their hands to the coiled wires. "When you squeeze those down"—he demonstrated compressing the springs—"the monkey disappears. The lid holds it down, but when the lid opens, this pops up." Myron let go, and the monkey bobbed around.

The boys watched intently as he repeated it.

"You have to hold it out far enough so it doesn't punch you in the nose," Myron warned.

John giggled. "The monkey almost banged David."

They took turns pushing it down a few times before they closed the lid and turned the crank.

At their belly laughs, Myron choked back his regret. If he'd been this patient years ago, his nephew might have enjoyed the jack-in-the-box instead of being terrified. After the first time he'd turned the crank and been scared, Tim had refused to go near it.

By the time Jed and Lloyd arrived, the boys had explored several more toys, and the workday began peacefully. Myron loved hearing John and David's chatter and giggles.

Once David burst into tears because he missed his *daed*. John put an arm around him and tried to be brave, but tears glimmered in his eyes. Myron hurried over and used Abby's listening and sympathizing technique. Once he'd calmed them, he let his assistants know he'd be taking an early lunch break, and he took the boys outside to the picnic table. They were thrilled with the playground and basketball court.

"After you eat, you can play out here."

He'd built a ten-foot-high fence around the lot after Ivy disappeared. Tim couldn't scale it, and nobody could see in. His nephew had spent most of his time outside, saying he hated the smells in the shop.

Myron couldn't understand it. He'd always loved the scents of sawdust and varnish. And inhaling the subtle fragrance of freshly cut wood soothed and relaxed him.

He often wondered if his nephew pretended to dislike everything just to hurt or get back at him.

He bit into his sandwich and closed his eyes to savor the tang of mustard on the ham's smokiness. The boys gobbled their food and begged to play basketball.

Myron dragged the plastic container of balls outside, and they went wild, ricocheting from football to soccer to basketball to kickball and back again. Tim had never had a playmate. Would he and Ivy have played together if she'd been around to grow up?

It had never occurred to Myron to invite friends for Tim. Amish families didn't do that, probably because they usually had plenty of siblings and cousins, so they never lacked for company. But Tim must have been lonely out here by himself. Being around these small boys brought up many things Myron wished he could go back and change.

The day flowed smoothly, and the boys kept busy. Cathy had packed granola bars, so Myron took time in the afternoon for a snack break with them. Afterward, he showed them how to use the wooden construction wall. Myron had poured his heart into designing this long wall for Tim with screws, nuts and bolts, hinges, doorknobs, latches, pegs, and various tools. The boys danced from one thing to another, thrilled to open and close, twist and turn, and try grown-up tools.

After Ivy had disappeared, Tim had turned his back on the wall and refused to have anything to do with woodworking or construction, so Myron enjoyed seeing these boys using it. He only wished Tim had liked it. If Myron had known then what he'd learned today, perhaps his nephew would be working beside him in the shop. That thought filled Myron with sadness.

His brother Hank must have taken time with Tim when he was young to show him how to milk cows. That might explain why Tim had taken to it so quickly now. How had Hank known what to do? He'd done the same with his sons, and his youngest, Abe, had stayed in the dairy business and remained close to his *daed*. All Hank's children had grown up obedient and loved spending time with their father. Why hadn't Myron developed those same parenting skills?

Cathy struggled to wait on customers while making more donuts. Ever since she'd arrived that morning, she'd been behind. Mixing the yeast dough at home and letting it rise and then cutting the donuts and allowing them to rise on the way to the market had been a mistake. She'd stayed too long at Myron's watching Abby handle the boys, so the dough had overproofed, leaving her with a batch of misshapen donuts that didn't brown right and probably had a coarse grain. She sold them for half-price, which meant she hadn't covered the cost of ingredients. Starting tomorrow, she'd have to figure out a better way to do this.

She hadn't had enough time to finish another batch of yeast dough before the market opened, so her regular customers had to settle for bad donuts or wait until a new batch fried. That wasn't a problem for the market vendors. They could stop back later. But *Englischers* on their way to work got upset. Cathy hoped she hadn't destroyed her business reputation by staying closed and then serving inferior products. What if she lost customers over this?

Wiping sweat from her forehead with the back of her hand, she lifted a fryer basket. With practiced flips, she turned those donuts before moving on to the next batch. The donuts on the other side were ready to be turned out and glazed. She let them rest while she filled the empty baskets.

Long days like this one were frustrating because she had to gauge how many more yeast donuts to make in the late afternoon to have enough to last through the evening. She could whip up extra batter for cake donuts, but a lot of people liked to grab a box of donuts on the way home or for a get-together like an evening Bible study or a book club. Most of them preferred her assortment of glazed and chocolate-iced yeast donuts. Unfortunately, she had no way of knowing what groups might stop by for an evening treat.

In addition to fretting over her donut mishaps while she worked, Cathy kept running Myron's comment through her mind. She valued honesty in others, but hadn't his remark been rude? It had jabbed her. And so had seeing how easily Abby handled the boys. In a short while, she'd calmed both boys, stopped their crying, and brought smiles to their faces.

Ach! Cathy ground her teeth. That *youngie* made it appear so easy. Yet Cathy suspected if she tried the same thing, the boys would never respond the same way. Just like with making friends. People always shied away from her, but she didn't understand why.

"Try opening your heart."

Cathy whirled around to find Mrs. Vandenberg waiting at the counter. The elderly woman had an unnerving way of reading people's thoughts. It spooked Cathy how she'd answer questions you asked silently in your head.

Mrs. Vandenberg gave Cathy an innocent smile. "Love is the key that unlocks every door."

That made Cathy eager to change the subject. "Would you like a donut?"

She didn't really want advice on making friends. Staying away from others suited her just fine. If people got close, they poked and prodded, sticking their noses into your private business. Like Mrs. Vandenberg had just done.

Mrs. Vandenberg studied the display case. "I'll take a strawberry iced. Is that coffee icing? My eyes aren't so good, so I can't read the label."

"Yes, it's coffee." What an odd comment about her eyes. Everyone called her eagle-eyed.

"Then I'll take those two."

While Cathy grabbed bakery paper and removed the donuts from the case, Mrs. Vandenberg pursed her lips as if deep in thought. As Cathy was about to put the last donut into the bag, the older woman asked, "How's it going with Myron?"

Cathy nearly dropped the donut. She recovered before it fell, but she squeezed a little too hard, leaving fingerprints on the airy yeast donut. Annoyed, she started to set the donut aside, but Mrs. Vandenberg stopped her.

"I'll take that one. Small imperfections don't change the flavor. Kind of like life. People are still worth befriending even if they aren't perfect."

Was that a dig? Cathy really wished for less advice, but either Mrs. Vandenberg didn't read that thought, or she chose to ignore it.

After waiting until Cathy had handed over the bag and counted out the change, the elderly woman reached out and patted Cathy's hand as if she pitied her. "Someday soon, you're going to learn to trust someone, and when you do, you'll find your lifelong burdens lifted."

As Mrs. Vandenberg hobbled away, Cathy stared after her. What had she meant by that?

CHAPTER 12

The boys were so engrossed in their play, their faces fell when Myron told them to put away the toys because they'd be leaving soon.

John's lower lip wobbled. "Do we hafta?"

David crossed his arms. "Are we going back to Cathy's?"

"Not yet. We're having supper at my house and ice cream with Abby."

"Ice cream?" David's pout turned into a grin.

"*Jah*, remember what Abby said? We can help churn." John picked up an armload of toys, hurried to the crates, and dropped them in.

David followed slowly with two more toys, but he beamed at his older brother. "And we get to eat it."

While the boys cleaned up, Myron did his last-minute checks around the shop and readied everything for the next day. He'd enjoyed having the boys here today. It filled a little emptiness in his heart to hear young voices while he worked. He'd never had that joy with Tim. For that, he blamed himself.

David sidled up next to Myron and took his hand. Myron's heart almost burst. He'd always longed for a father-son relationship like this. A trusting little boy who looked up to him. A child he loved with all his heart who responded in kind. Myron regretted all he'd lost because of his stubbornness and inexperience, but he had a second chance to redo his mistakes with these two boys, even if it only lasted two months.

When they got home, Myron let the boys rummage in the attic while he put the casseroles in to warm. After he set the table, he went up to join them. They exclaimed over a stick horse, some sock puppets, and a wooden barn with horses and cows.

"Why don't we bring those downstairs?" he suggested.

He helped them carry everything down, and they played happily until suppertime.

When they sat at the table, both boys looked somber. They bowed their heads for prayer, and when they lifted them, John had tears in his eyes.

"Is Daed in Mexico?" he asked, his voice unsteady.

"Not yet," Myron said. "The trip takes two days. The Melard bus has two drivers who take turns so the bus can keep traveling all day and all night." Ordinarily, he would have recited these facts and brushed aside the underlying concerns, but Abby had helped him realize this question wasn't really about where John's *daed* was.

"You miss your *daed*?"

Two heads bobbed.

"H-he always holds our hands when we pray." David's chin trembled.

John nodded.

Myron wasn't sure if they wanted him to hold their hands too, or if they meant they wanted to be holding their father's hand. Myron tried his best to get into a young boy's mind.

"It's hard to do things without him."

Momentary relief crossed John's face at being understood. Then his real fear came out. "What if he never comes back?"

His brother's mouth dropped open. "Never?"

Should Myron tell the truth and say it was always a possibility? *Neh*, they'd deal with that if it happened. Right now was not the time.

"More than anything, your *daed* wants to be with you. He'll do whatever he can to get back to you." For sure, that was true. Myron pushed the negative possibilities from his mind.

His *mamm* always said fears and doubts meant you weren't trusting God, but would the boys even understand that? While he'd raised Tim, Myron had never considered making his responses age-appropriate. He'd spouted whatever came to mind without wondering about the impact or if Tim would understand.

"We can trust God to help when we're afraid," Myron said.

"You get afraid?" David stared at Myron wide-eyed.

Part of him wanted to put on a show of strength, but he humbled himself and told the truth. "*Jah*, I do. Everyone does sometimes."

With a skeptical look on his face, John studied Myron. "Even Daed?"

"Your *daed*'s going to a new country, and doctors will give him treatments he's never had. Would you be scared to do that?"

John thought for a moment as if trying to imagine himself doing new things. "It scared me to come here."

"Me too," David said.

"What if we pray about everyone's fears?" Myron suggested.

When they agreed, he reached out and took their hands this time. They flashed him watery smiles, then turned serious as he prayed. After he finished, they each added a prayer for their *daed*'s and their own fears.

"And help Myron not to be scared," John added before saying *Amen*.

Ouch. That hit too close to home. Myron's mind flooded with memories of his recent conversation with Esther. He'd let his fears stop him from even considering marriage. Now that he'd spent time with these boys, he found himself yearning for a family. But to have children, he needed to have a wife. That would mean breaking down the barriers he'd erected to avoid getting hurt.

David startled Myron out of his reverie. "Are you sad? God can help you with that too."

"You're right." Myron reached over and ruffled David's hair. "*Danke* for reminding me."

Myron had no desire to think about his failed relationship and the impossibility of finding another one. He pushed it from his mind to concentrate on the mouth-watering meal in front of him. Pasting on a smile that became more genuine with each bite, he closed his eyes to appreciate each forkful.

When he opened them, the boys were shoveling in their food.

"We have to hurry," John said, "so we can get our ice cream."

"You're right." Myron didn't want to rush this meal, but he, too, looked forward to brownies and ice cream. And to spending time with his neighbors. He hadn't really met them properly when they'd moved in several months ago. He'd been so stressed about Tim and drugs that he'd had no energy left to visit or invite them over.

"I'm done." David waved his spoon in the air. "Let's go."

"We have to wait for everyone to finish." John examined Myron's plate. "You almost done?"

Myron hid a grin at John's parental tone. How many times had Myron asked Tim that question? This was the first time anyone had asked Myron that since he'd been a child.

Under the boys' eagle-eyed stares, he hurried to clean his plate. "Now we have to do the dishes."

They groaned, but they rushed to the sink to take turns cleaning their own cups, plates, and silverware. After they'd dried them and Myron had shown them where to put them away, they bounced up and down.

"Can we go now?" John wriggled with excitement.

"Let me get the brownies." Myron lifted the pan and inhaled the homey scent.

The boys beat him to the door, and at his nod, they

burst outside and shot across the lawn. Myron caught up to them as they banged on the back door.

"Abby? Abby? We're here," David called through the screen.

She poked her head out the door. "Oh my goodness, you're excited."

"We love ice cream!" David's excitement bubbled over.

"I can tell." She laughed. "We're finishing supper. Come on in."

Myron laid a hand on each boy's shoulder. "*Neh*, we'll wait out here until you're finished."

"It's fine," Abby assured him. "Mamm and Daed won't mind. They've been hoping for a chance to meet you." She opened the screen door wide. "Come on in."

The boys tore inside, but Myron, reluctant, followed. He'd prefer not to interrupt his neighbors' meal, the first time he officially met them.

Abby had no qualms about it, though. She swept through the mudroom and into the kitchen. "Mamm, Daed, this is Myron. And David and John."

Myron mumbled, "Pleased to meet you," as the family went around the table saying their names.

"It's so *gut* to finally meet you," Abby's *mamm*, Liz Huyard, said. "You always look so busy, we've hesitated to bother you."

"I'm sorry I didn't come over sooner." He could have introduced himself at church, but he timed his arrivals so everyone would be filing in for the service when he walked in the door. That way, he avoided talking with the men in the barn. And he ate rapidly after the service and left as soon as possible to prevent people from questioning him about Tim.

"We're glad you're here now." Liz motioned to extra chairs along the wall. "Please pull over some seats and join us. Would you like some—?"

Myron cut her off. "*Danke*, but we already ate." He stood awkwardly in the doorway, holding the brownie pan. Standing there, staring while they ate, seemed rude.

"Ben," Abby's father, Levi, said, "bring over a chair for our guest. And, Abby, why don't you set that pan on the kitchen counter?"

As his children scurried to do their tasks, Levi waved a hand. "Make yourself at home, Myron." He smiled at David and John, who'd crowded in beside a girl and a boy close to their age. "Looks like your children already have."

Myron took a seat in the chair ten-year-old Ben squeezed up to the table. "They're not my children. I'm watching them for a friend."

Liz gave her husband a fond grin. "You'll have to excuse him. He's so busy this time of year, he has no time to keep up with the neighbors." She patted Levi's arm. "Once fall comes and all the crops are harvested, he'll have more time to get to know everyone."

Abby turned to her *daed*. "These are the boys I told you about earlier. The ones miss—" She pressed a hand to her mouth and checked to see if the boys were listening. Seeing they were talking with her brothers, she relaxed. "I'll tell you later."

The family finished their meals, and Myron and the

boys helped clear the table. Abby and her *mamm* shooed everyone else onto the porch while they did dishes.

Levi hurried out the door. "Sorry, Myron. I take the supper hour off to be with my family, but I have to get back to the fields until sunset. My brother and I share acreage a few miles away. Nice to meet you."

"*Gut* to meet you too." Myron shook his hand.

Ben brought out the churn, and the boys helped pour in the ingredients and add salt and ice. The children took the first turns until it became too hard to crank. Then Ben and Myron finished it up.

It had been almost thirty years since Myron had churned ice cream. He'd forgotten how much fun it was. Too bad he'd never tried it with Tim. Maybe they would have bonded over a love for ice cream.

Meanwhile, Abby and her *mamm* cut and set out brownies. When the ice cream was ready, everyone took a plate and plopped a scoop on top. Ben brought out some kitchen chairs, and they sat and watched the fiery sunset fade to dusk. The children ran barefoot through the grass, laughing, calling out, and catching fireflies.

Contentment flooded over Myron. It had been ages since he'd enjoyed good food, cheerful company, and nature's beauty. He should take the boys back to his house soon, but Cathy wouldn't be home for at least a half hour—maybe longer, because she had to clean up after the market closed. May as well let the boys enjoy their fun for a while.

He relaxed back in the chair, inhaled a deep breath of fresh air, and smiled. Though he'd been tense and worried about the day, it had turned out *wunderbar*. He almost wished Cathy wouldn't come back and take the children home.

Following three large orders, Cathy ran out of donuts an hour before closing. She'd already washed all her mixing bowls, utensils, empty display case trays, and prep countertops between customers. Too tired and grumpy after her lack of sleep last night, she didn't want to mix up another batch of cake donuts and then have to redo all her cleaning. She hung her closed sign and wiped down the final trays, display case, and front counter. In less than ten minutes, she was ready to go.

Myron was probably dying for her to come for the boys. By picking them up early, maybe she could get them in bed sooner than last night. With luck, their crying jags would end at a decent hour, and she'd get more sleep tonight. Although she had no desire to face the boys' bawling, it wasn't fair to Myron for her to delay. If his day had been anything like hers yesterday, he'd be praying for her to arrive.

She hurried to her buggy and headed to his house. As each mile passed, her anxiety grew. She'd love to skip getting the boys, drive home, and crawl into bed. She could hardly keep her eyes open.

Another worrisome thought struck her. Suppose Myron wasn't a good person. After all, he hadn't been a good parent. His nephew made it clear he hated his *onkel*. What had she been thinking to let Myron take care of Wayne's *sohns*? Wayne would never forgive her if anything happened to his boys.

The farther she drove, the more this idea whipped her into a frenzy of fear. She'd made a terrible mistake. She shouldn't have left the boys. Myron couldn't be trusted with children. Why hadn't she thought this through?

Right before she reached his house, she pulled into a small graveled turnaround. She'd sneak up to his house, peek inside, and catch him unawares. She often spied on people to learn more about them. This wouldn't be hard. As long as they didn't hear her buggy coming up the drive, they'd never know she'd arrived.

Her unease increased as she approached the house from the road. No light shone from any of the windows. The neighbors' children were awfully rowdy. Cathy avoided that side of Myron's house, although she was unsure what she could see through darkened windows. Maybe she should go to the door before someone spotted her skulking around.

She knocked on the front door, then pressed her ear to the wood. With all the noise the neighbors made, she could barely hear, but she didn't make out any footsteps. She banged harder and longer. No response. Panic set in.

Myron's shop had closed hours ago. Suppose they'd been in an accident and were at the hospital. What if Myron had brought the boys home, but they'd eaten something poisonous from his refrigerator? Who knew how long those condiments had been in there? They all could be lying ill from food poisoning.

Cathy couldn't wait any longer. She had to do

something. Did Myron leave his door unlocked? She twisted the knob, and it opened. Cathy barged in and called for Myron and the boys. Still no answer. She had to check all the rooms.

A DeWalt light sat on the hall table. Cathy grabbed it, turned it on, and went from room to room, shining it into every corner, crevice, and closet. She even checked under beds and furniture with enough room for the boys to hide. The part of her that loved to find out juicy information about others longed to open drawers and look more closely at closet contents, but she had to find David and John. As she finished examining every room on the first floor and headed to the staircase, her fear grew along with her ire at Myron.

CHAPTER 13

Levi pulled into the driveway and jumped out of the buggy. "Ben," he called, interrupting the children's lively game of tag, "take care of the horse." He rushed toward Myron. "When I passed your house, the front door was ajar, and someone seems to be prowling around inside. I saw a light going room to room as if searching for something."

Myron jumped up from his chair, but Levi gripped his arm. "Don't go in. It could be a burglar."

Liz's face creased with worry. "A woman in our old *g'may* surprised an escaped convict about a year ago. And he—he . . ." She covered her face with her hands.

Levi went over and squeezed her shoulder. "Let's call the police."

Before Myron could object, Levi had already started running to the phone shanty at the edge of the *Englisch* neighbor's property next door.

"Please," Liz begged, "don't go in until the police come."

Myron agreed to wait, and ten minutes later, a police

cruiser showed up at the Huyards' house. Levi pointed out the open door, and Myron identified himself as the homeowner.

"Look," Liz said, "there's a light in the attic."

Until this point, Myron hadn't been frightened. Now he felt violated. The intruder must have gone through the whole house to reach the attic.

"Anyone live in the house who might be in there?" the policewoman asked Myron.

"*Neh*, I'm the only one who lives there." Myron hesitated over mentioning Tim being in New York, but he didn't want to remind them of his nephew's run-ins with the law. He should tell them about Abe, though. "Oh, and my nephew's visiting, but he hasn't gotten home yet."

"You sure?"

"Positive. He'd come in his buggy."

"You keep anything valuable in the attic?"

Myron shook his head. "Only old toys and some broken furniture."

"Your nephew do drugs?"

"Of course not. Abe would never—" Myron stopped. *Please, God, no.* What if Tim had hidden drugs in the attic?

The officer studied Myron's face. "Something wrong?"

Tim never would have left drugs in the house while he was away, would he? Myron stuttered out, "I, um, don't think so."

"You don't sound too sure."

"I have another nephew, but he's not here right

now." *And I'm pretty sure he'd take his drugs with him if he had them.*

Judging from her expression, the policewoman didn't quite believe him. "Since they don't seem to have a vehicle to transport large items, most likely they're looking for something specific or finding a place to hide," she said. "Possibly looking for money or drugs. Or it could be a runaway. We'll check it out."

"Call all the children inside," her partner advised. "If we surprise an armed trespasser, shots may be fired."

That hadn't occurred to Myron. He hoped whoever was in his house hadn't put his neighbors in danger. At least he and the boys hadn't been inside when the intruder entered. And thankfully, Abe wouldn't be back from Anna Mary's for an hour or two.

Levi whistled, and his children came running. John and David joined them.

Ben made a face. "*Ach,* Daed. Already? We haven't finished our game. It's still early."

Liz held open the back door. "Get in the house now, and we'll explain."

As the children trooped inside, the policewoman turned to Myron. "How many other exits do you have to the outside?"

"Just the back door. Oh, and the exterior basement steps. The lid to them is right by the back door."

"Okay. Go inside with this family until we've caught the intruder and secured the premises. Then you can go through the house with us to see what's missing or damaged."

Myron followed Levi into the house. Liz had gathered all the children in the room farthest from Myron's house, and she explained about the burglar.

"Can't we see?" Ben started to bolt from the room, but Levi blocked his way.

"The police asked us to all stay in here."

Ben's face fell. "Aww. I want to see them catch the burglar."

"We need to let them do their job." Levi closed the door and sat in a chair to block it.

"Why don't we all play a game?" Abby said brightly. "Let's do I Spy." She helped John and David until they understood the game.

Myron hoped nabbing the intruder wouldn't take long. Both boys looked tired. Cathy had gotten them up early, and they should be in bed.

Cathy! Ach, what if she pulled in while this was going on? He had to warn her, but how?

A slight shuffling behind her frightened Cathy. People sneaking up on her made her nervous. If this was Myron's idea of a joke, he'd gone too far. Unless he'd gone off the deep end . . .

Before she could whirl around and confront him, a voice barked, "Don't move. Put your hands in the air."

Definitely not Myron.

"You can't tell me what to do." She pivoted in one swift movement and aimed the flashlight beam in the man's eyes.

Ach, not just any man. A policeman. With a gun pointed right at her.

Cathy's hands shot in the air. She lost her grip on the DeWalt, and it crashed to the floor.

At the clatter, he jumped. "You make another move, and I'll shoot."

His warning sent shivers through Cathy. Another officer came up behind him and slipped past.

"I'm going to pat you down," she said.

"What's that mean?" Cathy longed to back up as the woman approached, but she didn't want to get shot. She couldn't risk that. She had two boys to look after. Two missing boys.

"It means I'm going to be feeling for weapons," the policewoman told her.

"I don't have any."

The woman ignored her and ran her hands down Cathy's body.

Cathy squirmed away. "Get your hands off me. Stop touching me."

The man in the doorway growled, "Stay still or else."

The threat in his tone kept Cathy motionless.

The policewoman finished and stepped back. "First time I've ever frisked an Amish woman."

"Hope it's the last time." Her partner seemed to find it amusing.

"Hold your hands out in front of you," the policewoman ordered.

Though she longed to resist, Cathy obeyed. Handcuffs clanked shut around her wrists. The policewoman clamped a hand on Cathy's arm.

Panic coursed through her. "What are you doing?"

Instead of answering, the woman recited some

gobbledygook about a right to remain silent. Cathy's brain whirled. What was going on?

"Is anyone else here with you?" the officer in the doorway asked.

"No, but there should be. Myron's taking care of my kids. Not my kids, my nephews. They're not really my nephews, they're my nephew's sons. But they aren't here."

"I'm not sure what she's babbling about," the policewoman said to her partner.

"Maybe she's drunk or—"

"I'm not drunk." Cathy stamped her foot, jerking her arm away from the officer's grip.

She grasped Cathy's arm tighter. "If you don't settle down, we'll charge you with resisting arrest."

"You don't understand. I'm supposed to be watching the boys, but I was at work."

"Boys? How old?"

"Five and six."

"You left them alone while you went to work?"

"No, I left them with someone I thought was trustworthy, but he kidnapped them. You should be looking for him."

A terrible thought occurred to her. The news had stories of missing children who later turned up dead. What if Myron's niece hadn't disappeared? Suppose he . . .

"You have to find him," she burst out. "Maybe he killed his niece and the boys."

The two officers exchanged glances. They didn't believe her.

A third officer appeared in the doorway. "We did a sweep of the house. Everything seems to be in order."

"After I take her out to the car," the policewoman said, "you can bring the owner through to check."

"The owner? Myron?" Cathy's voice rose in a shriek. "You know where he is? Ask him what he did with my grandnephews."

"Calm down, ma'am." The policewoman led Cathy to the stairs.

"But you don't understand." Cathy had to convey the direness of the situation. "I have to stay here. I need to find the boys. I'm supposed to take care of them."

"We'll talk about all that at the station." The woman's tone reminded Cathy of Abby's coddling of John and David.

Rather than soothing Cathy, it infuriated her. She was not an upset six-year-old. But she had to act rational. Make this woman listen. "You have it all wrong. I'm not a criminal. I just came in to find my grandnephews. I left them with Myron. He's the criminal."

The policewoman's face stayed impassive. She strode to the car, never loosening her hold on Cathy's arm. After opening the door, the officer nudged Cathy inside while protecting her head.

This had to be a nightmare. Cathy squeezed her eyes shut. *Please let me wake up.* But when she opened her eyes again, nothing had changed.

Instead, she sat inside a car, facing a metal mesh partition backed with glass. They'd arrested her and put her in a cage. John and David were missing. And she could do nothing to rescue them.

* * *

Myron had to protect Cathy. "Levi, I can't let Cathy get caught in gunfire when she comes to pick up John and David. I need to watch out a window that looks out on the street."

"It's not safe," Levi said, but he moved his chair so Myron could exit. "We'll pray for both of you. Bring Cathy in here once she arrives."

"*Danke* for the prayers." Myron, too, asked God for Cathy's safety. He hoped he'd be fast enough to stop her before she reached his driveway.

Although he wished he could go out to the street to flag her down before she reached the Huyards', he heeded the officer's warning and stood at the window beside the front door so he could rush out. From here, he couldn't see his house, but so far, all remained quiet. The police cruisers remained parked out front. Their lights whirled, sending red and blue beams flickering across the Huyards' grass. Myron hoped Cathy would slow when she saw them so he could race out and stop her. He asked God to keep her safe. He also prayed for the officers' safety.

A short while later, a policewoman led a protesting woman to the cruiser. Myron could hear them before they came into view, but he couldn't make out what they were saying. When they finally appeared, the policewoman blocked his view.

As they neared the car, Myron caught a glimpse of an Amish skirt and apron. He couldn't believe an Amish woman had broken into his house. Then, as the officer stepped aside to open the door, Myron caught sight of the woman's face and froze in shock. *Cathy?*

He yanked open the door and sprinted across the lawn.

An officer intercepted him. "We'd like you to come with us to see if anything's missing or—"

Myron sidestepped the man and dashed to the car. "Cathy," he called.

She whipped her head around. "Myron?" She burst into tears. "What have you done with the boys?"

Chapter 14

Half an hour later, the police had departed, and Cathy sat at the Huyards' dining room table, enjoying a brownie with ice cream as everyone shared stories about their days. She tilted her head skeptically as Myron recounted his time with the boys.

The angels he described bore no resemblance to the screaming, crying brats she'd dealt with all day yesterday. "I find it hard to believe they were good the whole day."

"Really, they were," he assured her. "We had the best time. The boys were very well-behaved, and they seemed to enjoy themselves."

John told her about the jack-in-the-box, the tool wall, and all the balls.

"We were good," David told her. "And we had fun. Can we go back tomorrow?"

Cathy couldn't possibly ask Myron to watch them again. "We'll see."

"The day after that?" John begged.

"Why don't you come on the days your *aenti* works?"

Myron beamed at him. “I’d love to have you starting next Tuesday.”

“I don’t think—”

Nobody responded to Cathy’s sputtered protest.

“And can we play here too?” John waved a hand toward his new friends.

“Sure.” Abby glanced at her mother for confirmation.

Liz nodded. “You’re all welcome anytime.” Her gaze included Myron and Cathy.

Despite her unease at the way plans seemed to be spiraling out of her control, Cathy’s heart warmed at Abby’s *mamm*’s invitation. For the first time in ages, Cathy felt accepted and part of a group. Warmth flowed through her. It was nice to be included rather than having people change seats to sit near someone else or duck into another aisle when they saw her coming.

“So, tell us what happened when the police went into the attic,” Liz said.

They all turned to Cathy, eagerness written on their faces. Embarrassed, she gave a brief account of the main events, but glossed over her reactions.

John leaned forward. “What do handcuffs feel like?”

How could she ever explain the dread of being confined, the loss of freedom, the terror of being in someone else’s control? “They’re chilly and hard metal. When they snap them shut, it’s scary.”

“Did you have to go in the police car?”

Cathy bit her lip before answering. “*Jah*. It’s like being in a cage.” And if Myron hadn’t come out when he did, they’d have whisked her to the station and locked her behind bars.

The boys made her describe every detail. As she did, she fought down the fear of being trapped. It brought up horrible old memories. Darkness threatened to overwhelm her.

Abby must have noticed, because she interrupted the boys' questions. "Why don't you tell Cathy about the games we played and about catching fireflies?"

This teen girl seemed to have a sense of what people needed. And Cathy badly needed a break. She shot Abby a grateful look, and Abby smiled back.

After the boys finished their excited chattering, Cathy stood. "*Danke* for the dessert and for playing with John and David, but I'd better get them home to bed."

David's eyes filled with tears. "I don't want to go."

"Me either." John's mouth set in a mutinous line.

"Wait." Abby hurried out of the room and returned carrying a book of Bible stories. "I promised to read them some stories, but why don't you take this with you?" She handed it to John and bent to hug David. "Cathy will read them to you, won't you?" Abby glanced up at Cathy with a question in her eyes.

One more thing to do tonight. Cathy sighed inwardly, but she did want to encourage her grandnephews' faith. "*Jah*, I will."

Abby knelt in front of the boys. "The faster you go to sleep, the faster Tuesday will come, and we can play again."

This girl was a wonder. She'd made the nighttime routine so much easier. Cathy could almost hug Abby. Except Cathy wasn't a hugger.

Myron stood. "I'll walk you out. I need to go too." He turned to the Huyards, thanked them, and said his goodbyes.

Cathy had been hoping to slip out unnoticed, but the boys tucked their hands into Myron's. At the thought of those dirty, sticky hands in hers, Cathy cringed. But he seemed to relish it.

He was a much kinder person than she was, yet he'd alienated his nephew. He'd explained some of it the other night, but she wondered if something more lay beneath it. Back when she'd gossiped about him, Cathy had created more disturbing reasons. Her imagination often ran away with her, like it had tonight, and she'd added those suspicions to the gossip she'd spread, but now, she wanted to know the real story.

Myron stopped and looked around. Then he asked the question she'd been dreading, "Where's your buggy?"

"I parked down the road." She waved vaguely in the direction of her buggy, hoping he'd head up his driveway rather than accompany her. "We'll be fine. I can take the boys from here." She reached out for their hands, but Myron didn't let go.

"It's no problem. I'll help you get them into the buggy."

"*Neh, neh.*" She hoped she didn't sound as frantic as she felt.

He turned to look at her. "Is there a reason you don't want me to go with you?"

Jah, there was. A big reason, an embarrassing reason. She should tell the truth, even if it humiliated her. But she didn't want Myron to know all the strange stories she'd concocted in her head.

Cathy squirmed for several long, uncomfortable seconds before she forced herself to be honest. "I-it's just that I worry about things. A lot. Things that don't actually happen. I don't want you to think I don't trust you. Because I do, but—"

"Just tell me. Don't worry about hurting my feelings."

"I—I parked way down the street and walked to your house." She couldn't believe she had to admit this next part. "I, um, worried you might be mistreating the boys." She pushed the words out in a rush.

"You planned to spy on me?"

Cathy hung her head. She would have just called it *checking up on the boys*. *Spying* sounded so . . . so sneaky and underhanded. But he was right.

"*Jah,*" she admitted.

Myron sighed. "I guess I deserve it. I wasn't a model parent with Ivy or Tim."

She didn't want him to blame himself. "It-it's not that. I just— Well, pictures come into my mind of all the bad things that might happen and then I get anxious and then . . ."

"You really don't trust people, do you?"

Once again, Myron's bluntness stabbed her. "You wouldn't either if you'd been through what—" She pinched her mouth shut. What was she doing? She couldn't believe she'd come this close to spilling a secret she'd kept hidden for years.

"What is it, Cathy?" His voice didn't have its usual rough edge. Instead, he kept his tone gentle and caring.

That almost broke her. Almost.

But she clammed up and shook her head.

Mrs. Vandenberg's words came back to her. *Someday soon, you're going to learn to trust someone . . .*

Was this what she'd meant?

Although Mrs. Vandenberg was the wisest person Cathy knew, she couldn't tell Myron. Trusting someone meant telling the truth about herself and her life. She'd never, ever let anyone know about her painful past.

David stumbled and almost fell. Myron bent and scooped the small boy into his arms. David was so sleepy, he rested his head on Myron's shoulder and drifted off as they walked.

That ended his deeper conversation with Cathy. He suspected she'd been about to reveal something important.

Lord, if there's anything I can help her with, please give her the courage to confide in me.

"So how was your day at work?" The desperate note in her voice signaled she wanted to avoid finishing their more personal conversation.

He sighed. She was wound up tighter than that jack-in-the-box spring. Sooner or later, pushing down those deeper problems wouldn't work, and they'd pop up and frighten everyone around her. Myron hoped it wouldn't happen in front of the boys.

"My day was fine. I already told you about most of it." He took a chance on switching the conversation to her. "How was yours?"

Chattering like a magpie, Cathy recounted all the problems of her day, seemingly grateful to turn the spotlight away from her deeper issues. She described her morning struggles with the dough over-rising, being behind for the rest of the day, and closing early after running out of donuts.

"You could drop them off at my house earlier and go in at your usual time."

"*Neh*, it's way too early."

"I wouldn't mind. I'm an early riser." Although he never rose quite that early, he'd really like to watch the boys. "With Tim gone, I have nothing to do in the evenings, so I go to bed soon after supper."

Cathy shook her head. "I can't wake them that early. They need their sleep. Maybe I just need to close the stand."

Myron's opportunity to spend time with David and John, to hear their joyful laughter, to redo old errors was slipping away. He couldn't let that happen.

"I have an idea. Why don't I drive to your house in the morning? That way, you could leave on time, but the boys would get their rest."

"That's ridiculous. I can't ask you to do that."

"I don't mind. Besides, it's on my way to work." It would make more sense than her coming to his house and then backtracking.

"I couldn't do that."

She seemed determined not to accept help. He never thought he'd admit this to anyone, but he wanted to convince her. "My life has been very lonely for a long while now. Tim's troubles distracted me, but since he left, I've been alone. Being with your boys filled a hole in my heart."

Cathy's face crumpled, and she blinked hard. Had he hit a soft spot? Maybe she, too, faced loneliness. She didn't appear to have many friends.

They'd reached her buggy. She slid open the door, and Myron laid David on the back seat.

"There's no room for me," John complained.

Myron settled the front seat in place. "You can sit here."

John eyed Cathy warily.

Abby's words came to mind. Myron pointed to the book he clutched tightly against his chest. "The faster you get home, the faster you'll get to hear a Bible story."

With a reluctant expression, John let Myron boost him up. Then Myron turned to Cathy. "I'll be there at four thirty Tuesday morning."

He turned and hurried away before she could protest.

Cathy stared after him. She couldn't let him do this. "Don't come," she called after him.

He stopped and turned. "Did you put up a sign closing your stand for Tuesday?"

She couldn't lie. "*Neh.*"

"Then I'll be there. It's only for a few weeks." He waved and jogged toward his house.

If John hadn't been in the front seat, she could have offered him a ride. He must have sensed she planned to argue. He veered onto the front lawn of a nearby house and angled himself away from her. She couldn't speak to him unless she pulled over and chased him. She couldn't even imagine the gossip that would cause.

Guilt troubled her as she drove past him. She had to discuss this with him tomorrow. If he showed up, she'd have another problem to deal with. What would her neighbors think when they woke to find his buggy in her driveway so early in the morning?

If she saw something like that, she'd jump to certain conclusions. Especially after Cathy had been in Myron's arms—accidentally, of course—in a public place a few days ago. His desire to help her might destroy her reputation—and even worse, his.

Both boys had fallen sound asleep before she reached home. She thanked the Lord for that blessing. By the time she lugged them into the house and up to bed, she had no energy to do anything tonight.

To her surprise, the boys dressed themselves for church without a fuss. Perhaps they expected to see their new friends there. Cathy didn't want to shatter their good moods by explaining Myron and the Huyards' lived in a different church district, but after the service, they surprised her by playing with other children.

And for once, dirty, messy *buwe* didn't disgust Cathy the way they usually did. Instead, she found herself thanking the Lord for the ones who'd invited her grandnephews to join them in games. Better filthy clothes than bawling boys.

On Monday, she faced sniffles and sobs, but she fought her instincts and tried Abby's listening technique. That and a reminder they'd see the Huyards tomorrow helped dry many a tear. After several Bible stories, both boys fell asleep.

With a lighter heart, Cathy, too, drifted off quickly but woke with a start at three thirty. Only an hour to dress, mix and shape dough, and prepare three meals for all of them. She also wanted to have her horse hitched up and ready to go so she could take off the minute Myron arrived.

That way, her neighbors, if they were up that early, wouldn't see her with a strange man in her house. Even if she explained it to Barb, would her next-door neighbor believe the truth? Barb had already convinced herself that Myron liked Cathy. This might provide more proof.

Cathy had everything packed in the buggy, and she'd put meals, including an oven-ready egg casserole for breakfast, in the refrigerator. She'd left notes and taped instructions to all the containers. Now all she had to do was finish a few last-minute chores and calm her nerves.

She needed to relax and trust the Lord, but her worries overshadowed her peace of mind. She didn't like letting anyone into her house. Myron was right. She'd never trusted people. All kinds of possibilities flitted through her mind, mostly negative ones. Not only did she have to worry about all those potential disasters, she also had to deal with her *onkel*'s scolding voice in her head—*Don't shirk your duties. Don't be lazy. Stand on your own two feet—*

Cathy slammed a mental door on those criticisms, the same way she'd cut her *onkel* out of her life years ago. And now that he was dead, she needed to rid herself of these old recordings that repeated his every negative remark. She didn't intend to throw away her morals, only to get rid of the rejection and shame he'd used to enforce them. But how did you stop the thoughts that popped into your mind automatically all day long?

She tensed at hoofbeats and the clatter of wheels on the driveway. Myron was here. Five minutes early. She had a few more small jobs she wanted to do, but she shot out the door with the containers of donuts she'd just cut. Everything else was ready to go.

"Make yourself at home," she said when he emerged from his buggy.

Myron waved. "*Guten tag.*" His bright greeting made Cathy feel uncomfortable.

"I can see you're in a hurry, so I won't keep you. We'll see you after work."

"*Danke.*" Worrying it sounded ungracious, she added, "I appreciate it."

"No problem. It's a pleasure." He smiled as if he meant it.

How could she ever repay him? She couldn't, but she hoped the food she'd left would at least make a dent in the huge debt she owed.

* * *

Myron headed into the house to find notes everywhere. He read all the instructions, including the ones on the casserole dishes. She really was bossy. The delicious food she'd left softened his irritation a little. But only a little.

He yawned. He had no idea how she kept this schedule day after day. He'd gone to sleep later than usual last night because his mind kept replaying the last time he'd seen Cathy, his shock at seeing Cathy in the police car, and later discovering she'd intended to spy on him and the boys.

That whole ordeal must have been terrifying for her. Not just the encounter with the police, but also finding her grandnephews missing. She'd left the boys with a strange man and returned to find him and the children gone. He could only imagine her panic as she moved from room to room in an unfamiliar house with only a flashlight beam to guide her. Then she'd found each room empty. His desperation over Ivy's disappearance swamped him. The frantic searches. The dead ends. The hope after finding a clue. The despair when it led nowhere.

At least in the end, she'd found the boys, but only after being arrested and dragged out to a police car. Myron's search, however, had never ended. He'd never experienced that relief.

As he always did, he whispered a prayer. *Lord, please keep Ivy safe wherever she is and help us find her.*

His eyes drooped. Getting up this early wasn't easy. Cathy had said to make himself at home. Myron removed his shoes and stretched out on the sofa to rest a bit.

Next thing he knew, small fingers poked him.

"Is he dead like Mamm?" David's words wobbled.

"I don't think so. He's making a funny noise." John didn't sound confident, though.

"But we put Mamm in the living room."

"*Jah*, but she was in a box."

Myron's eyes popped open. They both leapt back and stared at him with the same terror they'd shown when the jack-in-the-box jumped out at them.

"It's all right. I was just sleeping." Myron stretched and swung his legs to the floor.

David studied him with a furrowed brow. "How come you didn't sleep in a bed?"

"I, um . . ." What could he say? He'd never dream of sleeping in a bed here? He hadn't intended to sleep? "Let's get breakfast."

He led them out to the kitchen. *Ach!* If the wall clock had the right time, he'd be late for work if they ate now, because the casserole took a half hour to cook. Cathy had left donuts, but the boys should have a hearty breakfast before they rushed out the door.

Myron had promised his employees a chance to take over the store sometimes. They both had keys. Would they think to use them to open the shop? Or would they wait around for him? He weighed the options—put the boys' needs first and open his business late, or put his business first and let the boys eat donuts while he went straight to work?

Back when Tim was young, business always came

first. Tim often went hungry or waited hours for meals, and then the meals consisted of whatever Myron threw together at the last minute. If taking care of these two boys provided a chance for Myron to make up for the past, he had only one choice. He strode to the refrigerator and took out the casserole. He'd trust his employees to figure out what to do when he didn't show up. And if they didn't unlock the shop and get to work, Myron would deal with missing customers and orders, knowing he'd done the right thing.

Chapter 15

Cathy's morning went much better than it had Saturday. The donuts had risen perfectly during the buggy ride, and she'd fried them while preparing batter for cake donuts. She'd stocked her shelves completely before the market opened.

Gratitude for Myron's kindness filled her. After yesterday, she had confidence she could trust him with her grandnephews. That took a big load off her mind, but a niggling worry bothered her. Would he poke and pry into things at her house the way she would in his if she had the chance? Not that she had many private things, but the thought of him peeking into her drawers and closets made her edgy.

Even before the market doors opened, she had a run on donuts. Other stand owners lined up at her counter, and the line snaked down the aisle and out the door by the time the market officially opened. She ran out of donuts within an hour.

It galled her, though, that most people hadn't come for the donuts, but for the gossip. They didn't spend time choosing a flavor. Rather, they focused avid eyes on her and pointed carelessly to the nearest donut. Then they got to their main purpose—asking nosy questions.

"So, what was it like being arrested?" "Did you really break into Myron King's house?" "What's going on with you and Myron? I hear the two of you got pretty cozy the other day?" "Are you and Myron courting?" "When's the wedding?"

Englischers and Amish alike glanced at her askance and peppered her with questions based on wild, outlandish theories. Some people came to lecture her about sinfulness or warn that her behavior might warrant a visit from the bishop. She struggled to fend off the intrusions.

After a while, she clamped her mouth shut and refused to answer. Not that it mattered. The stories grew as people passed her answers or nonanswers down the line, embellishing them every time. They regaled customers who hadn't heard the news with crazy conjectures, and the newly informed listeners gleefully shared the information and added their own twists.

By midafternoon, while Cathy struggled to keep up with the demand for donuts, horrified customers and members of her *g'may* stopped to commiserate over her business closing due to her pending jail sentence.

"We'll miss you." "We'll all be praying." "Our Mennonite church has a prison ministry. We'll be sure you get on the list."

People patted her hand and stared at her with sorrowful eyes. A few quoted Scripture verses:

"Be sure your sins will find you out." "Abstain from all appearance of evil." "Resist the devil, and he will flee from you."

Cathy wanted to throw back the Bible admonition, *Even so the tongue is a little member, and boasteth great things. Behold, how great a matter a little fire kindleth!*

Around three, she ran out of donuts for the sixth time that day. She debated about closing early, but if she did, the blabbermouths would win. She kept her stand open to defy those who might say she turned tail and ran. Besides, a closed sign could start fresh rumors that the police had dragged her away and locked her up. So she suffered the tongue-lashings and worked until the bitter end.

Then she endured stragglers from other market stands who hadn't been able to get away during the day. They interrupted her while she cleaned her bakery cases and baking supplies. To avoid requests for donuts, she packed up the remaining leftovers in a large bakery box. She'd give them to the Huyard children.

By the time she'd finished the final mopping, Cathy had turned into a volcano about to explode. Why were people allowed to get away with such lies? How long would she have to live with these made-up blots on her reputation? Would she ever live this down?

She headed home frazzled and out of sorts. When she reached her house, Myron wasn't there. Immediately, she panicked. Had they been in an accident? Did Myron—?

Stop it! Don't be like the rumormongers at the market.

Determined not to let her mind spin out worst-case scenarios, Cathy tried to come up with logical explanations. He might still be at work. Or maybe he took the boys to his house or to play with the Huyards.

A little calmer, she berated herself for not stopping at Myron's in the first place. To her relief, his open barn door revealed his buggy inside. She picked up the box of donuts and headed for the front door. Her face heated as she remembered yesterday's events. She hoped no neighbors were watching her.

When Myron didn't answer her knock, she went next door. As she reached the Huyards' back porch, John and David burst through the door with Ben on their heels.

"Abby's It," John yelled. "Faster, David."

Cathy opened her mouth to yell at them to settle down and come now, but Abby's name stopped her. What would Abby do? Something to get their attention.

She had the perfect distraction right in her hands. "I have donuts for everyone."

All the runners screeched to a halt and turned to surround her. As the other children banged out the door, they joined the group.

"Are those for us?" the youngest girl asked.

"If you've had your supper and it's all right with your mother."

"We already ate," the girl said.

"So did we." John grinned and eyed the donut box. "We had fried chicken and macaroni and cheese. It was yummy."

His words soothed Cathy's irritated mood. He'd liked the meal she'd made.

David jostled John out of the way to be first in line. "*Jah*, it was *gut*. Myron said it was the bestest chicken he ever ate."

Cathy's heart swelled. They'd all enjoyed it. After the rough day she'd had, this compliment just about brought tears to her eyes.

Then Myron stepped onto the porch and spied her. His lips curved into a welcoming smile that set her heart fluttering.

She pinched her lips together to prevent her mouth from returning his cheerful grin. Quickly, she looked away. She didn't want him to get the wrong idea. After all the accusations she'd faced today, that was the last thing she wanted. Or was it?

The stress lines around Cathy's mouth bothered Myron. Her eyes held unhappiness, but when he smiled to try lifting her mood, her eyes widened as if he'd surprised her. Then they shuttered like a blind going down to block out the light; she compressed her lips into a forbidding slit, and avoided his gaze.

"These are for you and the Huyards. To thank you." Even her words sounded clipped and dutiful. She thrust the box at him.

He started to say, *You don't have to thank us. We're happy to do it.* But something about her frostiness made him hesitate. He could tell she disliked imposing on people and needed to do something to repay others' kindness.

"*Danke.*" He reached for the box. Then, before he could think better of it, he added a teasing response, "This will more than repay all of today's hardships."

Her gaze shifted to his face in alarm.

"I'm kidding. The boys were good." He was so busy studying her reaction, he didn't pay attention to the box. His hands brushed her fingers as he took the donuts. A jolt ran through his arm.

She jerked back as if burned. The box almost fell, but he managed to catch it.

He hoped she didn't think he'd done that on purpose. After what had happened in her stand . . .

Myron yanked his mind away from that memory, but impressions of her softness, her womanliness still haunted him and left him longing for the closeness and tenderness he'd denied himself for decades.

Not that he'd want that with Cathy. She definitely wasn't his type, but maybe he should consider dating again. Someone sweet and gentle and kind. Having a relationship, though, would mean facing his inner demons. He'd pushed Anna Mary's mother to get over her fears, but he himself stayed trapped in the past.

Cathy whirled away from him. "I should get the boys and go. It's been a long day."

Myron shoved his wayward thoughts away and focused on the donuts. "I'm sure John and David won't want to miss out on these. Do you have time to come in and have a donut with everyone?"

"I don't want to impose." Her response came out as stiff as her back.

He should just let her go, but he convinced himself his only concern was making sure the boys didn't miss out on this treat. "Liz and Levi love company. They were just planning to come out on the porch after dinner. We could all enjoy the donuts together before you leave."

"They don't mind you inviting random people to join them?" Sarcasm edged Cathy's words.

"Not at all." Liz walked outside carrying two chairs. "I brought your chair, Myron." She turned and called through the screen door, "Ben, bring an extra chair for Cathy."

"I—I didn't plan on staying." Cathy blushed and appeared agitated.

Liz's smile radiated understanding. "I'm sure you're quite busy. Can you stay until the boys have dessert?"

With obvious reluctance, Cathy sat in the chair Ben brought out for her while everyone exclaimed over the donuts. The children clamored for favorites, but some wanted the same donut. To solve that problem, Liz advised them to break the donuts in half.

"One person divides. The other gets first choice of halves." She shared a secretive smile with Myron and Cathy. "Amazing how well that works in making sure they both get the same-sized pieces."

"Smart idea," Cathy agreed. She seemed to be making a mental note of it.

Once the children had their donuts, Abby handed the box to the adults. Even though Myron had vowed never to eat one of Cathy's donuts, when they passed him the box, he took one.

After he bit into it, he closed his eyes to appreciate the taste and texture. Like everything else she cooked, it was fantastic. He now regretted giving away the two boxes of donuts she'd given him when they'd first met.

As soon as everyone had finished their donuts, Cathy rose. "John? David? It's time to go."

Once again, Myron took her departure as a signal he should leave too. He stood. "*Danke* for everything, Liz and Levi. You too, Cathy, for the scrumptious donuts. I'll head home now."

He accompanied Cathy across the lawn to her buggy. The tension in her face and posture concerned him. "Is everything all right?"

"Why wouldn't it be?"

Myron bit back a sigh. Why did she get defensive over well-meaning questions? "Do you always have to be so prickly?" The words popped out of his mouth before he could stop them. Something about Cathy made him more likely to spit out thoughts that he'd normally hold back.

She stopped and looked taken aback. "That was rude."

"I know." Myron didn't intend to back down. "But it was true."

They reached her buggy, and she opened the passenger door. He lifted both boys into the buggy, then stepped back to find Cathy glaring at him.

"You're upset because I put the boys in?"

She huffed. "*Neh.* Because you hurt my feelings."

"Sorry. You hurt mine too." He didn't mean to turn this into a tit-for-tat argument, but he felt like she should know how her behavior affected other people.

"Oh." Cathy stared at the ground. "Nobody's ever told me that before." Her voice quivered with hurt. "They just run away from me. Or they act polite to my face and then talk about me behind my back."

As he had so often lately, Myron felt sorry for her.

"I guess it's better to have someone tell me the truth even if it hurts."

He was amazed that with her bluntness, no one had ever confronted her before. Yet, he couldn't help admiring her for speaking her mind. "I prefer honesty too. It often hurts, but it helps you see your faults."

"Exactly." Cathy's lips lifted in what might have been a smile.

At least he'd be sending her home in a somewhat better mood than when she'd arrived. With Cathy, that counted as a major victory.

Cathy had spent the day getting slammed by gossip and criticism. Now Myron had gone after her, but for some reason, his comments hurt less. Maybe it was his direct, no-nonsense manner.

As she rounded the buggy, he stopped her. "You didn't answer my question. Are you all right?"

She wanted to shout at him to leave her alone and mind his own business. Instead, she went into attack mode. "Would you be all right if everyone made up lies about you? If they thought you were heading to jail or having an affair?"

The minute she said that, it dawned on her that those rumors were about him too. "Never mind. I shouldn't have said that." She pressed a hand over her mouth, wishing she could stuff her words back inside. She turned her back to hide her burning cheeks.

"So, we're the subject of gossip at the market?"

"*Jah,*" she admitted. "Customers stopped by to warn me about living in sin or to tell me to avoid appearances of evil or to let me know they were praying for me."

"It's too bad people jump to conclusions about things they see. It's even worse when they spread those mistruths to others."

Cathy gasped and straightened. He must have intended that as jab against her too. She'd been guilty of the same thing. Still, he didn't have to point it out right now when she was hurting. "Are you talking about me?"

"That's not what I meant." But the quirk of his mouth indicated he was thinking, *If the shoe fits, wear it.*

To her shame, she realized it didn't just fit; it fit perfectly. Over the years, she'd done this to others, including Myron.

He turned conciliatory. "Look, I'm sorry if I hurt you. I feel bad that people are spreading rumors about you. About us. If there's anything I can do to stop the gossip, let me know."

She longed to snap at him, but curbed her impulse to attack. Pointing a finger at someone else wouldn't absolve her of her own part in all this. Her conscience wouldn't let her wriggle out of the guilt. If anything, it nagged at her even more. Besides, he'd apologized. She should be gracious, but she struggled to find the right words.

When she didn't respond, Myron said hesitantly, "I don't know if it helps to know this, but I understand a little of what you went through today. My shop was extra busy today, and not with customers. I had my share of lectures and shocked faces."

Cathy wanted to cover her face with her hands, but she clenched fistfuls of her apron to keep them by her sides. She couldn't believe this. It had never occurred to her that people would also criticize him. She'd been so focused on herself, she hadn't even considered how this might affect him.

These rumors were all her fault. She'd started them by asking for parenting help, and he'd gone out of his way to take care of the boys. He didn't deserve any of this. Well, except maybe for grabbing her in public. But that had been an accident.

She turned to him. "I'm so sorry." And she really, truly meant it.

He looked surprised at her sudden meekness. Then he offered a half-hearted grin. "I guess we're in this together."

That last word echoed in a hollow and lonely place inside Cathy. *Together.* She repeated it silently to herself. *Together.* She'd never heard a more beautiful word. Her whole life, she'd always been outside looking in. Right now, this very minute, Myron had included her on his team.

She blinked her stinging eyes. Her voice raspy, she

managed to say, "*Danke.*" Her heart overflowed with gratitude for all he'd done for her, but most of all for making her feel like she belonged. She had no words to express it, and if she didn't get away from here now, she'd break down.

Cathy scrambled into her buggy before any telltale tears slipped out. "Goodbye," she choked out before shutting the door and trotting off. But she couldn't outrun her churning emotions.

Tears trickled down her face as she drove home. This wasn't like her. She'd always been strong and stoic, withstanding blows and circumstances that would have destroyed others. All those tears had been cemented behind a wall. A wall that kept her from feeling the pain and sorrow, except sometimes late at night when she was alone.

Never in her life had she cried. Not once since she'd been a lost and lonely child. Yet, in the short time since meeting Myron, she'd cried twice. What was happening to her?

Myron stared after the departing buggy. He'd never met anyone who was such a bundle of contradictions. She flip-flopped from grouchy and sharp-tempered to insecure and guilty. Tonight, if he wasn't mistaken, she'd been close to tears.

He went back over what he'd said, but couldn't find anything that might have provoked that response. Unless it had been a delayed reaction to his comment about gossip that she'd taken personally.

Something inside him still wanted to reach out to her, to help her, to lift the clouds enveloping her. He had no idea what more he could do besides take care of the boys. She hadn't told him not to come, so he assumed that plan was still on.

As he headed for his house, he thanked the Lord for that opportunity. He really enjoyed having the boys at the store. They'd been a spot of brightness amidst all the rumor-hungry shop visitors. He'd spent more than two decades reestablishing his reputation after Ivy disappeared, only to still have to deal with Tim's rebellious antics. Myron was no stranger to criticism and lectures, but associating with Cathy had inflamed all the talk from a bonfire to an inferno. And he had no idea how to douse these flames.

Abe pulled into the driveway just then. His smile and wave lifted Myron's spirits. He'd been headed to bed, but he went into the kitchen, pulled out the peanut butter pie Cathy had sent for that night's supper, and cut two slices. He also poured them each a glass of milk, wondering if Cathy would object to milk with this fluffy pie. Myron pushed aside the question. For some reason, Cathy invaded his thoughts frequently. Too much, in fact.

"Want some pie?" he asked when Abe came inside.

His nephew groaned. "I ate a lot at Anna Mary's." But as if sensing Myron wanted to talk, he sat at the table. "*Mmm*, this looks delicious."

Despite being full, Abe polished off his whole piece as Myron shared his dilemmas with Cathy. Myron wasn't sure what he expected Abe to do about the problems. It felt good, though, to spill all the issues weighing on his mind.

"Sounds like quite a pickle." Abe leaned back in his chair. "I don't know what you can do to stop the rumors except marry her."

"What?" Myron shot bolt upright in his chair. "Perish the thought."

Abe chuckled. "Relax. I was only joking. The two of you would grate each other to shreds."

"We're not that awful," Myron protested.

His nephew's eyebrows shot up. "Are you defending her?"

"*Neh*, of course not. It's just that she made this pie we enjoyed."

"She makes great desserts. I have to give her that. Also, her donuts are *wunderbar*."

Myron nodded. "*Jah*, they are."

Abe gave him the side eye. "Really? When did you taste one? You gave away both boxes and refused one at Anna Mary's."

"I had a chocolate one at the Huyards." He waved a hand toward the back door. "My neighbors."

"I see." Abe's lips twitched. "Sounds like you're not only softening toward her donuts."

"Don't be ridiculous." Myron shoved back his chair and gathered the plates. He turned his back on Abe, but his nephew's words bothered him.

They stayed with him as he headed up to bed. Was he really softening toward Cathy? He supposed he had, at least a little. Definitely not in the way Abe had implied, though. Myron felt sorry for her and wanted to help. But he had absolutely no interest in a relationship.

Later as he tossed and turned, unable to fall asleep, Abe's suggestion kept running through his mind. Marry her? Ugh, no way. But every once in a while, a softer side of her peeked out from her thorny personality, and it intrigued him. She was a fabulous cook, and he'd miss her meals once the boys went home. But you didn't marry someone for their cooking. Or because you felt sorry for them. Or to stop gossip from spreading. Or . . .

Myron drifted off before he could come up with more excuses. He didn't need any. The answer was a loud, emphatic *neh*.

CHAPTER 16

Over time, the rumors died down, and people found more exciting things to gossip about. They accepted that Myron was caring for Cathy's grandnephews, and Cathy rushed out to the driveway each morning as soon as he arrived.

They only talked to each other outside and limited their time together, but their connection to each other grew deeper over time. Because they didn't have long conversations, they made those they had meaningful. Some of their discussions concerned the boys, but they also covered deeper topics than they would as casual acquaintances.

Although sparks flew between them that sometimes flared into irritation, they each appreciated the other's honesty. Over time, they learned to communicate their most important messages with their eyes. Myron tried to convey caring and support when Cathy doubted her parenting abilities. She expressed her appreciation for his help with a smile or a shared look.

Once Abe went back to Fort Plain, Myron adjusted his schedule to sleep soon after dinner and rise early on market days. He washed and returned all Cathy's dishes to her house in the mornings while he kept an eye on the sleeping boys. Cathy left daily meals for the three of them in the refrigerator, which Myron appreciated.

After John started school, Myron dropped him off and took David to work with him. They picked John up after school and ate the dinner Cathy had prepared. Afterward, they often played with the Huyards, but Myron collected them so they'd be at his house before Cathy came to pick them up after work. After the run-in with the police, Myron didn't ever want her to panic about the boys going missing. He'd endured too much agony over Ivy to inflict that misery on anyone else.

When John and David heard her buggy, they went outside to meet her. That way, Cathy didn't come into his house, and Myron and Cathy spoke for only a short while in the driveway, surrounded by the boys and in full view of the neighbors.

Once in a while, all four of them would spend the evening at the Huyards, the adults sitting outside on the porch while the children played games or chased fireflies. No matter what they did together, Myron went out of his way not to tarnish Cathy's reputation.

Because he spent so much time with the boys, he grew attached to them. He did everything with them he wished he'd done with Tim. God truly had given him a second chance to parent and to get it right, for which

Myron was grateful. And John and David filled Myron's life with joy and laughter.

Both boys came to his shop on Saturdays. He especially liked teaching them to work with wood. They were always so proud of themselves when they accomplished a task or helped him with a job. He'd miss them when they went home. And that time was soon approaching. They had only a few more days together. Wayne had made it through the treatments and was doing well, so on Thursday he'd be boarding the bus for the two-day trip home. Myron wanted to make the rest of this week count, so he'd made special plans for each day he had the boys.

On Thursday, Cathy's long day at work, they were going to make ice cream with the Huyards again, only this time at his house. He fed the boys one of their favorite dinners—Cathy's scrumptious baked macaroni and cheese with a buttery cracker crust along with corn on the cob and green beans from Levi's harvest. After helping with the dishes, they headed over to play with their friends while Myron removed desserts from the refrigerator. He cut and laid out an assortment of leftover pie and cake slices that would taste good with ice cream and added today's raspberry-rhubarb crumble bars to the choices on the counter. He had plenty for everyone.

He'd just started for the Huyards to call everyone over when Cathy's horse galloped up the driveway straight at him. Myron jumped back and pinwheeled his arms to stay upright.

What was she doing? If he hadn't leapt out of the

way, she'd have flattened him. He opened his mouth to yell at her, but she emerged from the buggy with panicked eyes.

"Where are the boys?" she demanded.

"At the Huyards. We're getting ready to—"

"I need them right away." Her rapid-fire words bumped into each other.

"Cathy, calm down. What's wrong?"

Digging her teeth into her lower lip, she squeezed her eyes shut. "It's Wayne. He—he—"

She swayed, and Myron raced over to support her before she collapsed. "Easy. Why don't you come in and sit down? You can tell me inside."

"I can't," she wailed. She opened her eyes and gazed at Myron with desperation. "I have to get the boys."

He kept a firm grip on her arm. "What happened to Wayne? Was there a setback? Does he need to stay longer?" If so, that would be fine with Myron, but he hoped it didn't mean something worse for Wayne.

Cathy shook her head. "*Neh, neh.* He—he died. But not of cancer. Sudden cardiac arrest."

"*Ach*, I'm so sorry." Poor Cathy. Poor David and John. They'd lost their *mamm* and now their *daed*.

"I don't know how to tell them. Remember how they cried when they first got here? I won't know how to help them."

She sounded ready to burst into tears. Myron didn't know what to do. He realized he hadn't let go of her arm. She appeared steadier on her feet, so he released her, praying nobody had seen them.

Abby bounced across the yard. "Myron, are you

ready for us yet? Everyone's so excited about the ice cream. Cathy, are you going to join us?" She drew closer. "Is everything all right?"

"Cathy needs to talk to John and David," Myron told her. "Can you bring them over?"

"Of course." Abby scanned Cathy's face. "Can I do anything to help?"

Her face sorrowful, Cathy shook her head. "I—I have to tell them their *daed* died."

"*Ach*, how awful." Abby's face crumpled. "They're orphans? They told me they'd lost their *mamm*." She glanced from Cathy to Myron. "Could they have their ice cream first? They've been looking forward to it all day. I know that probably seems silly when you have such bad news, but . . ."

"Actually," Myron said, "it would be nice for them to do something positive first."

Cathy's jaw tightened. "It's my decision. I think it's best to get bad news over as soon as possible. They may as well get used to things being hard. I had to, and it—"

"Oh, Cathy." Sympathy oozed from Abby's words. "Did you lose a parent?"

"Two of them." Cathy's curt answer made it clear she didn't want to talk about it.

But Abby ignored her. "How did you deal with it?"

"A stiff upper lip."

"You didn't cry?" Abby pressed.

"Absolutely not. That wasn't allowed. My *aenti* and *onkel* said it was God's will, and I needed to trust Him.

They believed doing chores kept you from dwelling on it, so they gave me plenty of work."

"Even Jesus cried," Abby pointed out.

Myron was pretty sure Abby wouldn't change Cathy's mind about crying. He'd be willing to guess Cathy hadn't cried since her parents' deaths. It might explain her tough exterior. She seemed to have put up a wall to protect the hurting little girl she once was, but she'd ended up blocking everyone out.

He didn't want her to do the same thing to John and David. Myron knew from experience it didn't work. Cathy was fragile right now and grieving herself, so he tried to express his opinion gently. "I wish I hadn't forbidden Tim to cry. I think it's one of the reasons he ended up so rebellious."

Cathy stared at him as if he'd betrayed her.

"I'm not criticizing you," he said. "I'm only offering my mistake as an example."

"And implying that I'm making one."

She was right. "I'm trying to prevent you from making the same error I did."

"Fine," she muttered. "Have the ice cream party. If you think having fun is more important than dealing with reality, I'll sit in the buggy until it's over." She stalked past them and climbed inside.

Myron suspected she'd retreated to the buggy because she was struggling to hold back tears.

In a low voice, Myron said to Abby, "Why don't you go and get everyone while I see if I can convince her to join us?"

Abby hurried across the lawn to do his bidding, and

Myron trudged toward the buggy. "Cathy, I'm sure your heart is breaking right now. If you want to cry, we'll understand."

"Myron, I know you're trying to be helpful, but just leave me alone."

"Sometimes sorrow is easier if it's shared."

Cathy's whole body went rigid. "I don't have anyone to share it with."

Her plaintive words made Myron ache for her. "You have us. The Huyards are very understanding. And we can tell the boys together."

"We? This isn't your responsibility. Or the Huyards."

"But all of us care about you and the boys."

"I'm in this alone, just like I've always been all my life."

"God didn't mean for us to be by ourselves. That's why we have a community. We're supposed to support and encourage each other."

She semi-snorted. "Can't say I've ever had that."

Myron wanted to tread gently, but he also wanted to speak the truth. "Is it because others didn't reach out to you or because you wouldn't accept their help?"

Cathy glared at him. "You love to put me in the wrong."

"Can't say I love it, but I suppose I do it more often than not."

A wan smile appeared on Cathy's face. "And I guess I deserve it."

Her eyes, filled with grief, but also lit with a tiny ray of hope, met his, and he longed to take her in his arms to comfort her. Taken aback by his reaction, he retreated a few steps. Where had that thought come from?

Cathy had fled to her buggy to avoid everyone's scrutiny. Myron and Abby made her feel guilty for wanting to tell the children right away. Wasn't it better to get it over with? They'd have to face the truth sometime. Why not now?

The longer she waited, the harder it would be to get the words out. And the longer she held back her own pain and pretended to be all right when she was falling apart, the more likely she'd be to break down when she tried to tell the boys.

Wayne had been the only one left from her family who'd been on her side when she'd broken with her family. He didn't know why she'd done it, but after he'd grown, he hadn't cut her off like the rest of them. Nobody knew what had happened except her *aenti* and *onkel*. And God.

Cathy trembled now the same way she'd quaked the day she'd told them all the truth. Back then, nobody had believed her. They'd given her an ultimatum—admit to lying or leave. Cathy had walked out the door and never gone back.

But as she'd crossed the lawn, young Wayne had run after her and begged her not to go. When she insisted she had no choice, his voice quavered, "I don't know why they're sending you away. I'll never stop loving you. You'll always be my friend and my favorite aunt."

That had touched her. It had been the only bright spot in that horrendous day.

Wayne had kept his promise. Even if his parents punished him, he found ways to communicate with her until he'd grown and gone out on his own. Then Cathy and Wayne had visited whenever they could, and later, after their busy lives and jobs kept them apart, they sent letters.

Now she had no one. No family. Except her two nephews.

Myron startled her by appearing outside her buggy. She wanted to ignore him, but at his pleading look, she opened the window. His compassion and understanding, his invitation to join them, and his offer to share her sorrow had hit all the right notes. Even their sparring had reassured her that he meant what he said.

All that kindness and caring vibrated a chord deep within Cathy, setting off a tiny trill that made her pulse flutter despite the deep undertones of sorrow in her heart. Her somber song interspersed with his upbeat tones created an unexpected melody. Cathy's soul had always responded to music.

The way their notes blended reminded her of his statement two months ago. *We're in this together.* Ever since that day, the word *together* had echoed through her mind. Everything they did to take care of the boys was like well-ordered teamwork. He'd been there for her and supported her every step of the way.

In the depths of her being, she knew she could rely

on him. But could she share her heartache and her burdens?

Just when she'd made the decision to try, he backed away. She didn't blame him. Nobody could help her. Her whole life, she'd been left alone to cope on her own. Why should now be any different?

As if regretting his earlier retreat, Myron moved closer. "Is there anything I can do to help? Anything at all?"

Without meaning to, she burst out, "What am I going to do? Wayne asked me to take care of his boys if anything happened to him."

Myron stared at her, stunned for a moment. "You'll be their guardian?" he finally managed. Then his eyes took on a faraway expression, and his shoulders sagged as if he were carrying a heavy weight. Perhaps he was recalling being as staggered as this back when he'd been saddled with his niece and nephew years ago.

His eyes filled with sympathy. "It's a lot of responsibility."

If anyone would know, Myron would. He'd been through it. And that's what she dreaded. Not the day-to-day chores that came with feeding and housing two children, although that wouldn't be easy, but the emotional and moral obligations of parenthood.

"I won't be a fit parent. I've barely been coping the past two months. Only knowing they'd be heading home in a few weeks kept me going." Cathy's words wobbled. "I don't know how to do this. You know what an abrasive personality I have. I'm not the right person to help them grow up properly."

"You must be. God's leaving them in your care." Myron tried to encourage her, but he didn't sound any more confident than she felt.

She didn't like clichés, especially from him. "Is that how you felt when Ivy and Tim suddenly became your children?"

Myron hung his head. "*Neh*, I didn't. I felt overwhelmed and saw them as a burden. Not that I didn't love them, but I was totally unprepared."

"So, maybe you know a little about what I'm feeling right now. I'm frightened of making mistakes, not sure I can mother them properly, and I feel like I'm drowning."

"I can understand that. I'm sorry, Cathy."

His apology meant a lot. So did his understanding. But they hadn't even covered the biggest hurdle she faced today. Telling John and David the devastating news. And trying to comfort them.

"Why don't you come inside?"

"*Neh*, I can't go in." Cathy didn't want to tell the boys this devastating information in front of others. And she wasn't sure she could do it without breaking down.

There might have been a time when she could deliver a cut-and-dried message with no emotion, but since caring for the boys and spending time with Myron, some of her walls had crumbled. She'd cried twice already. What if she did it now with everyone watching?

"I can see why you'd rather stay out here," Myron

said, "but maybe it will help to have others around when you . . ."

It wouldn't help her, but what about John and David? They'd grown attached to Myron and Abby, who might be a comfort. Doing this in front of an audience would be much more difficult, but Cathy had to think about the boys' well-being.

"All right. I'll go in."

"I know it won't be easy, but we'll do what we can to help."

Cathy believed he would. She also needed to trust God for guidance.

Myron was glad Cathy had agreed. She tried to do everything on her own. Over the past two months, she'd gradually begun to trust him and the Huyards a bit more. Liz beamed when they walked through the door, but her eyes radiated compassion and caring. Abby must have told her parents the news.

Levi dipped his chin in acknowledgment. "Hope you don't mind we got started, but the young ones were so eager."

"*Gut* idea." Myron breathed a sigh of relief to see the boys occupied and having fun. He ached for what they'd have to face shortly.

Cathy took a seat in the corner far from the excited children, who were taking turns churning the ice cream. She gazed off into the distance, misery etched into her features.

Myron longed to ease her pain, but all he could do was pray. He sent up petitions for God's comfort for her and for the boys.

All the adults' smiles held a touch of sadness, knowing what was coming next, but they tried to stay cheerful and encourage the children to have fun.

When the ice cream was ready and everyone had plates except Cathy, John studied her with concern. Then he bounded over. "Don't you want some?"

"Not really." Her lips curved into a forced smile. "*Danke* for asking."

"But I helped make the ice cream."

"I know."

John looked disappointed. "Don't you even want to try it? It's really good."

David hurried over. "I helped too."

"All right, I'll have a little bowlful." Cathy sounded as if she were forcing out each word.

Myron went to the cupboard for a mug and scooped out a small amount. He remembered how hard it had been to swallow and how queasy his stomach had been after his fiancée's and his brother's deaths. Cathy might be feeling the same.

She noticed what he was doing and gave him a nod. *Gut.* He'd guessed right.

"Do you want pie or cake?" John seemed determined to cheer Cathy up.

"*Neh*, just ice cream."

Myron called to him. "Do you want to take this to Cathy, John?"

"*Jah.*" He collected the mug. Holding it with two hands, he took careful steps across the room and handed the ice cream to Cathy as if it were a precious gift.

She thanked him with a stiff smile that didn't reach her eyes. He fidgeted, waiting for her to take a bite.

Cathy dipped the tip of the spoon into the cup and licked it off. "It's delicious."

John beamed at her compliment and didn't seem to notice the tremor in her voice.

But Myron did. Interacting with the boys had taken a toll on her. He didn't want this added pressure to cause a breakdown before she gave them the news.

"Hey, John," Myron called, "want to help me clean the dasher?"

"Can I lick it?" John raced to the ice cream maker.

David scurried over. "Me too."

"As long as you share with your brother," Myron agreed.

Cathy sent Myron a grateful glance, but she looked exhausted. Maybe he shouldn't have insisted on letting the boys make ice cream tonight. He lifted the dasher and held it out to John.

To Myron's surprise, John carried the dasher around and offered some of the last blobs of ice cream to everyone else first. Myron's heart warmed. He'd been trying to teach the boys to share with each other, but John had just demonstrated that lesson. Myron's chest expanded like a proud *daed*'s, even though the boys weren't his.

After everyone had finished their treats, Levi stood. "Why don't I take the younger ones home for bed?"

He gathered his children and sent Liz an *I'm-with-you-in-thought* message of support that she returned with a special glance.

Myron had often observed their private silent conversations, and that's what had given him the idea to use that technique with Cathy. Their messages weren't as intimate or lovey-dovey as Levi and Liz's, but Myron and Cathy managed to convey a lot of information as well as understand each other without words.

As Levi headed out the door with the children, he turned to Cathy. "I'll be praying."

She choked out a *danke*, and Myron asked the Lord to guide her through this ordeal.

Chapter 17

While Myron and the boys cleaned the dasher and emptied the churn, Abby and Liz washed and dried the dishes. Cathy should get up and help, but an overwhelming sorrow pinned her to the chair. And she needed to settle on the right way to tell two small boys their *daed* was never coming back.

As Myron slotted the pieces back into the clean ice cream maker, David rubbed his eyes and yawned. Cathy worried the boys were getting too sleepy. They should be home in bed.

Myron turned to her and mouthed, *Are you ready?*

Although his eyes expressed compassion, she responded like a cornered animal, hunching in on herself for protection. *Neh*, she had to be strong. The children needed her. With great effort, she lifted her chin, straightened her spine, and signaled she'd do it now. *Lord, please give me the words to say.*

Myron sent her a brief look of encouragement to brace her. Then he and Abby took the boys' hands and led them over to the corner where Cathy sat. They lowered themselves to the floor in a semicircle around her.

In a halting voice, she told them the news. At first, the boys sat there, confused and stunned.

"Like Mamm?" a dazed John finally asked.

When Cathy nodded, he threw himself into Abby's arms and sobbed. David wrapped his arms around Myron's neck and clung to him as he bawled. Myron held him close.

Cathy had gotten out the terrible, painful words. Words that sank like heavy stones into a pond. Words that had destroyed the lives of two small children. Her children now.

What hurt her most was that neither of them came to her for comfort. They clung to Abby and Myron.

Cathy sat there bereft. Alone. Isolated.

As she'd been all her life. And would be now that her only family was gone forever.

A hand descended on her shoulder. Cathy jumped. She hated when people walked up behind her or surprised her with a touch. She wanted to know they were there ahead of time.

She took a deep breath to calm her racing heart.

Liz's concerned expression also radiated strength and encouragement. "This must be hard on you," she murmured.

Cathy bit her lip. Harder than anyone would ever know. But if she answered, tears might spill out. She'd gotten through the speech she'd rehearsed in her head without revealing all the emotions swirling inside.

She nodded wordlessly, and Liz squeezed her

shoulder. If only Cathy were a child who could cry in someone's arms. But she'd never had that opportunity in her life, not even when she was three years old. The year she'd lost her parents, and her *aenti* and *onkel* took her in. They insisted she call them Mamm and Daed, but those names never fit. Although they forbade crying, Cathy couldn't stop the tears that leaked out at night when she lay by herself in the dark, trying to make sense of her loss.

That topsy-turvy time of her life had become a blur. The sharp pain, helplessness, disorientation, fear, and loneliness still haunted her, but the details had been buried under a gray cloud of grief. Much of it had been locked away and overshadowed by later tragedies.

She shook off the past. She had enough distress in the present without dredging up old burdens. Today, she'd lost the last family member she'd grown up with. Now it was up to her to raise the next generation. A task she didn't have the skills to do. And how could she show the boys how to heal their loss while struggling with her own grief?

She never had anyone comfort her the way Abby and Myron were doing for John and David. The lonely young child inside her longed for someone to hold her and let her cry. Myron had said he forbade Tim to cry, yet right now, he'd wrapped his arms around David and let him spill out his grief. Cathy yearned to take David's place in Myron's arms and have him console her like that.

She banished the thought. That could never be.

When his crying slowed to hiccupping, John lifted his

head and asked the question Cathy had been dreading. "Where are we going to live?"

David wailed, "We'll be all alone in our house. No Mamm. No Daed." He collapsed back against Myron.

Myron hugged David, rubbed his back, and whispered something in his ear. Then Myron looked up, and his eyes met Cathy's with an inquiry. *How are you doing?*

They'd often communicated with gazes, but this time, the empathy in his soft, caring brown eyes almost undid her. Her eyes grew so misty, she almost missed his second question.

Do you want me to tell them?

She swallowed to dislodge the choking feeling in her throat. If only she could take him up on that, but this was her responsibility. She'd worked hard these past months to banish her *onkel*'s criticism, but now his harsh voice scolded her for letting others do her duty. She had to do this herself.

Cathy shook her head and tried to send a thank-you message to Myron. *I have to answer his question.*

Her words quavered as she forced them out. "You'll be staying with me."

John's mouth rounded into an O. "But I want to go home."

That declaration led to a fresh spate of crying and tore Cathy apart. They didn't want to stay with her, which only added to her inadequacy and her sadness. It brought back memories of the upheaval in her own childhood.

"I want . . . my toys . . . my bed . . . my quilt," John

gulped out. "My *da—*" Then, realizing the truth, he crumpled into a heap on Abby's lap.

She gathered him in her arms again and murmured soothing words as he huddled against her. "I'm sure you can bring your things here." She sounded about ready to cry, but she looked to Cathy for confirmation.

"Of course you can get your things." Something she hadn't been allowed to do as a child. She'd make sure John and David had the things that were most important to them. Whatever she could do to make their transition easier, she'd do.

Ach. She hadn't even thought about all the things she'd have to handle. How would she do it all? *Lord, please help me.*

The next morning, Cathy opened her market stand as usual. She'd been planning to hang a closed sign, but Myron had convinced her to keep the boys' schedule as regular as possible. They'd had one big disruption by losing their *daed*, so they needed a familiar structure they could count on.

Turned out he'd been right. Making the donuts had helped her too. The automatic steps of mixing and kneading occupied her mind and kept her from wallowing in grief. The repetitive motions of her daily routine calmed her, but they also gave her a chance to think and plan. And most of all to pray.

God sent an immediate answer to her petitions. The person who showed up before the market opened solved most of Cathy's problems, except for the hole in her heart.

"Only God can take care of that," Mrs. Vandenberg

said briskly, as if she'd read Cathy's mind. She ordered one donut, then whipped a pen and tablet from her purse along with her phone.

"I know you have a lot to do right now, so I thought I'd help unravel the legal tangles so you can concentrate on other things. Here's what I need to know." She went down a rapid-fire list of questions.

After she jotted down Wayne's information, she made several phone calls to give out assignments—everything from getting all the necessary legal papers to contacting the embassy and funeral home for returning Wayne from Mexico to hiring a small moving van for items the boys wanted from their New Wilmington house to getting the house listed for sale.

By the time Mrs. Vandenberg finished, Cathy's head was spinning. She hadn't even known half of those things would be necessary.

"*Danke*," Cathy said weakly. "I could never have done all that."

"Sure you could, but why should you when I have people who know how to do all of it? Might as well use my connections to cut through all the red tape and get it done quickly. This way, you can spend your time on more important things, like caring for those two adorable boys."

Cathy had to be honest. "I'm not so sure I can do that either."

"Nonsense. Give them plenty of love and good guidance. And pray for wisdom." Mrs. Vandenberg's eyes grew unfocused as if looking into the distant past.

"Children grow up so quickly. Before you know it, they're grown and gone."

Cathy wondered if Mrs. Vandenberg had children and grandchildren. Or even great-grandchildren, at her age. Cathy had never heard about any, but Mrs. Vandenberg's nostalgic expression seemed to indicate she might have raised a family. Cathy waited, hoping for more advice, anything to help her do a better job of parenting.

After a while, Mrs. Vandenberg returned to the present and added, "Oh, and trust the others in the boys' lives to do their part."

"I can't expect Myron and the Huyards to keep doing this. I've imposed on them long enough."

"Myron's never been happier. The boys are healing old wounds in his life. And John and David need a father figure."

Cathy gulped. Surely Mrs. Vandenberg wasn't implying . . .

Images flashed into Cathy's mind like blinking yellow lights on the roadway. *Caution*, they warned. But no matter how hard she tried to erase them, a series of snapshots of her and Myron together as a couple flickered by, making her wish they were true.

Her face burning, she pulled herself up short. She truly hoped Mrs. Vandenberg hadn't been reading her thoughts.

The elderly lady laughed. "Neither of you are ready for a relationship at this point. You both have deep-seated pain you need to address."

Cathy had plenty of that, but her instinctive nose for

gossip set her wondering what Mrs. Vandenberg knew about Myron.

"You'll find out in good time," Mrs. Vandenberg advised. "Be gentle with him. He has to face several fears and heartaches."

"I know about his problems with Tim. But what other things—"

Mrs. Vandenberg cut her off. "You'll have to find out for yourself. Use your detective skills."

Although Cathy racked her brain to come up with possibilities for Myron's secrets, nothing came to mind. Now that she thought about it, she hadn't been creating many stories about people lately. She hadn't had time. But also, being the recent subject of rumors had dampened some of her enthusiasm for spying and sharing.

Mrs. Vandenberg nodded vigorously. "You've made some strides too." She reached out and patted Cathy's hand, which was clenched around a cleaning cloth, scrubbing the countertop. "The path to true love is never smooth, but in the end, the journey is worth it."

Is she talking about me? Or about Myron? Pain shot through Cathy at the thought of him finding true love. All along, she'd been telling herself she wasn't interested in him, but the thought of losing him to another woman filled her with a deep ache. With that added to the pain of losing Wayne, negative emotions threatened to capsize Cathy's shaky emotional ship as it navigated choppy waters.

"Steady, dear. Don't let your guesswork gallop ahead of reality."

Mrs. Vandenberg's warning righted Cathy's tipping

boat, and a different thought struck her. *Did Mrs. Vandenberg mean Myron and I should be together?*

For a second, the idea thrilled Cathy. Myron had even used that word, *together*. Did it have a special meaning?

No sooner had she rejoiced over that possibility than worrisome thoughts punctured her happiness. Even if Myron asked to court her, she could never agree to marry him. She couldn't marry anyone. Love was not in her future.

"Trust God for the days ahead. He has a wonderful plan for you. One your active imagination can't envision."

With the darkness of her present life, Cathy had a hard time believing Mrs. Vandenberg's words.

The elderly woman cleared her throat. "Now I have a favor to ask of you."

After all Mrs. Vandenberg had done, Cathy would be happy to repay her.

"You know my project with the STAR center? The one where I've been placing trainees in market stands?"

"*Jah*," Cathy said warily. The trainees came from a program for ex-gang members.

When Mrs. Vandenberg had first proposed the idea, Cathy railed against it to everyone in the market. What if the ex-gang members stole from the market stands? Slit their throats? Or did other horrible things?

She'd imagined knife battles in the aisle. Or gunfights, where they'd all be flat on their stomachs cowering from flying bullets. Police would storm the market searching for criminals.

With an odd sense of relief, Cathy realized that since she'd been spending time with Myron and the Huyards, she didn't picture quite as many of those horrible scenarios.

Mrs. Vandenberg nodded. "When you spend a lot of time alone, the mind tends to awfulize."

Awfulize? That was a great word to describe the way Cathy automatically assumed the worst.

Before she might have blurted out her objections to this program, but one of Myron's digs reminded her to hold her tongue. After all, Mrs. Vandenberg had placed many of these trainees at market stands, and so far, nothing bad had happened. But Cathy didn't want to be a part of that experiment.

"I have a trainee in accounting and business management who used to work for a donut franchise. She knows about mixing dough, cutting and frying donuts, and waiting on customers. I think Tahiri would be a perfect fit for your stand."

Cathy tried not to wince. She couldn't possibly allow an ex-gang member access to her stand. How could she ever trust her? What if the girl got angry at Cathy and knifed her in the back?

She couldn't express her fears to Mrs. Vandenberg, so she grasped for another excuse. "I don't make enough to pay a worker."

"Not a problem. My charity pays the wages for all the trainees who work at the market. You'll get qualified help for free."

"That's so nice of you, but my stand's too small for two people."

"Not if one works in the back and the other handles the counter."

Through gritted teeth, Cathy said, "I prefer to work alone."

"I know you do. But I think you've been finding that having friends is a big help. And they add joy to your life."

Cathy couldn't argue with that, but she couldn't possibly imagine making friends with a gang member.

"You know, sometimes a blot on your past can be caused by someone else's actions rather than your own." Mrs. Vandenberg's gaze sliced through Cathy.

Does she know about mine?

"Maybe you should talk to Tahiri and find out her story before you decide."

No matter what this girl said, Cathy wouldn't change her mind. But after all Mrs. Vandenberg had done this morning, Cathy couldn't possibly refuse outright. "I-I'll think about it," she managed at last.

"You'll have to think fast." Mrs. Vandenberg glanced at her watch. "The market opens in five minutes, and Tahiri will arrive then."

Cathy's heart sank. How could she possibly get out of this? "I, um, don't really need help. I can manage well on my own."

"But it would be helpful if you didn't have to come in so early in the mornings. Tahiri could mix up the dough for you so Myron wouldn't have to get up at three a.m."

That hit Cathy in a sore spot. She felt guilty about him missing out on his sleep to help her.

"In fact, you could drop John at school and get here soon after the market opens."

Doing that would mean Cathy would miss all the early-morning rumors about other people circulating around the market. It surprised her to find she didn't mind the idea of that as much as she once would have.

And she'd love to see John off to school in the mornings. Now that she was his parent, she wanted to keep a closer eye on him and do all the regular motherly duties. Plus, if she stayed at her house, he could walk to school like the other children.

Because Myron lived outside her *g'may*, he had to drive John in the opposite direction and then turn around and drive past his own house to head to work. That had bothered Cathy ever since school started.

This whole plan was starting to sound *wunderbar*, except for one major catch—leaving a gang member in charge of her stand.

Mrs. Vandenberg hadn't finished trying to convince Cathy. "You'll also need someone here during the funeral and when you're moving the boys and—"

Cathy waved that away. "I can close the stand."

"You dislike doing that, don't you?"

Squeezing her eyes shut, Cathy rubbed her temples and nodded. She hated it. She'd listen to her *onkel*'s streams of criticism the whole day long.

But which would be worse—her *onkel*'s ghost screaming at her about her faults or having a criminal working in her stand?

"Not every gang member is a criminal."

Had Mrs. Vandenberg been following Cathy's

thoughts all along? Her cheeks heated. People always said you couldn't hide anything from Mrs. V.

"Ah, here comes Tahiri." Mrs. Vandenberg turned to greet a pretty girl with a million braids clanking with multicolored beads, a sparkling nose stud, and orange, jewel-bedecked fingernails that extended so far out Cathy wondered how she could possibly pick up anything.

Mrs. Vandenberg barely had time to introduce them before people flooded to Cathy's stand. She didn't normally have so many customers at once, except when people had come to find out the latest gossip about her encounter with the police or her relationship with Myron. Both of those no longer held people's interest.

Cathy apologized to Mrs. Vandenberg and Tahiri. "Sorry, but I need to wait on everyone."

"Your stand's real busy."

Tahiri's observation made Cathy want to retort, *You think so?* Instead, she mustered a smile and gave an honest reply. "Lines aren't usually this long." With a final nod, Cathy rushed to fill orders, hand over bakery boxes and bags, and make change.

She didn't have time to catch her breath for almost forty-five minutes. By then, her display case was almost empty, but the line still extended down the aisle. She needed to make more donuts, but when would she get the time?

Cathy almost regretted turning down Tahiri's help.

At a sizzling sound behind her, Cathy wheeled around. Tahiri was dropping donuts into the fryer. On the counter, rows of precut donuts were rising. Cathy's first instinct was to yell at the girl and tell her she had no business in the stand.

For once, Cathy held her tongue. She needed help. And from the way Tahiri handled the fryer and cut out the donuts, she had the skills. And Mrs. Vandenberg would be sure anyone she brought into the market was honest and upright.

Cathy had no doubt she could trust Mrs. Vandenberg's judgment. Maybe it was time Cathy learned to trust more people. And let them help her. Right now, she had no choice.

She turned back around and continued serving customers, humbled by Tahiri's willingness to jump right in and do what needed to be done despite Cathy being less than welcoming.

Forgive me, Lord, for judging Tahiri and rejecting her. Give me the grace to admit I'm grateful for her help. And thank you for sending help when I need it even though I don't always appreciate it.

CHAPTER 18

With Mrs. Vandenberg's assistance, Tahiri's competence, and Myron's support, Cathy managed to get through all the heartbreaking events that month. If it hadn't been for all three of them, she'd have fallen apart. They'd done so much for her, and so had the Huyards. Cathy wished she could find a way to pay them all back. She made meals for Myron, Tahiri, and Abby's family, but it seemed so insignificant compared to what she'd received.

Cathy confided that to Mrs. Vandenberg, who pointed out Tahiri was thrilled to have a job and to be able to move out of the city and into a place of her own. "You've also given her self-confidence by letting her run the stand on the days you've taken off."

Nobody would ever know how much Cathy had agonized over that. She'd suffered stomach pains the first time she left Tahiri in charge for two hours. The whole time Cathy was gone, her mind conjured up awful scenarios—everything from Tahiri stealing all her money to a fire burning down her stand. None of which happened.

Cathy had returned to happy customers, dough rising, a donut-filled display case, and a smiling Tahiri. Although that calmed some of Cathy's fears, she still hesitated to leave. But she had to make trips to New Wilmington, which meant she needed to turn the business over to Tahiri several times for full days.

Mrs. Vandenberg noticed Cathy's tension as they rode in the van together. "Relax, dear. Tahiri will do fine."

It always surprised Cathy the way Mrs. Vandenberg read her mind. "How did you know that's what I was worried about?" Cathy said defensively.

"I can tell by the way you're gripping your apron that you're nervous. And I can sense why. God gives me nudges."

Myron sat behind her with John strapped into a car seat beside him. Mrs. Vandenberg had asked Myron to come along to help with the boys. "Why don't we pray about it?" he suggested.

He had a way of grounding Cathy when her imagination began awfulizing.

"You're right. I need to turn this over to the Lord."

After they all prayed, Cathy calmed a little. She had trouble letting go of complete control. Vivid pictures of Tahiri's skills flowed through Cathy's mind. Tahiri did everything so well and quickly. She'd even shown Cathy ways to streamline her work. Of course, Cathy had resisted at first. Being open-minded didn't come easily to her, but Tahiri had persisted. And her suggestions had improved the business and saved time. *Jah*, Cathy could count on Tahiri to do a good job of running the business.

Letting go of that anxiety, though, only opened the door for grief to pour in.

Myron must have sensed it, because he reached forward and set a hand on her shoulder. "We can pray about that too."

Once they'd finished, Myron squeezed her shoulder and let go. Cathy turned her head to convey a *danke*. Beside Myron, tears dripped down John's cheeks. Myron pulled out a pack of tissues and wiped John's face with such gentleness for a man with big, strong, calloused hands that Cathy's eyes welled with tears.

Expressing emotion still made her uncomfortable, but Myron's acceptance of her changeable moods allowed her to let some of those walls down. He made it safe for her to show sadness and fear, two feelings she'd always kept locked away.

When Myron set his hand on John's head and whispered something soothing, Cathy's tears trickled out. Myron held out the packet of tissues. She took several. It amazed her how he always seemed to anticipate what she needed. Right now, he'd offered her the two things she needed most—prayer and tissues—along with emotional support.

Myron wished he could comfort Cathy like he did John. He longed to wipe away her tears and enfold her in his arms. Something about seeing her so vulnerable made him want to protect and shelter her.

With a watery *danke*, she turned back around and followed his lead, placing a comforting hand on David's head, even though he was sound asleep. Maybe that touch would console her. He hoped so. He'd been through this depth of grief himself, although his had been tinged with shame and guilt. Still, he understood her pain.

John's sniffles made Myron wish he could wrap his arms around the small boy and hold him close. If they'd been in a buggy, he could have. In an *Englisch* van, though, the car seat prevented that. He'd have to wait until they arrived at their destination.

These trips to New Wilmington brought up the same distress Myron had endured when he'd moved Tim out of the home he'd grown up in. Back then, Myron had insisted Tim keep a stiff upper lip. Ivy, as a bewildered two-year-old, hadn't comprehended the situation. She walked around, dazed and confused, when they left her familiar home and moved to his.

The only piece of furniture they'd moved to Myron's place had been Ivy's crib. He'd let her keep the baby blanket she rubbed against her face when falling asleep. And he'd allowed Tim to bring his ratty teddy bear.

This time, he encouraged Cathy to let the boys bring their beds, dressers, and toys.

She frowned. "You gave them plenty of toys."

"At least let them take some of their favorites."

Her jaw tightened, but she relented. Though she

obviously hadn't been expecting how many favorites the boys had.

"I can pack up some of mine and return them to the attic. Or, better yet, give them to someone else." Myron couldn't say why he'd held on to Tim's toys in the first place. Maybe to remind him of Tim clinging to his hand back before Ivy disappeared, back before the terrible tantrums began.

Myron shook away the nostalgia. He needed to concentrate on the two small boys, who were having meltdowns. Instead of dealing with them the way he'd done with Tim, Myron had mastered Abby's technique of listening, sympathizing, and hugging.

Sometimes, he ended up with two sniffling boys in his arms and a soaked shirtfront, but they cuddled close afterward or slid down and held his hand. Then they went back to the projects they needed to accomplish. Eventually, they managed to whittle down the toy collection to one container apiece. Afterward, the three of them supervised the movers and played in the backyard between bouts of bawling.

Meanwhile, Cathy and Mrs. Vandenberg met with lawyers, signed papers, made phone calls, and dealt with arrangements. Whenever Myron passed them, Cathy appeared stressed and on the verge of tears. He sent her a smile he hoped might uplift her. From the spark that lit her eyes, she seemed to appreciate it.

The only thing that bothered him was Mrs. Vandenberg's knowing grin. He hoped she wasn't reading too much into it. Even more troubling, he hoped she hadn't set her sights on him as a match for Cathy. Myron might like her as a friend, but they'd clash constantly if they had to live in the same house.

After the first successful trip with Tahiri left in charge of the stand, Cathy relaxed a little more when she had to leave. Even though traveling to New Wilmington reminded her of Wayne and all she'd lost, she had to admit Myron's company had proved to be a godsend. He had developed an instinct for what the boys needed most, and he guided her, helping her understand them better.

His warmth also thawed some of Cathy's frozen memories. She'd never forget how lost she'd felt after burying her parents or her pain at moving and leaving her beloved home behind. Uprooting the boys filled her with guilt and a deep sadness for them, so she tried to be as understanding as possible. It would take a while for them to adjust to losing their *daed* and to moving to Lancaster permanently. Cathy only hoped they'd come to accept her house as their new home and her as their new parent.

She'd never force them to call her *mamm* the way her *aenti* had. She'd give them time to grieve. Maybe in time, they'd come to see her as their *mamm*, but if not, she'd allow them to call her Cathy.

She marveled that she'd relaxed some of the rigid standards she used to insist on. Abby had taught Cathy to pick and choose which rules to enforce. Morals were nonnegotiable. But she could let lesser issues slide. Accepting that made her life so much easier.

The more she spent time around others, the more she softened, but in a good way. And the less judgmental she became. Tahiri had been a big help with that too.

The most amazing thing about Tahiri was that she never bragged or took credit for her successes. Through Tahiri's humility, God gave Cathy daily lessons in *demut*.

Cathy had also been humbled after she'd heard Tahiri's life story. Tahiri had joined a gang when she was twelve to keep her younger sisters safe. She'd given up her own childhood in exchange for theirs. Once you were in a gang, there was no escape. If you ran, they'd track you down, and you'd pay for your disloyalty. Tahiri didn't go into detail about all the terrible things that had happened to her, but the horror of that time showed in her eyes when she described her past.

Like hearing Myron's story, learning about Tahiri's past taught Cathy not to jump to conclusions. It made her sad she'd passed along rumors of people's lives without understanding what they'd been going through. She'd observed their actions from the outside and guessed at the rest. She'd never gotten to know the person or taken time to find out the deeper truths of their circumstances. Her gossip must have only added to their burdens, the way the gossip about her and Myron had been hurtful and so unfair, and sometimes still was. Often, those false impressions stayed with people longer than the actual facts.

Now that Cathy had no time to pry into other people's

lives, the church members had become friendlier. They went out of their way to welcome John and David, and several young mothers invited Cathy to their get-togethers. Because of her work schedule, Cathy could rarely attend, but she appreciated them including her. For the first time in her life, she began to feel part of a group.

She opened up a little, but kept her deeper emotions and struggles hidden. She could never share those with anyone, except Myron, and she came to depend on him more and more. If he hadn't accompanied them on all the heartrending trips back and forth to New Wilmington, Cathy wasn't sure she would have made it through the dark days. He'd even had his two shop managers help him move and rearrange all the bedroom furniture at her house after work one night. She owed him so much and had no way to return his assistance and support. Same with Mrs. Vandenberg, who'd taken care of so many details and organized all the travel to New Wilmington.

"I wish I could do something for you and Myron after all you've done for me," Cathy said to Mrs. Vandenberg after they returned from their final trip.

"As for me, you don't owe me anything. It makes me happy to help people. But you've done a lot for my program by hiring Tahiri. If you really want to do something, you could convince a few reluctant stand owners to take on some of my trainees."

"I can do that. Just give me their names."

If anyone had told Cathy a few months ago she'd be volunteering to bring more ex-gang members into the market, she'd never have believed them. Now, she'd do it with happiness and conviction.

She gave Mrs. Vandenberg a rueful smile. "I might be the best person for this job because I understand the reasons why people are reluctant to participate."

Mrs. Vandenberg's eyes twinkled. "You certainly do. And you know a lot about everyone in the market, so you can tailor your presentations perfectly."

Cathy lowered her head. Was that a nice way of calling her a snoop?

"You know, dear, God can turn our faults into assets if we let Him. You've made quite a turnaround. Trust Him for His leading, and you'll be a blessing to many people, including me."

Lord, Cathy begged, *please make me a blessing rather than a curse.*

"Back to Myron, I suspect if you asked him, he'd tell you that you've more than repaid him. He raves about the meals you make. And I don't think I've ever seen him as happy as he is right now. You and those boys have given him a new life."

Although Cathy didn't feel as if those were gifts she'd given either of them, it gladdened her heart to know she'd made a difference in their lives. Still, she wanted to do something more. But she wasn't sure what.

* * *

The November wedding season came and went, and winter set in. Myron had never been so content. The boys and Cathy had brought so much joy to his life.

Because of the icy weather, they couldn't talk out on the driveway. He'd invited Cathy inside to warm up. All four of them sat at his kitchen table, sipping hot chocolate.

John beamed over the rim of his mug. A brownish milk mustache edged his upper lip. "Guess what, Myron. I learned my part for the Christmas program at school. Want to hear it?"

"Of course." Myron loved finding out what they were doing at school.

John set down his drink and hopped off his chair. He stood straight and tall, holding an imaginary sign while he recited a short poem.

Myron smiled. "Great job."

"Will you come and see me?"

"Umm." Myron glanced at Cathy. They'd managed to squash most of the rumors flying around months ago. He didn't want to risk starting them up again.

She hesitated. "I don't know if that's a good idea."

"But . . ." John's lips wobbled. "I don't have a *daed* to watch me." He hung his head and mumbled, "And I wanted to ask Abby and Ben and—"

Myron cleared his throat to dislodge the huge lump choking him. He couldn't let John down. "Why don't I come with the Huyards? I'm sure they'd enjoy attending."

Cathy breathed out a soft sigh. "That might work."

With a teary-eyed smile, John threw his arms around Myron's neck and hugged him hard. "*Danke.*" Then he gulped down his cocoa and turned to his brother. "Want to play with me?"

David nodded and jumped down.

"Mugs, boys," Myron reminded them, and they rushed to put their cups in the sink.

"Don't pull out too many toys," Cathy warned. "We need to go home soon."

"That reminds me." Myron rose and headed for the living room. He returned with a bolt of fabric. "John's teacher sent this home with him for his shirt."

Cathy groaned and rubbed her head. "I'm not sure when I'll have time to sew it. I have so many orders to fill for holiday donuts, including on my days off. Do you know who the fabric goes to next?"

"No, but I can drop it off at the school when you're done."

"That would be helpful. *Danke.*" She stood, carried her cup to the sink, and started running the dishwater. "I'd better get going. I'll have to at least lay out the pattern tonight. If I get the fabric cut in the morning before I leave for work, I can send it on tomorrow."

"Leave the dishes," Myron told her. "I'll get them. You have a lot to do."

"I don't want to make more work for you."

Myron went over and took the mug from her hands. Their fingers brushed. Heat rushed through his arm. He stood stock-still. Cathy sucked in a breath and jumped back. Had she felt it too?

His face burned. He tried to keep his voice steady, but his words came out hoarse. "After you . . . I, um, mean you and the boys . . . When you leave, I don't have anything to do." His house seemed like a lonely, empty shell at night. "This will keep me from being lonely." *And from missing you. All of you.*

Chapter 19

Christmas carols filled the air as Myron walked down the street to his shop every day. Lights and holiday displays decorated every window. Myron had placed several battery-operated candles and some pine boughs on the furniture in his display window, but a hand-carved nativity set by Luke Bontrager held a place of prominence on a table centered close to the glass.

Later that evening, Myron whistled "Away in a Manger" as he locked up his shop, took David's and John's hands, and headed for the buggy. Although he had so many orders to fill before the holiday, he'd left work early because he had an important event to attend.

As he lifted the boys into the buggy, they were both bursting with anticipation.

John puffed out his chest. "It's my program tonight."

"For sure and certain, it is." Myron smiled at him.

"I did a good job in the afternoon program. You're coming to see me, right?"

"I promised you I would, and I always keep my promises."

"*Gut.*" John breathed out a sigh of relief. "I want you there."

"Don't worry," Myron reassured John. "I'll be there with the Huyards. They're as excited as I am to see it." Myron remembered how excited—and nervous—he'd been at his first program ages ago. He debated discussing stage fright with John, but he decided against it. No point in putting ideas in his head. At the moment, John seemed thrilled and confident. But it wouldn't hurt to rehearse.

"Want to say your poem for me?" Myron prompted.

John lifted his chin and repeated the words in a loud, clear voice.

"Sounds like you're ready." Myron reached out and patted John's shoulder before steering the horse to the shoulder of the road to let a line of cars pass.

The buggy vibrated as they zipped by. Once the single lane had cleared, Myron encouraged the horse to return to the road and keep up a brisk pace. Ordinarily, he let his horse meander home, but today he needed to meet Cathy at his house. She'd be taking John to the schoolhouse.

When they arrived at Myron's house, Cathy was already waiting, pacing impatiently up and down in the driveway.

"About time," she said. "I was afraid we were going to be late."

He wished she didn't always work herself into a

frenzy. "I said we'd be here a little before five, and we are."

"I went in and put a casserole in the oven so we can eat quickly."

Myron's eyebrows rose. "You're eating with us?"

Cathy ducked her head and shuffled her feet. "I, um, thought it would be faster if I eat here."

"I see." Myron tried to sound noncommittal, but for some reason, knowing she'd be joining them for the meal made his pulse jump.

Cathy backed up a few steps. He was right to be hesitant. They'd been struggling to put out the flames of gossip. "I don't have to eat here. I can wait outside until the boys are done."

"Don't be silly. It's cold out. Come inside and join us."

"If you're sure." She surprised herself at how much she wanted him to welcome her company. But she didn't wait outside, in case he said something to make her feel like an interloper. She hurried ahead of him and the boys. "I need to check on the casserole."

"Go ahead." He led his horse toward the barn. "I won't completely unhitch him, just feed and water him."

His *go ahead* hadn't exactly been gracious, but they were in a hurry. Cathy bustled into the kitchen, herding the boys in front of her. "We'll need to eat quickly." She'd already set the table, so she removed the side dishes from the refrigerator and the casserole from the oven.

Outside the window, Myron was taking care of her

horse too. If only he wasn't so unfailingly thoughtful. It made it hard to steel herself against falling for him. The more kindness and understanding he directed her way, the more she—

Cathy jerked her thoughts from the path her yearnings were taking. "John," she said sharply, "fill the water glasses." She rummaged through the drawer for serving utensils and settled the boys in their seats by the time Myron walked in and sniffed the air.

"Mmm. Smells *wunderbar*." He headed for the sink to wash his hands. "Nothing like walking into a kitchen hungry and breathing in warmth and spices."

A flush slid up Cathy's neck and burned her face. Flustered, she kept her back turned to him and continued digging in the drawer as if she hadn't found the serving spoons yet. Myron's simple observation made her heart ache for what she couldn't have. She waited until she had enough control over her emotions before turning around.

She stole quick peeks at Myron while he pulled out his chair, then focused on putting spoons in each side dish. She had to almost reach across his shoulder to place the final one. Her hands shook a little at their closeness.

Cathy scolded herself. Why hadn't she just handed him the spoon and let him put it in the casserole?

All these unexpected feelings tumbling inside threw her off balance. She welcomed the chance to bow her head and close her eyes for prayer. But after she opened them, she avoided looking in Myron's direction.

"Hurry, boys. We need to leave."

"Relax, Cathy," Myron said. "You should get there in plenty of time."

Although she always worried about being late, her main reason for getting out of here was her jittery nerves around Myron. As much as she hated to admit it, she had to flee her sudden attraction to him. It had been building gradually the more she spent time around him and the better she got to know him.

She should never have suggested eating together. That had been a mistake. Being in this confined space with him at the table made her long to be on his left as his wife. She jerked her mind from that fantasy. It could never be. Never. Never.

Myron inhaled the aromas of Cathy's delicious supper. Every bite fed his senses as well as his stomach. He thanked the Lord for this blessing of three *wunderbar* meals every day. Even the days he didn't watch the boys, he had her leftovers. He'd never eaten so many *gut* meals since he'd moved out of his family home in his twenties. Maybe the intervening years of choking down his own cooking had blurred his memories, but he believed Cathy's cooking was far better than Mamm's.

Cathy rushed the boys through dinner, and again, he insisted on doing the dishes so she could leave for the *schulhaus*. For once, she didn't even protest. She hustled John into his program shirt, brushed his hair, wiped his face, and practically pushed him out the door. David trailed behind.

Soon, the buggy clattered down the driveway, and

Myron gathered the dishes and stored the leftovers. Cathy had been jumpy tonight. Almost as edgy as she'd been when he first met her. Was she concerned about the program? It was a shame she let herself get so worked up about unimportant things.

Over the past months, she'd softened and relaxed a little. The prim, tight lines around her mouth and eyes had disappeared. At times, she even smiled when they met to exchange the boys. Her eyes still held sorrow from Wayne's passing, but she seemed to find joy and satisfaction more days than not. He hoped the tension was temporary, because it made her short-tempered with the boys.

After the Christmas program was over, he'd see if she unwound. If not, he'd try to discover the cause of her stress and do what he could to alleviate it.

He'd put away the last plate and wiped the table when Ben knocked on the door.

"Everyone's ready to go," he announced.

Myron couldn't wait. He was as excited as if his own children were in the program. In a way, they were. He'd gotten so attached to David and John, his heart swelled like a proud father's.

Several chattering Huyard children had already piled into his buggy, eager to head off. Levi and Liz followed behind him with the rest of their family. Liz had brought several platters of cookies and treats to share. Myron should have thought to bring something, but Liz assured him she'd made enough to cover his contribution too.

As he drove, Myron couldn't help drifting back to the years when a sullen Tim sat beside him in the buggy on the way to his Christmas program. Tim had balked at changing into the shirt Myron had paid an elderly woman at church to sew for him.

Tim crossed his arms and pouted the whole way, complaining he didn't want to match his classmates and saying he disliked everyone in class, as well as his teacher. But he saved his greatest loathing for Myron. Up front at the program, he had scowled the whole time, purposely made mistakes, poked other children, and sung out of tune, drowning out the others.

Myron winced and tried to focus on the present. This would definitely be the most enjoyable Christmas program he'd ever attended. His spirit lifted even more when they entered a room filled with stars and snowflakes hanging from the ceiling. Two boys rushed over and hugged his legs.

John beamed at Myron and the Huyards. "You came."

"We wouldn't miss it for the world," Abby said, echoing the sentiment in Myron's heart.

The teacher clapped her hands, and the scholars rushed to their places and lined up, facing the audience. Smiling parents, relatives, and friends took their seats or stood in the back of the room.

Up front, each child held a sign with their name and, below that, their parents' names. Myron's heart ached for John. His was the only one who had only one name under his. Poor kid. That had to be hard.

The children went down the line introducing themselves.

The boy beside John smiled a gap-toothed smile.

"I'm Andy Schwartz, and my parents are Matthew and Lena Schwartz."

John looked out at everyone with sad eyes. "I'm John Zehr, and my parents are dead."

Everyone gasped. A tear slid down his cheek. Myron wanted to rush up to the stage to comfort him. Cathy sat a few rows ahead of him, where he could see her profile. She kept blinking, which she often did when she was trying not to cry.

The girl next to John stared at him, her mouth gaping.

He swallowed, took a deep breath. "I have a new *mamm*, Cathy Zehr."

The audience released a collective breath, and the girl beside John moved her lips to form an *I*, but John kept speaking.

"And I have a new *daed*, Myron King."

The room erupted in whispers. People turned around to stare at him. And at Cathy. The girl stood uncertainly, unsure whether to continue.

Myron sneaked a sideways peek at Cathy. She stared straight ahead, but her visible cheek had turned a deep rose. His own scalding-hot face probably matched hers.

The teacher stood, clapped her hands, and waited for the undercurrents to die down. "Emily, it's your turn."

Despite his embarrassment, Myron couldn't help feeling happy and proud that John thought of him as a father. Even if it could never happen in reality, Myron hugged the secret in his heart. The best Christmas present ever.

* * *

Cathy couldn't believe what John had just done—embarrassed her in front of the whole *g'may*. How could she look anyone in the face after that? They'd all be gossiping about her and Myron and their supposed relationship.

What hurt her most wasn't people talking about her behind her back, but that the rumors weren't true when she wished they were. Spending all that time with Myron when they'd traveled to New Wilmington, seeing him morning and evening every market day, watching his kindness in caring for the boys had drawn her to him. More and more often, she imagined a future with him, but he'd never be interested in her. She was too moody, too snappish, too bossy, too irritable . . .

Cathy jerked her attention back to the program. She couldn't dwell on impossibilities. Reality always smacked her in the face. She wasn't fit to marry anyone. And she never would be.

She needed to be grateful for what she had. God had given her children even though she'd never have a husband. Cathy thanked Him for the wriggly boy beside her and his brother standing on the stage wearing the shirt she'd sewn for him. Her first-ever sewing project for a child. Her child.

For tonight, she pushed away the sorrow and dwelled on the positives. She had two boys and two good friends, Tahiri and Myron. Well, three, if you counted Mrs. Vandenberg. And she supposed she could count the Huyard family too. Cathy also had gotten better acquainted with some of the young mothers, even if she was almost a decade older than most of them.

She wouldn't have a lonely Christmas or Second Christmas this year. Last year, the bishop and his wife had invited her for Christmas dinner, but sitting with all the other charity cases—several older folks with no family around anymore—had made Cathy feel even more lonely and left out than sitting at her table alone during the holidays. This time, she'd have two children at her meal.

Beside her, David giggled, startling her. She'd missed a funny skit. She joined in the laughter around her so people wouldn't think her grumpy.

John filed back onstage. Cathy leaned forward so she wouldn't miss his part. For the first time since she was three, she'd have a happy holiday. She whispered a prayer of thanksgiving for her many blessings, especially for the birth of the Christ Child, who'd come into the world and given His life for her.

As the program progressed, Myron couldn't help wishing he could be a father to John and David. Those boys needed and deserved a *daed* around at night and every morning when they woke, not just a caretaker several days a week. But that would have to include Cathy.

Myron yanked his thoughts away from that prospect. Although he liked Cathy better the more he got to know her, he couldn't imagine grouches like the two of them getting along well. And he definitely couldn't see her agreeing to marry.

Marry? The word choked him. He ran a finger around

his too-tight collar. All eyes had returned to the program, but Myron could still feel them focused on him. He'd been so busy thinking, he'd almost missed John's part. He forced himself to concentrate on the children.

Chuckles came from around the room as a humorous skit came to an end. Myron laughed with the audience, but Cathy's chuckles caught his attention. She looked almost pretty when she was so joyful. Too bad she spent most of her time tight-lipped and annoyed with the world.

Several different children lined up, with John in the middle. One by one, they each recited a poem. Myron held his breath when John's turn came.

Before he spoke, John picked out people in the audience as if checking to be sure they were paying attention before he began. David, Cathy, and Abby each received a smile, but John reserved his broadest grin for Myron. Myron's chest ached with love for the small boy, and he tried to convey that through his smile and his eyes.

Heads swiveled to see what was delaying the program. Once again, Myron was the object of curiosity. Even Cathy had turned to stare at him. He tried to avoid gazing in her direction, but he couldn't help himself.

The look in her eyes stunned him. Admiration shone in her glance, but also sadness and hurt. He read that message loud and clear. It bothered her that John preferred Myron to her. He tried to send an unspoken apology. He hadn't meant for that to happen. John only gravitated to Myron because he spent more time with the boys than she did. And perhaps because they were missing their *daed*.

The silent conversation took only seconds, but those seconds seemed to stretch into minutes with all eyes on them. Myron broke his gaze and nodded at John. Everyone turned back to the program, and John delivered his poem flawlessly. Myron beamed at the boy who meant so much to him.

Then he tipped his head in Cathy's direction. John got the message and grinned at Cathy. Her tense shoulders relaxed, and from what Myron could see, her whole face lit with happiness.

John heaved a sigh. Only then did Myron notice the sorrow in his posture and his eyes. The poor boy had to be missing his parents.

Abby leaned over and whispered, "He looks so sad."

Myron nodded. "*Jah*, this must be hard on him."

As the program droned on, Myron's thoughts drifted back to Tim standing up front for his Christmas programs. The first year, his head had drooped, and he'd mumbled his part so the audience could barely hear. Instead of sympathizing with his pain, Myron had been embarrassed, and he'd admonished Tim to lift his chin and talk louder next time.

With his newer understanding of people's feelings, Myron now saw how he'd failed Tim. His nephew had needed kindness and reassurance. Myron had given criticism.

With shame, he recalled each program over the years. The Christmas after Ivy disappeared, Tim had been watching a small girl in the audience and missed his cue. He ignored his teacher's whispered prompt. After her sharp *Tim*, he snapped back to attention and gave a stumbling recitation. Myron had lectured Tim all the way home.

The following years, Tim did a lackluster job or spoke in a loud, defiant voice while glaring at Myron. Every year, Myron shrank lower in his seat, ashamed of his failures as a parent, and spent the ride home scolding Tim. Never once did he think to ask Tim what was bothering him or try to understand his pain.

A huge wave of grief washed over Myron. He'd made Tim's performance mistakes all about himself rather than his nephew. Myron had scolded Tim because of his own embarrassment and fear people would think poorly of him as a parent. If only he'd treated Tim the way he did David and John, Tim might have searched Myron out in the audience, and they would have shared a connection. One thing was becoming increasingly clear to Myron. He owed his nephew an apology.

Cathy's cheeks still burned after the program ended. She struggled to overcome her hurt when John raced off after the program ended. Straight to Myron. Her heart ached as Myron squatted, set his hands on John's shoulders, and talked earnestly, both their faces alight with pleasure.

When Myron stood, John slipped his hand into Myron's and pulled him toward the dessert table. Then John stopped abruptly and tugged Myron in the opposite direction—right toward Cathy.

With all the eyes on them, Cathy exchanged a stilted greeting with Myron and bent to compliment John on his program. He wriggled with delight and reached for her hand.

"Let's get some cookies." John turned to his brother. "You want some too, David?"

David nodded eagerly and took Cathy's other hand. How awkward could this get? All four of them were holding hands like a couple with their two children. After John had included Myron in their family from the stage, Cathy couldn't do this. It seemed to her that everyone was staring at them.

Myron must have sensed her discomfort, because he disengaged his hand from John's. "I need to help Levi." He gestured toward Levi, who was trying to corral his two youngest sons. "I'll be back later. You go enjoy your snacks."

John's face fell as Myron loped across the room and intercepted the Huyards' toddler.

Cathy tried not to give in to hurt feelings at the way John gravitated toward Myron rather than her. John had done the same thing during the program. She was grateful Myron had taken the pressure off them. Now he was walking around with someone else's *sohn*. He looked good as a father.

John was still staring after Myron.

"Let's get some cookies." Cathy hoped to distract John, and it worked. He headed with her and David toward the refreshments.

The two boys chattered about their favorites while they waited in line for their turn to select desserts. Cathy smiled when their first choice was her lemon bars. They did love her cooking.

After they filled their plates and moved away from the table to nibble on their treats, Cathy tried to avoid glancing in Myron's direction, but her eyes kept straying toward the Huyards, who were now in line. Myron still held the small boy, and Cathy's heart thumped at the sight.

Once all the Huyards had their desserts, Abby led the group over to Cathy. Although she didn't want Myron to come over, he accompanied them. He stayed behind the group while Abby and Liz commented on John's performance. To Cathy's relief, John glowed and didn't single Myron out.

She hoped that would help the gossip die down. Yet, part of her was disappointed. In some ways, she hoped stories about them being a couple would continue to circulate. She secretly liked having her name linked to a beau.

Chapter 20

Apologizing to Tim was the first thing on Myron's mind when he woke the next morning, and the nagging thought stayed with him as he headed to Cathy's, dropped John at school, and headed in to work with David. He made up his mind to phone his brother during his midday break.

Myron didn't have time to brood over the phone call, because a steady stream of customers kept him busy with both orders and sly questions about last night's Christmas program. Coming up with excuses to fend them off didn't work because David kept popping out of the back room to ask for Myron's help or cling to his pant leg. Most of the conversations ended with nudges and winks connecting him to Cathy.

"I'm going to work in the back room," Myron told Jed as another gossipy group of ladies exited. "Don't disturb me unless it's an emergency."

Jed grinned. "Tired of being teased about courting and marrying, huh?"

Myron blew out a long, exasperated breath. Now even his employees were in on it.

"Sorry, boss," Jed said in a tone that didn't sound in the least apologetic. "Couldn't resist a little joke."

"Harrumph." Myron pretended to be annoyed, but Jed was loyal and wouldn't take the jabs too far. Before Myron could turn and escape, a young man burst through the door.

"Can you tell Tim the factory will be up and running by the end of next week? We're all supposed to report back next Thursday."

Myron's heart sank. Tim would be coming home so soon? Myron had gotten used to his peaceful life. *Jah*, caring for two small boys was exhausting and challenging, but it was also rewarding. Very rewarding.

Being around Tim was definitely not. It was stressful and upsetting and— Myron stopped himself. He intended to apologize to Tim today. Maybe God wanted Myron to prove he was sorry by mending their relationship in person.

"Tim hasn't been answering the messages we've left. Can you let him know?" the young man asked. "I need to go. I have to contact a few Amish workers without phones."

"I'll be talking to him during my break." Myron waved, and the kid dashed away.

After his employees finished their meals, Myron settled David at the small worktable he'd set up beside his own much larger workstation in the back room and laid out the delicious meal Cathy had sent. Myron's mouth watered, but he'd wait until he'd finished this important call. His stomach twisted into knots over talking to—or attempting to talk to—Tim.

"All set?" Myron asked David, although he should be asking himself the same question.

David nodded and bit into his sandwich. Reassured food would keep David occupied for a while, Myron picked up the receiver and forced himself to dial the number.

Some of his anxiety eased when Abe picked up. His nephew's cheery greeting and "*Wie geht's*" made it easy to hold a conversation. Abe told Myron that Tim was doing a great job.

After chattering excitedly about Anna Mary's recent visit, Abe told Myron to hang on. "I know my *daed* wants to talk to you."

Myron loved talking to his brother, but he had an important reason for this call. "I really need to speak to Tim."

"No problem. I'll go get him while you talk to Daed."

This phone bill would be huge, but Myron had to make up for years of mistakes.

Hank's voice boomed over the line. "Myron, I'm so glad you called. I have great news."

David tugged on Myron's arm. "I can't get this open." He held up a small container of applesauce.

"Just a second, Hank." Myron put down the receiver and opened David's applesauce. "Anything more you need help with?"

David shook his head. "*Danke.*" He settled back at the table and spooned applesauce into his mouth.

"I'm back," Myron said into the phone.

"Who was that?" Hank asked.

"David. Remember I told you about the two boys I'm watching?"

"*Jaaah.*" Hank drew out the word, evidently puzzled. "Last time we talked, you were taking care of them for two months while their *daed* got treatments."

Had it been that long since they'd called each other? "Sadly, their *daed* died, and Cathy is now their parent."

"Sounds like you're their other parent."

Myron bristled at Hank's conclusion. "No, I only watch them four days a week."

"Four days? Seems like it's almost a full-time parenting job."

Though Myron wished it were, he'd never be their parent. "Don't be silly. It's just part-time to help Cathy out."

"You're doing all this for Cathy, huh?" Hank's inflection made it sound like there was more to the relationship. "Does she pay you for your time?"

"Of course not. Well, she does make delicious meals for us."

"Us?" If Myron and Hank had been in the same room, Hank's eyebrows would be waggling.

"The boys and me." Myron came across too defensive.

"I see. You help with parenting, and she feeds you. Sounds almost like a marriage to me. Is that where it's heading?"

If one more person poked Myron about weddings

today, he was going to explode. "*Neh.*" The word blasted from Myron's lips so loudly, David jumped and cowered.

David's lips trembled. "Did I do something bad?"

Myron clunked down the phone and reached for David. "*Neh*, I'm sorry I scared you. I was talking to"—*more like yelling at*—"my brother." Shame coursed through Myron. He should be setting an example for David in how to treat his brother. "I need to tell my brother I'm sorry I yelled at him."

"*Jah*, you do," Hank said when Myron picked up the phone. "My ear still hurts. Sooo . . . did I hit a nerve?"

"What do you mean?"

Hank's voice grew gentle. "I know what it's like to be in love with someone who turns you down. I'm sorry. I shouldn't have poked you in a sore spot."

What? Hank thought Myron was in love with Cathy, but she'd rejected him? "Wait, you got the wrong idea. Cathy and I, well, we're not interested in each other. Not at all. We're both too old and set in our ways. We're not compatible. We're—"

"You're protesting a little too much. Maybe you'd like to ask her, but you're afraid she'd turn you down?"

"*Neh.*" This time Myron said the word quietly through gritted teeth. He didn't want to alarm David again. "I have absolutely no interest in this woman. If I ever decided to get married, which I have no interest in doing, she'd be the last person I'd think of asking."

"Wow. Sounds like you really don't like this woman. Why are you watching her children?"

Because I care about them and love being a parent.

"I—I, well, I feel like it makes up for being such a terrible parent to Tim."

"So, you're doing it out of guilt?"

Was he? At first, Myron had been. Now, though, his heart had gotten involved. How did he convey that to his brother?

He didn't have to. His older, wiser brother figured it out.

"You like doing it, don't you? I can tell."

"*Jah*, I do. It's nice to have another chance to do things right and to figure out where I went wrong with Tim." Myron swallowed down the sadness and regret choking him. "That's actually why I called. I need to apologize to Tim."

"I'll put him on, then." Hank placed a hand over the receiver, but it didn't quite muffle his voice. "Hey, Tim, phone."

Would Tim refuse to come to the phone? Maybe not. Wisely, Hank didn't say who was on the other end.

The pounding of running boots approaching carried across the phone line. Myron winced. If he'd called Tim to the phone, his nephew would have run the other way. Tim seemed eager to please Hank. Maybe Hank treated Tim the way Myron treated John and David.

"Hello?" Tim's cheerful greeting stabbed Myron's conscience. Was this how Tim would have turned out if he'd been raised by a loving, caring parent?

"Hello?" Tim repeated.

Myron cleared his throat. His insides scrunched into a tight ball of anguish. "Tim, it's me, Myron."

He pictured Tim's fist tightening on the phone, his

smile changing to a glower. "Yeah?" The old indifferent attitude had returned.

"First of all, the factory is repaired. They'd like everyone to report to work next Thursday."

"I'm not going back." Tim's flat, matter-of-fact assertion sounded definite.

"But—"

"Hank says I can stay here and help with the cows. I like it. I'm good at it."

All these years, Tim had probably been dying for someone to approve of him, appreciate him, encourage him. Myron regretted that lost time.

"I never want to go back to Lancaster." Tim's words rang with finality.

Myron could understand why. Before David and John had come into Myron's life, he'd have demanded Tim get on the next train or bus and return immediately. Now he only said, "I don't blame you. Life with me hasn't been easy."

Tim's sardonic laugh added to Myron's guilt.

"Ya think?"

Tim talking like his *Englisch* friends had always angered Myron. He clenched his fist tighter around the phone, but he wanted to build bridges, not burn them down. *Lord, give me patience.*

When his irritation simmered down, Myron said, "I not only think, I know. I wasn't the parent I should have been. That's why I called to apologize. I'm sorry for the way I treated you while you were growing up. Will you forgive me?"

"What's this? Are you hoping to be invited to the wedding?"

"You're getting married?"

Tim laughed. "Guess they didn't even tell you. Forget I mentioned it."

Someone in the family was getting married? Anna Mary and Abe?

Myron didn't want to ask and feel even more left out. He decided to refocus the conversation on his real reason for calling. "Will you forgive me, Tim?"

"I have to think about it." Tim paused. "And pray about it."

Pray? Tim would talk to God about this? His nephew had always fought against anything to do with the Lord and church. Had Tim had a change of heart?

"I won't lie," Tim continued. "I have a lot of resentment built up over the years."

"I understand. I wish I could go back and do things differently. I never listened or tried to understand what you were feeling. I yelled at you and punished you for crying when I should have comforted you. And forbidding you to speak about Ivy . . . I'm so, so sorry."

"Yeah, well." Tim sounded as if he were choking. "I'll think about it. Here's Hank."

Tim must have thrust the phone at Hank and run off because Hank's puzzled voice asked, "Myron? What's going on? Tim shot out of here like a race horse. I'm not positive, but I think he was crying."

Myron struggled to push out an answer. "I asked him to forgive me for . . . everything. The way I treated him and—" He couldn't go on.

He started when a small hand reached for his.

David stared up at Myron with concerned eyes. "Did your *daed* die, too?"

Until then, Myron hadn't realized he, too, had been crying. He brushed at his cheeks. "*Neh*, David. I'm all right." But the small hand in his larger one anchored Myron amidst the storm within.

"Want a bite of my cookie?" With his other hand, David held up a delicious-looking chocolate chip cookie.

If tears hadn't already been leaking from Myron's eyes, they would have started then. He could barely manage a *danke*. "Could you get me my lunch from the cooler?"

David squeezed his hand and scampered off.

"Myron?" Hank's concerned voice barked in his ear. "Are you all right? This phone call must be costing you a lot."

For once, Myron didn't care if it cost several days of pay. He'd connected with Tim and asked for forgiveness. An apology that had been almost fourteen years overdue.

When he didn't answer, Hank said, "Look, I have some news I've been meaning to call about, but I'll do it another day. I'm going to hang up now."

"Wait." Myron wanted to hear the news. Hank had said it was *gut*. "Tell me now."

"First of all, *danke*. If you hadn't helped, this never would have happened."

Huh? After his emotional conversation with Tim, Myron was having trouble following Hank. Myron lived in Pennsylvania. His brother lived in New York. It didn't make sense.

"Esther told me what you did. If you hadn't talked to her, she never would have told me our breakup wasn't my fault."

"She told you the truth?"

"*Jah*, all of it. Her fears. Her love for me. Why she ran away. They're moving to Fort Plain, all of them. And Esther and I are getting married in February. And I'll have a lovely new family of daughters. I still can't believe it."

"That's *wunderbar*." Myron was thrilled for his brother. And happy he'd been a part of it. Hank deserved a second chance.

"I hope you can come."

"I wouldn't miss it, but we'd better end. My break is over."

Myron hung up to find David waiting patiently, holding Myron's lunch. How long had the small boy been standing there waiting?

Taking the lunch in one hand, Myron ruffled David's hair with his other hand. "*Danke*."

"Did your brother forgive you?" David's furrowed brow revealed his worry.

"*Jah*, he did."

"That's *gut*." David broke into a relieved smile.

Myron smiled back at the caring little boy beside him. "*Jah*, it is. It's always good for brothers to forgive each other." And for *onkels* to forgive their nephews.

If only Tim had forgiven him as well. But Myron understood his nephew had endured years of anger and unkindness. Myron's own soul had been unburdened. Even if Tim chose not to forgive, Myron had begun to make things right. It might take years to prove his sincerity to Tim. All Myron could do was wait and pray. And treat Tim differently to show he meant what he said.

Chapter 21

February arrived with blustery gusts and frequent snowfalls. Myron had promised to attend his brother's wedding, but he wasn't sure he'd be able to make it. New York State stayed buried under more snow than Pennsylvania.

Some days, Myron struggled to make it to his shop. His horse strained through snow drifts, and the buggy wheels slid on black ice. He even had a few close calls with fishtailing cars. Lloyd and Jed kept the walkways outside shoveled and salted, but few customers braved the weather to come to town. The phone rang a lot, though, which meant they had plenty of orders to keep them busy. When a storm downed power lines and other businesses closed during the blackout, the woodworking shop operated as usual. Besides avoiding worldliness, not being connected to the grid had other advantages, like having heat and light when others didn't. He kept his shop open for neighboring business owners and employees to come in and get warm until the power was restored.

A week before Hank and Esther's wedding, an unusual thaw set in. Snowbanks melted into puddles. And one afternoon, a Bentley drew up outside the store.

Mrs. Vandenberg strode into the store, her cane tapping jauntily in front of her. "I need a wedding present," she said. "What do you think your brother would like?"

"My brother? You're going to the wedding?"

"I go to the weddings of all the couples I match."

"You matched them?" But Hank didn't even live around here.

Mrs. Vandenberg's expression hinted at many secrets. "For the second time. At least, for Hank. The third time for Esther." Her face pulled into sorrowful lines. "It's sad they've both lost other loves, but this union will last well into old age. God has given me that sign."

"You matched Hank with his first wife?" Myron found that hard to believe.

"I certainly did. He still lived here in the Lancaster area."

That was true. Hank had gotten married here and taken his newlywed bride to New York. Their parents had moved north for the inexpensive farmland in Fort Plain, and all their children were supposed to follow. Hank and Joe both went. Myron and his fiancée planned to follow, but she jilted him. She was killed heading home that day. Myron was too much of mess to follow his family.

Before he could get himself together, his other brother's wife left him for the *Englisch*. Soon after, his brother died, leaving behind two children for Myron to raise. Once Ivy disappeared, Myron decided not to leave the area in case she returned. He'd never made it to Fort Plain.

Mrs. Vandenberg gave him a sympathetic smile. "Your being here in Lancaster is no accident. God has a plan for your life."

Did it include ruining my nephew's life? Myron wanted to demand, but he kept his mouth shut.

Nevertheless, Mrs. Vandenberg must have read his thoughts. "You might be surprised at what good will come out of that experience. God has plans for Tim."

Myron doubted Tim would want to follow the Lord's plans, but his nephew had said he'd pray about forgiveness. That had to mean he'd become less rebellious and resistant to God.

"A wedding gift?" Mrs. Vandenberg reminded Myron.

"Right." He led her around the shop and pointed out possibilities.

She stopped him with a question. "Do you have anything like the blue bird cupboard you sold me?"

"I've been painting a smaller version of that in green. Let me show you." He took her into the back, where John and David were playing in the gated-off area.

"The perfect solution for your children," Mrs. Vandenberg trilled.

Myron snapped his mouth shut before he could protest, *I don't have children.*

"You will," she assured him.

He doubted it, but he wasn't about to argue with a customer, especially one who seemed to have a direct connection with God. Not that he quite believed in her "nudges from the Lord," but plenty of people he respected insisted she did get them.

"Here." Myron pulled off the sheet covering the cabinet. He only worked on the decorative furniture when the boys weren't in the shop. He didn't want spilled or smeared paint.

"Perfect." She leaned her cane against a nearby chest and clapped her hands together. She squinted and spread her arms as if measuring its size. "That should fit in the niche beside the kitchen cupboards."

"You've been in Hank's house?" Myron couldn't believe it.

"Of course. I have several romances to sort out in Fort Plain. Not all of them will be quite this easy to work out. But I thank you for your help on this one."

He took a few steps back. She was the second person who'd credited him with Hank's romance. "I didn't do anything."

"You talked to Esther and convinced her to tell the truth. All I did was provide transportation." She retrieved her cane. "Speaking of that, I'll be renting a van large enough to transport this cupboard to New York. If you have a gift you'd like to bring, there'd be room for it. And you, of course."

"*Danke.*" Myron had been wondering about how to take the rocker he'd been finishing. His usual driver wouldn't be able to fit it into his car. But did Myron really want to take such a long trip with a matchmaker?

"I'd be grateful for the company, although I must admit, I often sleep most of the way. Still, it's lonely when I'm awake. My driver prefers to keep his mind on the road."

Her request tugged at Myron's heartstrings. What would it be like to reach her age and live and travel by yourself? "I'd be happy to go with you."

"I'm so glad." She reached out and patted his arm. "Don't worry. I don't have any matchmaking plans for you." She turned and headed out of the workshop.

Myron wasn't quite sure, but he might have heard her murmur under her breath, "At least not yet."

He hoped he'd heard wrong.

Business had been slow at Dough-Re-Mi as snow piled up in February. But with the unseasonably warm weather this week, people flocked out of their houses and ran errands. That meant Cathy and Tahiri stayed busy.

A harried mother with two lively children rushed up to their stand as soon as the market opened. "Thank goodness you're open. My kids have bugging me for donuts every day the past few weeks."

She ordered a dozen donuts, handed one to each of her children, and asked, "Can you freeze donuts?"

Tahiri stepped forward. "Of course. Not the filled ones. The glaze on the yeast donuts can get crackly, but they still taste good. Cake donuts freeze best."

Cathy stared at her. How did Tahiri know that? Cathy had never even thought about freezing donuts, but she should have.

The mother smiled. "I'm sure the snowstorms will

start up again soon. Give me three dozen assorted cake donuts."

Both Cathy and Tahiri filled boxes. While Cathy rang up the sale, Tahiri handed over the boxes and explained how to freeze donuts.

"Set them inside a large plastic freezer bag with wax paper between each layer. If they don't touch each other, you can pull them out one at a time to thaw."

"You're a lifesaver," the mother exclaimed as she walked off with a stack of four bakery boxes.

Other people in line overheard the conversation and ordered extra donuts to freeze. Tahiri headed back to start new batches of donuts, and she kept the stand supplied with fresh ones as Cathy hustled back and forth to wait on customers.

Right before noon, they had a brief lull, and Cathy could finally catch her breath. She turned to head back to help Tahiri refill the bakery case and spotted a sign hanging on the support beam right beside her stand.

In big block letters, the sign said, *How to Freeze Donuts*, and it listed the steps. The words could be read easily by customers far down the line.

Cathy turned to Tahiri. "Is that why everyone kept ordering multiple boxes? And when did you have time to do that?"

Tahiri shrugged. "While I waited for the donuts to fry."

"You're amazing. Whatever Mrs. Vandenberg pays you isn't enough."

"Is that so?" a chirrupy voice asked behind Cathy.

Cathy whirled around to find Mrs. Vandenberg

standing at the counter. Her face heated. "I didn't mean . . ."

Mrs. Vandenberg laughed. "You didn't insult me. It sounds like Tahiri deserves a raise. And perhaps a promotion?"

"A promotion?" Cathy echoed. How did you promote someone in a business with only two people?

"Manager, perhaps? She can supervise employees here when you open a new branch of Dough-Re-Mi. Maybe a shop downtown."

"What? I don't think . . ."

Mrs. Vandenberg tilted her head to one side. "Sometimes it's better not to think but to trust the Lord. You never know what He has in store for you."

Cathy's head was spinning. First, Tahiri finding a new way to increase business. Now Mrs. Vandenberg suggesting Cathy open another store in town. She had enough to do keeping up with her present stand and caring for the boys. The last thing she needed was an additional project.

"You need to stop thinking about doing everything yourself and not only trust God, but trust others."

Mrs. Vandenberg's words brought Cathy up short. She did trust a lot of people. Well, three people at least. A new shop would require a lot more employees.

"You're not ready for an expansion yet," Mrs. Vandenberg mused, "but I'm planting a seed. I hope you'll keep an open mind."

"Sure," Cathy choked out, although having an open mind didn't seem to be one of her skill sets. "And, Tahiri, from now on, you'll be a manager."

A rather empty title when they had no one for her to supervise, but Tahiri beamed as if Cathy had given her a valuable award.

"A manager's pay grade is much higher than your present salary," Mrs. Vandenberg said to Tahiri. "Now you can look at that house you've had your eye on to restore."

Tahiri gasped. "How did you know?"

A knowing smile lifted Mrs. Vandenberg's lips. "It'll be the perfect place for you and Roberto."

Hands pressed to her flushed cheeks, Tahiri stared at Mrs. Vandenberg. "You think?"

"I know. Roberto has been itching to renovate a house in that area."

"But he doesn't even know I exist."

"He will once he starts working with you. And he'll definitely like what he discovers."

A starry-eyed Tahiri breathed out, "I can't believe this."

"Well, I'd better let you get back to work. You need to get ready for all the customers who'll be coming shortly." Mrs. Vandenberg nodded to Tahiri, who floated back to the fryers as if on air.

Mrs. Vandenberg called after the dazed girl, "Don't be surprised if all your dreams come true."

Cathy glanced around for all the customers Mrs. Vandenberg had mentioned. Normally, her stand was busiest during the noon hour. Having no customers, especially with the market as busy as it was today, seemed odd.

"Your lines will start soon and keep you busy until closing, Cathy. Don't worry."

"I'm not worried." As soon as she said the words, Cathy knew they were a lie. "I guess I am."

"It's all right. I just asked the Lord for a little quiet time with you. I'm so glad he granted my request."

"Because you had matchmaking business?" Cathy tried not to sound as incredulous as she felt.

"That and one other thing. I need to talk to you about Myron."

Cathy groaned inwardly. *Please don't try to match Myron and me.*

"I'm not playing matchmaker right now."

Great, because that's the last thing I want. Once again, Cathy's conscience bothered her. That wasn't true. She would like to be matched with Myron, and he'd be a perfect father for her boys. But she could never marry anyone. Sadness crept into her heart.

"Your future will be brighter than you think."

Mrs. Vandenberg's brisk remark brought Cathy's self-pity to an end. Ever since Christmas, Cathy had been making a point to count her blessings. She had so many. Mrs. Vandenberg was right. Cathy did have a bright future.

"About Myron. Has he talked to you about next week?" At Cathy's furrowed brow, Mrs. Vandenberg continued, "I guess not. He'll be heading to Fort Plain for three days."

"What days?"

"Thursday to Saturday."

"*Ach!* That means he can't watch the boys." The market was open all of three of those days. What would she do? Tahiri had been fine when Cathy left her employee in charge for a day here and there during the New Wilmington trips. But Cathy couldn't ask Tahiri to do three days in a row, especially not with Thursday being a long day.

Mrs. Vandenberg reached out and patted Cathy's clenched fists. "My dear, you need to learn to pray rather than getting so worked up."

The wise elderly woman was right, but Cathy always jumped right in with all her worries the minute she faced a problem. Right then and there, she bowed her head and closed her eyes.

Lord, I don't see a solution to this. I can't bring David into the shop during the day or have both boys here for Thursday's long hours. And Tahiri— Cathy cut off her complaining. *I'm thankful for all you've done for me. Please help me to figure out a way to handle this.*

She lifted her head and met Mrs. Vandenberg's compassionate eyes.

"Ah, Cathy, do you know Matthew 6:8? *Your Father knows what you need before you ask him.* I came here to tell you that Abby Huyard is willing to babysit while Myron's away."

Cathy couldn't believe she'd wasted her time in worrying when she could have just let Mrs. Vandenberg finish her message. *If my brain didn't jump to awfulizing, my life would be much less stressful.*

She almost missed the rest of Mrs. Vandenberg's suggestion.

"So, I thought it might be best if she stayed at your house. That way, she wouldn't have to get up at three in the morning. She could sleep until the boys wake, and she'd be able to take John to school and put supper in the oven before you come home. If you wouldn't mind a houseguest for a few days."

As usual, Mrs. Vandenberg had come up with a perfect solution.

"*Danke.* That would be *wunderbar*. I can't thank you enough." Cathy wasn't sure how she felt about a houseguest, but she'd try to be thankful about how much easier it would make her work schedule. And she wouldn't have to stand outside in the snow to meet and speak with Myron.

"Good. Well, I need to be going. I have several other people to talk to. Thank you for talking five stand owners into hiring STAR center trainees."

"I was glad to do it. Tahiri has been a godsend."

"You'll need more trainees when you open your new shop in town."

Cathy only smiled and didn't contradict Mrs. Vandenberg. No way could she handle two locations. One was more than enough.

Mrs. Vandenberg hobbled away. The minute she disappeared into another aisle, customers flooded to Dough-Re-Mi.

Cathy's mouth opened in astonishment. Where had

all these people been hiding while she'd talked with Mrs. Vandenberg? Cathy didn't have time to wonder. The line wound the length of the aisle and around the corner. Cathy couldn't see the end of it.

She shook her head. Mrs. Vandenberg really must have a direct line to God. But that didn't mean Cathy would be opening another branch of Dough-Re-Mi. Or did it?

Chapter 22

By the Monday of wedding week, Myron had trained Lloyd to cash out at the end of the day and to handle bank deposits and daily accounting records. Jed could open and close the business as well as troubleshoot problems with the battery-powered tools.

Myron would only be gone three days, but he had confidence that his managers could handle any problems that might come up. He'd also lined up woodworking help from two older men at church, who'd be willing to fill in as needed. Now that he'd gotten his business in order, he had to figure out what to do about watching John and David for Cathy.

As usual, Mrs. Vandenberg was one step ahead of him. She stopped by his shop to finalize plans for the Fort Plain trip and check on her gift for Hank and Esther. After exclaiming over the green painted cupboard, which Myron had stayed late to finish, along with the rocker Myron was giving them, she pulled a notebook from her purse and set it on the counter.

Myron watched, fascinated, as she riffled through tabs with names of projects, labeled in bold block printing. The notebook had everything from "STAR Center" to "Homeless Housing" to people's names. She stopped at the tab titled "Hank King Wedding," but not before he'd glimpsed a title that made his mouth go dry. What was listed under the heading "Cathy & Myron"?

He forced himself to focus on Hank's list and the items Mrs. Vandenberg was busy checking off. Even upside down, Myron could read the tasks. As she flipped through several pages of entries, she had plenty of checkmarks next to earlier planning, such as "Convince Esther to visit New York" with a variety of steps underneath. Under "Gift," she'd checked off "ordered" and added a date beside it with a description. Now she marked "completed," wrote down the date, and followed it with "Beautiful!!"

That lifted Myron's spirits. She liked the cupboard. He couldn't help noticing some of the notes on the facing page. Beneath "Transportation," she'd written the date a van had been booked, along with all the information, including payment and pickup time. But what really caught his eye was the heading "Babysitting for Cathy."

"I've been worried about that." Myron pointed to those words.

"Oh, that's all settled. I visited Cathy at the market last week to finalize the arrangements. I just need to jot it down." She tilted the notebook to a different angle, checkmarked it, and recorded "Abby Huyard" along with the date.

"Abby's going to babysit?"

"Yes, we decided she should sleep over so she doesn't have to get up as early as you do."

As usual, Mrs. Vandenberg had come up with a brilliant solution. But if Abby worked out as a babysitter, maybe Cathy wouldn't need him anymore. The thought depressed Myron. He'd miss spending time with the boys. Picturing his life without them chilled him more than the winter weather outside.

Mrs. Vandenberg studied his face. "You know, sometimes we have to go through winter to get to spring. Never give up faith when things seem dark."

Myron agreed with her wisdom, but it didn't seem to apply to the boys. He'd never see them again if Abby took over his role. He and Cathy didn't go to the same church. Their paths didn't cross, so he'd have no chance to spend time with John and David. Would the boys miss him the way he'd miss them?

"Sometimes you have to get creative when you can't think of an immediate solution."

Had Mrs. Vandenberg been reading his mind again? Myron had never considered himself creative, so he wasn't sure if he'd be able to come up with a plan.

She interrupted his thoughts. "I have a busy morning, but I want to confirm the trip time. I've rented an extended-length cargo van with extra seating. The dimensions will accommodate both pieces of furniture." She ran her finger over the details. Her pickup time and his. "If you can be ready by six, we'll pick you up at home and swing by your shop. The driver can help you load the furniture."

"I can do that." Myron looked forward to getting on the road early in the morning. He'd gotten used to rising before dawn to head to Cathy's.

"Perfect." She beamed at him. "We'll return in three days, but we'll drop you at home since it'll be evening. Oh, and I've made reservations for us at Delores's bed-and-breakfast. She's Esther's cousin, and Anna Mary works there now to be near Abe."

And, just like that, Myron's whole trip had been arranged. The woman was a wonder. But her efficiency also worried him. One tab in her notebook niggled at the back of his mind. It might be innocent notations about Cathy's new worker, Tahiri, and him taking care of her boys, but why would she have paired their names like that? She didn't plan to match him and Cathy, did she?

Cathy had panicked last week when she'd learned about Myron's trip to New York for his brother's wedding. That shock made her realize how much she'd come to depend on him. And how much she'd miss seeing him for three days next week.

Ever since the Christmas program, she'd been daydreaming about the ways they shared parenting duties. She'd longed to make it a reality, despite knowing it would never work out between them. She and her past stood in the way of any future relationship. Myron would never consider her, not with her grouchy personality. Still, she put love into every meal she made for him, and she let her mind conjure up impossible fantasies, especially as she drifted off to sleep at night.

On Tuesday morning, Mrs. Vandenberg dropped by Dough-Re-Mi. After ordering two donuts, she'd smiled at Cathy and patted her hand. "You need to stop worrying and start trusting."

That word *trust* raised Cathy's hackles. A privileged, rich woman like Mrs. Vandenberg would never understand Cathy's struggles. Not her childhood woes or her present-day stresses of making enough to pay the bills.

But she had so much to thank Mrs. Vandenberg for, such as providing Cathy with such a great assistant—well, manager now. Day after day, Tahiri proved to be one of Cathy's most valuable helpers. Ever since she'd come up with the sign about freezing donuts, many of their customers bought an extra dozen or two to freeze for the days the market stayed closed. They'd made more in one week than Cathy usually made in a month.

Mrs. Vandenberg studied Cathy. "I'm glad things are working out for you. But I mean it when I say you need to trust. Not only God, but others."

Cathy crossed her arms. "I have learned to trust. I trust Tahiri." Cathy also trusted Myron, but she'd never mention that to Mrs. Vandenberg, or she might find herself matched up. Her trust for Myron didn't extend to a relationship.

"You've cracked your heart open to others, which is a start."

A start? Cathy had made herself very vulnerable.

"My dear, you've done well in taking the first steps. Someday you'll need to open your whole heart, including everything you've hidden for years."

Inwardly, Cathy scrunched into a ball. Some parts of

her could never see the light of day. The past was over and gone. She had confided some of it to Myron. Dredging up the rest would only bring up sadness, loss, and unbearable pain.

She tried to keep the sharpness from her tone, but she wasn't quite successful. "I don't see the point."

Mrs. Vandenberg's eyes filled with pity. "Perhaps someday you will. Then, and only then, can you fully accept God's healing and forgiveness."

Gideon, the market manager, strolled by to open the doors for the customers. Cathy prayed she'd have a huge crowd of customers to sweep away the memories Mrs. Vandenberg's words had stirred up.

"Listen." Mrs. Vandenberg leaned closer. "You'll be busy shortly, but I want you to think about my words. Watch for the right time. And the perfect person. When it comes, don't run. Face it with courage."

Cathy gulped, unable to respond.

"Oh, and I forgot the main reason I came."

Squeezing her eyes shut, Cathy braced herself for another jab.

"I know you've been concerned about your relationship with Myron."

Cathy's eyes flew open. Mrs. Vandenberg seemed to know every detail about Cathy's life.

"Don't worry, he'll still want to care for the boys when he returns. I know having Abby to babysit might seem like the best solution, but I hope you won't turn your back on Myron. He needs you. The boys are special to him, and it's worked wonders in his life. Please don't cut him out of their lives. Or yours."

Cathy had no intention of doing that. She relaxed as she realized what Mrs. Vandenberg meant about Cathy's relationship with Myron. The elderly lady only wanted to ensure Myron had time with the boys. Cathy's secrets could remain safe and hidden.

More than twenty-five years had passed since Myron had traveled these roads north to Fort Plain. Much had changed since then. He marveled at the differences, but many saddened him. New neighborhoods and business complexes had sprung up in areas that had once been farms or woods.

True to her word, Mrs. Vandenberg slept most of the trip, leaving Myron alone with his memories. He'd been younger then, bursting with hopes and dreams. Spurred on by the pioneering spirit of his ancestors, he'd accompanied his parents to look for farmland to establish their family homestead. He'd also recently started courting Dorcas, and he couldn't wait to bring her to New York State to start a new life and a family.

Myron could barely remember being that thrilled *youngie*, back before Dorcas had passed, back before his brother had died, back before Myron had been saddled with two youngsters. Guilt rolled over him in waves. Instead of seeing raising children as a privilege, he'd viewed it as a yoke around his neck, an onerous responsibility. And he'd made a mess of it all.

To be fair, he'd been grieving Dorcas and his brother, but Myron had bottled up his sadness and grievances and let it fester into resentment. He'd lost his freedom, his happiness, and his future in the space of few short months. Now, he had an opportunity to put it right. Maybe seeing Tim face-to-face would allow them to heal the past. If only Myron could go back and change his guilt over Dorcas.

Mrs. Vandenberg's head popped up in the seat in front of him. "Excited about returning to Fort Plain?"

"Nervous is more like it," Myron admitted. "I'm not sure how things will go with Tim. I am looking forward to seeing my brother and to attending the wedding."

"Go easy on Tim," Mrs. Vandenberg advised. "Give him time to get used to the new you. He may not trust your change of heart will last."

Myron could understand that, but he wanted to be relieved of this huge blot on his conscience that only forgiveness from Tim could erase.

Mrs. Vandenberg's eyebrows rose. "Depending on human forgiveness instead of God's is a mistake. Put the emphasis where it should be."

That brought Myron up short. Had he ever asked God's forgiveness?

No matter how Tim reacted, Myron needed to lean on the Lord. "*Danke,*" he said to Mrs. Vandenberg. Her wisdom always brought him back to where he should be in his walk with God. Myron hoped someday he'd be able to guide others that way.

"You will," she assured him.

Myron shook his head. He still couldn't get used to her guessing his thoughts.

After they crossed the New York border, he sat up straighter, eager for the trip to end. He couldn't wait to see Hank and the rest of his family. And to face Tim for the first time since he'd altered his attitude toward his nephew.

Mrs. Vandenberg said to the driver, "We'll drop our bags at the B and B, then head to Hank's to give them their presents."

Less than an hour later, they pulled into the circular driveway of an elegant three-story mansion with marble columns. Myron's mouth dropped open. He'd never seen an Amish bed-and-breakfast this fancy.

"Not very Plain, is it?" Mrs. Vandenberg chuckled. "Delores's husband bought this property for the farmland, but they lived in that house, which has no electricity. At least so far."

"She's planning to put it in?" Myron tried not to sound disapproving and judgmental.

"Delores is in an ongoing dispute about that with her contractor. The two of them are proving to be one of my most challenging matches. Although I have others that require a lot more patience."

The notebook tab "Cathy & Myron" flitted through Myron's mind. He hoped Mrs. Vandenberg didn't see that as one of her matches. Although . . .

"Oh, there he is." Mrs. Vandenberg rolled down the window and called, "Hello, Peter," to an older man who was spritzing WD-40 on the hinges of one of the cathedral-sized wooden doors and wiping the hinges with a rag.

"Welcome, Mrs. V. Just trying to get rid of some squeaks." He wiped his hands on the cloth and tucked it into one pocket of the carpenter apron strung around his waist. All the rest of the pockets bristled with tools. Underneath the apron, his broadfall pants were spattered with stains and paint drips. So were his graying hair and beard.

He crunched across the gravel drive. “Let me help you with your bags.”

The driver circled to the back of the van and opened the doors. Myron hurried around to help. Peter stepped forward, greeted each man, and shook their hands. He stopped to admire the green painted cupboard.

“Excellent craftsmanship.” He ran a hand over the wood and slid a finger over the drawer joins. They’d taken the drawers out for the trip and laid them beside the cupboard with thick padding between.

“*Danke.*” Myron shuffled, uncomfortable at the praise.

Peter’s eyebrows shot up. “You made this? The rocker too?” When Myron nodded, Peter’s smile broadened. “I always like meeting other woodworkers.”

“You’re a woodworker too?”

“Grew up in the family business. Since then, though, I’ve branched out into contracting, but I spend most of my time repairing this old girl.” He gestured toward the mansion, where a middle-aged woman bustled down the steps, wiping floury hands on her apron.

“You’d better not be referring to me that way, Peter,” she said tartly, plonking her hands on her hips.

“Huh?” He stared at her blankly.

“I heard you say ‘this old girl’ and wave in my direction.”

Peter chuckled. “Those who eavesdrop can’t expect to hear only good about themselves.”

The woman, whom Myron assumed must be Delores, glared at Peter.

Then his face softened, and his eyes held love. "I'd never say anything bad about you. Besides, you're a spring chicken. I meant the house. She's an elegant old girl."

Delores narrowed her eyes suspiciously. "You sure?" She looked at the others for confirmation.

Mrs. Vandenberg stepped forward. "It's true, Delores. Peter's still as in love with you as ever."

Peter's cheeks glowed crimson, and he stared down at his work boots. Delores sniffed and turned her attention to her company.

"Welcome, everyone. I'm Delores. Come on in, and I'll show you to your rooms. Only family will be staying here through the weekend."

As she led the way into the high-ceilinged foyer with embossed decorations and a chandelier with crystal teardrops, she continued to chatter, but Myron didn't hear a word she said. He gawked at the marble floor and the intricately carved mahogany newel post and spindles on the sweeping staircase. Unlit gold sconces decorated the walls, and antique furniture graced the niches on either side of the stairs.

When Delores opened the doors to various bedrooms, Myron bit back a gasp. Each one was more beautiful than the next. Antique poster beds, intricately carved Victorian furniture, and priceless Aubusson rugs filled every room.

"All the furnishings are original. Most date back to the late eighteen hundreds. Everything came with the house. My husband decided it would be more economical to keep it rather than replace it."

In studying his craft, Myron had spent time in museums and antique stores examining the way old-time woodworkers had created their furniture, so he recognized quality when he saw it. Delores could start her own museum right here.

Stunned by their accommodations, Myron trailed after Peter and the driver to set bags in the various rooms. If Myron had a chance, he'd love to explore the whole house, including the wainscoting, cornices, and decorative moldings, along with the furniture. All those intricate details intrigued him. Perhaps he could even find a way to incorporate some of them into his own designs.

"Anna Mary is across the hall." Delores pointed to a room with two single wrought-iron beds. "Sarah stays here, too, now that Tim's visiting."

Sarah? Mrs. Vandenberg must be referring to Anna Mary's younger sister. Myron couldn't figure out what that had to do with Tim. Mrs. Vandenberg had said Tim was visiting. Had Tim told anyone of his plans to remain in Fort Plain permanently? Or had he made that up to jab Myron?

Delores beckoned them toward the stairs and sailed ahead. "I imagine you'll want to get to Hank's now. Tell them I'll join you later. I have the wedding cake in the oven."

They trooped downstairs, and Delores sniffed the air. "I'd better go." With a brisk wave, she took off for the kitchen.

Peter gazed after her disappearing figure. "Delores is always busy. She's quite a woman." His eyes blazed with admiration and love.

Mrs. Vandenberg patted his arm. "She'll come around."

"I hope so." The light in his eyes dimmed, and he sighed. "Doesn't seem like it, though."

"Keep the faith." Mrs. Vandenberg's words expressed a deep certainly. "You might be surprised what the next few months bring." But even as she said it to Peter, she glanced toward Myron.

Had she been directing that to him too?

When Cathy woke on Thursday, two emotions warred inside. One was gratitude that Abby had arrived yesterday evening and helped Cathy get the boys ready for bed. Now Abby was sleeping upstairs and would be here all day to care for the boys. It relieved Cathy not to have to wait in the cold for Myron to arrive. She could prepare her dough, move everything out to her buggy, and leave when she was ready.

But as she pulled out of the driveway, she fought sadness and a sense of loss. She hadn't expected to miss Myron. Nor had she realized how their brief daily encounters added happiness to her life. She shook off her gloom, but somehow her morning started off wrong and seemed to stay akilter the rest of the long day. Everything seemed off, and small problems snowballed. Even Tahiri's calm tackling of the glitches didn't set Cathy's inner compass right.

To Cathy's relief, they ran out of donuts forty minutes before their eight o'clock closing. Tahiri offered to make more, but Cathy waved aside her suggestion.

"Let's close early." Cathy hung her closed sign and began *redding* up.

Tahiri's eyebrows rose. "You sure?"

"Positive." Cathy rushed about, eager to get home. "I have a babysitter watching the boys."

"Oh, yeah. Myron went to a wedding out of state, right?"

Neh, it wasn't right. It was awful. But Cathy couldn't say that. She just nodded. He'd only be gone two more days. Surely she could last that long without him. Actually, with Tuesday being the next day the market opened after his return, she wouldn't see Myron for four days. Four long days.

She shook herself. This was ridiculous. It wasn't like she was in love with him or anything like that. And she didn't ever see him on Sunday and Monday, so why was she making such a big deal of it? Yet, him not being around today had turned her whole life upside down.

Cathy had to get control of herself. To erase him from her thoughts, she scrubbed the inside of the counters with vigor.

"Are you okay?" Tahiri stood staring down at Cathy, who was scouring the display shelves inside the glass bakery counter.

"Why wouldn't I be?"

Tahiri shrugged. "I don't know. Maybe because you've been acting weird all day, and now you look like you're trying to sand those shelves instead of wiping them."

With a huff, Cathy lightened her pressure.

"Can I ask you something?" Without waiting for an answer, Tahiri said, "Seems like you miss Myron. You like him or something?"

"What makes you think that?" Cathy regretted her waspish response. She shouldn't be taking out her off-balance feelings on Tahiri. Plus, she didn't want an answer to her question. "Never mind. Let's get cleaned up so we can get out of here."

"If you say so." Tahiri returned to her usual rapid cleaning, and soon the stand was spotless.

Cathy walked out the employee exit with Tahiri and waved goodbye to her, hoping to dispel some of her early grumpiness. Cathy prodded her horse to move faster than usual despite the black ice on the roads. The thaw this past week created puddles of melted snow during the day that froze when temperatures dropped at night. Cathy scolded herself for taking chances and slowed. She didn't need to get in an accident. If she did, who would take care of the boys?

An immediate answer came to mind. *Myron.* And that brought her back full circle to missing him.

CHAPTER 23

After all their bags had been deposited in the assigned bedrooms, Peter escorted them back out to the van. "Everyone's at Hank's house waiting for you. They've been cleaning and preparing the house for weeks to get ready for the wedding."

Delores smiled at Myron. "Esther and the girls have been staying here, but they'll move into Hank's house after the service tomorrow, so I hope you're ready for some heavy lifting."

"I get plenty of it at work," he assured her.

"I'll see you all later tonight." Delores, with Peter standing beside her, waved until they were out of sight.

When the van pulled into the driveway at Hank's, relatives swarmed out to greet Myron. His eyes stung to see all his sisters and brothers and nieces and nephews together in one place. Esther sent him a grateful smile, but she and her daughters hung back as he talked to each of his family members and met children he'd read about in letters, but whom he'd never seen.

After bending down to speak with every one of the

children, he straightened and rubbed his aching back. His heart overflowed with love for his family. And he tried not mind the one person who was missing from this happy reunion—Tim. His nephew was nowhere to be seen. Myron tamped down his hurt and focused on the pleasure of being with his siblings for the first time since his brother had died.

Esther beckoned them all into the house. "*Kumme esse*."

Before they ate, Myron and the driver unloaded the green cupboard and rocker. Esther cried tears of joy when they set the painted cupboard into the kitchen niche where Mrs. Vandenberg had envisioned it.

"It's so beautiful." She ran a hand over the birds and flowers. "I've never had such a pretty piece of furniture. It will bring springtime into the kitchen even when snow piles up outside."

They, too, had experienced unseasonably warm weather in New York, but more snow had been predicted for the following week.

After everyone exclaimed over the rocking chair, they headed downstairs to the basement, where some wedding benches had been converted into tables.

After they all sat, with Tim as far away from Myron as possible, they bowed their heads for prayer and passed around delicious dishes. Being with family made the food taste even better, but even in the midst of the bounty, Myron's thoughts kept drifting to Cathy.

Her red beet eggs were a mite tangier, her applesauce a touch more cinnamony, her fried chicken a bit crispier and spicier, her green bean casserole a little tastier . . .

He brought himself up short while sipping his milk. No way could hers be creamier than his brother's fresh-from-the-cow milk, yet Myron could have sworn it was. Or maybe the fact that Cathy had made the meals or poured the milk to go with her delicious cookies that added to his pleasure.

Myron wished he could have brought her and the boys to meet his family. John and David would have loved to play with all the children. And Myron would have liked to watch his siblings interacting with Cathy. Would they like her? Would she get along with them?

What in the world is wrong with me? All the excitement about the wedding had pushed his thoughts into a strange—and unwelcome—direction. He'd been acting as if this were the prelude to his own wedding instead of Hank and Esther's. He reined in his musings and focused on the here and now.

He gazed around the table at the faces, so familiar but older, and it brought back memories of meals they'd shared when they were younger. "You know," he said, "this is the first time we've all been together for a meal since—since . . ." His words faltered, and his throat closed up.

Myron regretted bringing up that final meal in Lancaster. The meal before the whole family, except him, moved to Fort Plain. He'd been thrilled that day too. He'd intended to marry Dorcas in a few months, then sell his house, and join everyone.

Hank picked up on Myron's sentiment. "You're right. We celebrated buying this farmland we all share now.

It was an exciting day, and it proved to be a wonderful decision. We've been happy and prosperous here."

Maybe they had been. Myron had spent those years in loneliness and misery.

As if sensing Myron's sadness, Hank turned to his brother. "We've missed you, though. I wish you didn't live so far away." Hank looked thoughtful. "Now that Tim's here to stay, why don't you consider joining us?"

Across the room, Tim's eyes widened in horror, ripping a hole in Myron's heart. Tim appeared ready to get up and flee. He'd found a home here with Hank. Myron couldn't destroy Tim's contentment and security.

Besides, Myron didn't want to leave John and David. Or, to his surprise, Cathy. But Myron couldn't confess that to his extended family, so he only said, "I couldn't leave my business. I've built up a strong customer base over the years. And my church . . ." He trailed off at Tim's relieved expression.

"Just think about it," Hank urged. "We'd help you get established up here, wouldn't we?" He turned to their siblings, and everyone agreed.

Myron nodded, but in his heart, he had a conviction he'd never move away from Lancaster.

After dinner, while the women washed dishes, the men moved furniture out of the front room and set up benches for the next day's service. With it being a second marriage, it would be a smaller and shorter ceremony, only a half day, rather than a full-day event.

As always when he was faced with weddings, sorrow curled inside Myron. Hank had enjoyed a *wunderbar* first marriage until his wife had died. Now he would embark on another long-term relationship, at least according to Mrs. Vandenberg. Myron's brothers and sisters each had spouses and children. He stood apart from them, alone and unmarried. No children of his own. And the one boy he'd raised—or attempted to—wanted nothing to do with him. Myron shied away from thoughts of the small girl he'd been entrusted with. Gone forever.

The idea of heading into old age without a partner or a family sent a chill through him.

"Hey, *bruder*." Joe, one of his older brothers, clapped Myron on the shoulder. "You look so gloomy staring off into the distance. What's on your mind?"

Myron couldn't bare his soul to anyone on this happy occasion. He didn't want to put a damper on everyone's happiness.

Joe didn't seem to notice Myron hadn't answered. "Hank tells me you have a lady friend. Are you missing her? I hope you'll invite us to your wedding."

Lady friend? That sounded like something his *Englisch* customers would say about someone they were seeing but had no intention of marrying. Surely Hank couldn't possibly have said that about Cathy.

"Hank got it wrong. I'm helping out a woman by caring for her two boys while she works." As soon as Myron said it, he realized how it sounded.

"*Jah*, that's what Hank said. The boys go to work with you?"

Myron tried not to sound defensive. "I have a play area I built for Tim. They don't distract me from my woodworking." *Actually, they make my days happier.* But he couldn't say that without giving Joe the impression he was interested in Cathy.

"What does Tim think about that?"

The only answer Myron could give was a shrug. Probably not much. Although he doubted his nephew even knew. Tim wouldn't expect Myron to be a good caretaker.

"You think you're up to it?" Joe's question, though gentle, implied Myron didn't have the best parenting skills.

Myron bridled. "I've learned a lot since I messed up with Tim."

"Hey." Joe held up his hands to express innocence. "I didn't mean—"

"I know exactly what you meant. *Why is someone who did such a bad job of parenting taking care of other people's children?*"

"It's not that. It's just that parenting always seemed such a struggle for you, so it's hard to believe you'd volunteer to do it unless you're sweet on this Cora or whatever her name is."

"Cathy." Myron had no idea how to explain caring for John and David when he didn't have feelings for Cathy. He did have some, he supposed, in that he wanted to help her, but not the marrying kind of feelings. That was a whole different story. "I'm not interested in her. We're both too sharp. We'd cut each other to pieces with our tongues."

"Hmm. You always did have a problem with that.

I still remember some of the nasty jabs you took at me. So do the girls."

Myron assumed by *the girls* Joe meant their sisters. Myron did spend a lot of time teasing them as they grew up.

"Being the oldest, Hank probably didn't deal with as much of it as the rest of us. He says you've changed over the years."

"Maybe not as much as you'd think. I'm sure Tim could tell you that."

Joe shifted uncomfortably. "*Jah*, he does seem to have some scars."

Scars? That hit Myron hard. He did have a temper, but he hadn't physically hurt Tim. "I didn't hit him." He might have spanked him from time to time, but . . .

"I didn't mean it that way. I meant the scars inside. Sometimes those hurt as much or more than a whipping."

Myron had never thought about that. Realizing his words could have done that much damage added to the guilt he already carried.

He'd never considered his tongue a weapon, but Dorcas had. The day she broke up with him, she said she couldn't bear his cruelty to her and to others. He yelled at her then, shouting that he'd never been mean to her and how could she say something so awful?

She'd turned and fled. He'd run after her, screaming nasty things as she sprinted away from him, climbed into her buggy, and galloped off. The buggy had careened from side to side, she'd been driving so erratically. He'd even chased her partway down the road, spewing hateful accusations after her. She'd glanced over her shoulder to see if he was gaining on her, and then—

Myron covered his eyes as if he could block out what happened next. She never saw the cars of teens drag racing each other. She didn't halt her horse at the stop sign, but raced across the intersection to get away from him.

The lead car had plowed into the buggy. With a screech of brakes, the other car had swerved around, gone up onto the curb, and hit a lamppost.

Myron had rushed to Dorcas's side. He'd blubbered apologies and begged for forgiveness, but Dorcas's eyes never opened again. Several of the teens had bad injuries, but they'd recovered.

"Hey, you all right?" Joe grabbed Myron's arm, dragging him back to the present.

"A bad memory," Myron mumbled. "Hank's right. My temper's not as bad as it once was." But it had been bad enough to leave scars on Tim.

"Sorry, I shouldn't have brought up the past." Joe shot Myron a teasing smile. "Don't worry. We survived your temper. We all got good at running and hiding." Joe chuckled. "Bet I can still outrun you."

Myron pasted on a halfhearted grin as Joe went over to help Hank set up another bench. Instead of going for one more, Myron stood rooted to the spot and ached inside at the damage his temper had done over the years. He'd softened a lot since he'd been caring for John and David. One thing he'd learned from Abby was how to listen to other people's viewpoints. If he'd learned that years ago, Dorcas might still be here. Maybe they'd be married and have a family.

In a blinding flash, Myron saw that anger was selfish. It was imposing your will on someone else, an attempt to control them. It stemmed from thinking your needs and feelings were more important than another person's needs or feelings. But deep down, under all that, it came from fear.

Myron didn't know what to do with that insight. Yet, it had a rightness about it. The older and more secure he got, the less he needed to intimidate others. He wished with all his heart he'd had this epiphany when Tim was young. It would have saved them both years of heartache.

Usually on Thursday nights, when Cathy returned home, Myron had dinner warming in the oven, and he came outside to take care of her horse, insisting she go in and eat. Because David and John had gone to sleep by then, Cathy and Myron had a few minutes in the barn together to talk about their workdays and about the boys. The barn door stayed open so neighbors could see them occupied in different tasks.

Tonight, Cathy did all those jobs alone. It worried her how much she'd come to depend on Myron's company and his help. When she went into the house, the oven was empty and cold, and the boys were crying.

Cathy bounded up the steps. "What's wrong?"

Abby sat on the bed, her arms around both boys. "They're worried something happened to Myron."

"He's fine," Cathy assured them, though she didn't know that for a fact.

"Did he"—David's voice wobbled—"die? Like *Daed*?"

"Of course not."

"Then why isn't he here?" John asked.

Hungry and grumpy, Cathy snapped, "I told you he was going to New York for a wedding."

John scrubbed at his eyes with his fists. "Is that as far as Mexico?"

"*Neh*. He'll be back on in two days."

"We can't sleep. He didn't pray with us."

Abby's calming presence didn't seem to be working. "Is there any way you can reach him?" she asked. "Maybe it would reassure them, and he could pray with them."

Cathy shook her head. "I couldn't do that. He's probably busy with preparations for the wedding and spending time with his family. I don't want to interrupt him." But deep inside she did. She longed to hear his voice as much as the boys did.

"I probably shouldn't do this." Abby pulled a cell phone from her pocket. "But Mrs. Vandenberg gave me this to use for emergencies. She fixed it so I could push the number one, and it'll call her. She'll know if Myron's too busy to talk."

Before Cathy could stop her, she hit the number.

As they finished assembling the tables in the basement, the women decorated them and set a small gift at each place. Myron stretched and yawned. He'd gotten used to going to bed very early. He hoped he could keep his eyes open a little longer.

Mrs. Vandenberg appeared exhausted. Maybe he could use her as an excuse to go back to the B and B.

He headed over to her. "You look ready for bed. Should we go?"

She held up a finger. "Shortly." Her phone dinged, and she pulled it from her purse. After listening for a few seconds, she said, "He's right here." She held out the phone to Myron.

He frowned. *Who is it?* he mouthed. He'd given his employees this number, but they closed the business at five. It was almost nine. They wouldn't be calling this late.

With one of her secretive smiles, she thrust the phone into his hand.

"Hello?"

"Myrrrooonn." A loud wail sounded in his ear.

"John? Is that you?"

Loud sniffles came from the other end. "Me and David was scared you were dead."

"*Neh*, I'm fine. I'm at a wedding."

"Myron?" a quavering voice asked.

"David, I'm all right."

"Wait a minute," Abby's voice interrupted. "Mrs. Vandenberg showed me how to push this button. Then both of you can hear at the same time."

"We need you to tell us a Bible story and pray." John's words sounded steadier.

Myron glanced around. Everyone in the room had

their gazes glued on him and seemed to be listening avidly to every word. "Um, just a second." He headed upstairs to the living room and sank into a chair with his back to the closed basement door.

"You want to hear David and Goliath?"

That suggestion elicited cheers, so Myron recounted brave David's fighting the giant.

"How come David gets to be brave, but I don't?" John whined.

"The Bible has a story about Jonathan being a *gut* friend to David."

"Tell us that one."

Myron was too tired to recount the whole story. "Not tonight. It's time for you to say your prayers and go to sleep. It's way past your bedtime."

"Will you tell us tomorrow?"

"We'll see. If not, I'll tell you when I get back."

"But we want to talk to you tomorrow."

Myron repeated, "We'll see. My brother's getting married tomorrow. Now let's pray."

They all prayed together, and Myron couldn't believe how much he missed them. He wished he could tuck them into bed.

In a husky voice, he said, "Now I want both of you to go right to sleep. It's late."

"We will," both boys promised.

Myron wanted to be back in Lancaster. New York seemed so far away from them. He regretted not asking about Cathy. For the first Thursday night in months, he hadn't seen her and talked to her.

With a sigh, he stood up and turned around to find

everyone standing in the living room behind him or on the stairs. How long had they been listening?

Mrs. Vandenberg's eyes twinkled. "We heard the end of the Bible story and your prayer. How are the boys? I guess they're missing you."

Myron cleared his throat. "They're doing fine." He couldn't meet anyone's eyes.

Tim pushed his way through the group and pounded up the stairs, leaving Myron's spirit weighed down with guilt. He'd given two boys he barely knew all the love and attention he should have given Tim.

CHAPTER 24

Cathy's eyes were misty by the time Myron hung up. She'd never sat in on his Bible story and prayers with the boys. He'd done such a *wunderbar* retelling of David and Goliath, it made her heart ache. David and John deserved a father who prayed with them like that every night.

Although she read from the book Abby had given them, it came across as much more powerful when Myron told it. They were missing out on a lot by not having a *daed*.

Lord, help me to find a way to give them the father figure they deserve.

Even if she could marry, which she couldn't, Myron would never be interested in her that way.

For now, all she could do was to have him around on market days for as long as he was willing to watch the boys. She disliked depending on him that way when she couldn't pay him back, but Mrs. Vandenberg kept assuring her the boys were helping Myron as much as he was helping them.

He did seem to genuinely like the story and prayer time. Either that, or he was excellent at pretending. He didn't seem like a man who would bother to fake enjoyment. He'd been straightforward with her when she bugged him. Cathy suspected he'd have shown his annoyance if the boys' request tonight had bothered him. She had to trust he wanted to do it.

Abby helped Cathy put the boys to bed. After talking with Myron, they settled down and fell asleep.

"*Danke* for taking care of them today," Cathy said before she skipped supper to head for her own bed and fall into dreams about Myron that could never come true.

The joy of being together as a family increased the next day as they prepared for the wedding. Myron enjoyed being with his siblings and their families, but it made him miss David and John. Watching Esther and Hank stare at each other with starry eyes brought an aching tenderness to Myron's heart and soul.

As he and the rest of the church members gathered around the happy couple and agreed to support them, the joy in Myron's chest expanded until it hurt, but it also brought a pang of sadness. Myron had never experienced the happiness of being united with a woman he loved. And he never would.

The sting of loneliness overwhelmed him as they filed downstairs for the meal. The happy chatter of strangers from Hank's church made Myron even lonelier and more isolated.

Joe came up behind Myron, elbowed him, and asked in a joking tone, "You going to be next?"

"I already told you I'm not." The words came out almost savagely.

"Whoa." Joe stepped back and held up his hands. "I was just kidding."

Myron couldn't believe how upset the question had made him. His brother had stabbed Myron in a sore spot. A very sore spot.

But that didn't give him the right to respond so angrily. "I'm sorry. Will you forgive me?"

Joe nodded. "Of course. But why did that make you so upset?"

"Because . . ." Myron didn't want to admit the real reason, but he should be honest and not let *hochmut* stand in the way. He gathered his courage and said, "I'm happy for all of you with your partners and children, but it also pains me that I'll never have a family of my own."

His brother took Myron's arm and drew him off to the side as people milled around talking to each other and finding seats. "We all heard you last night telling a Bible story and praying. That's more than just watching those children. You must be an important part of their lives. You sounded like a father to those boys."

Myron had only wanted to ease John and David's grief. Most of the time, he thought about how much he missed the boys, not that he'd taken on the role of *daed* in their lives. Last night, he'd been overjoyed that they'd missed his usual Thursday night ritual of stories and prayers, but maybe he shouldn't get them accustomed to that. If Cathy married, her husband would take on that responsibility.

That thought sent a sharp pain through Myron. He sucked in a breath. It had never occurred to him before that she might—

"Myron?" Joe studied him with concern. "Are you all right?"

Neh, Myron definitely wasn't. He was *ferhoodled.* The idea of losing Cathy and the boys had spun him upside down and inside out.

Joe pulled Myron off to the side, where they had a little more privacy. "Look, I don't know what's going on with you, but something's wrong. What is it?"

Myron desperately wanted to get away from his brother. He didn't know how to deal with his topsy-turvy thoughts. "We should sit down. They're about to start serving the meal."

"Fine," Joe agreed. "But afterward we're going to talk."

Myron sank into his chair and ate the food on his plate, but he didn't taste the chicken and filling the church women had been preparing since early that morning. Bite after bite went into his mouth, but with his mind whirling, he chewed and swallowed without paying attention.

One burning question stood out to him. If he didn't have romantic feelings for Cathy, why did the idea of her marrying someone else bother him so much? And it didn't just bother him. It devastated him. He tried to tell himself it was because he'd miss the boys, but something deep inside kept insisting it was more than that. He hadn't fallen for her, had he?

After the festivities ended and all the guests departed, the family scurried around, cleaning up, folding benches and tables so the wedding wagon could pick them up tomorrow. After everything was in order, most of the family sprawled in the living room to chat, while Tim, Abe, and two of Hank's other sons did the milking.

Hank stood up to help, but they insisted he stay with his new bride.

"Enjoy your wedding day, Daed," they said, and a beaming Hank settled onto the couch beside his wife.

Myron envied that happiness. If only he could find the same joy.

"It's time." Joe dragged Myron into the other room. "Now you're going to tell me what's going on."

"How can I when I don't know myself?"

"Sounds like you're mixed-up."

"That's for sure and certain."

"So let's talk it out."

Maybe discussing the situation would help Myron sort things out in his own mind. Joe had always been a good listener, so hesitantly, Myron explained how he'd started to help Cathy and had become attached to the boys. He even admitted he wished he could be their *daed*, but he didn't like Cathy.

Myron paused. "Well, I didn't at first. We rub each other the wrong way. She's not my type at all."

"Who is your type?"

Joe's question brought Myron up short. In all the

years since Dorcas's accident, he'd avoided women. "I don't know," he admitted. "I've stayed away from them."

"So, Cathy's the first woman you've spent time with?"

"*Jah.*" Myron brightened. That might explain his odd reaction to the thought of her marrying someone else. Relief made him giddy. He hadn't fallen for her. It was only that he hadn't had a relationship in years, so he'd dislike losing this one. And he'd miss her meals and the boys.

Joe examined Myron's face. "How do you feel about her?"

Myron started with the things he was sure of—their many differences and how annoyed they made each other. It felt good to air all the complaints he'd been keeping to himself.

His brother chuckled. "She sounds like she's good for you."

"What? How can you say that? We get annoyed with each other a lot." At least they had. That had decreased somewhat over time.

"I don't want to be cruel, but you ran roughshod over Dorcas. She never stood up to you, and I think you crushed her."

Myron lowered his face into his hands. Dorcas had used those very words. She'd also called him a bully. It had taken a lot for a sweet, docile girl like her to stand up to him. Instead of listening, he'd exploded. And his temper had caused her death.

He'd never told anyone what had happened. It had stayed bottled up inside of him for decades. Maybe it was time to pull the plug and release the flood.

When Myron finished, Joe stroked his beard. "That's a lot of guilt to bear. Have you asked God for forgiveness?"

"*Neh.*" To Myron, his behavior had been unforgivable. He'd punished himself by staying away from women and relationships.

"I think it's time you brought it to God. I'll pray with you if you want."

Myron nodded, and they both bowed their heads. When he lifted his face again, he radiated joy. It flowed out from every cell of his being. He felt cleansed and free. "I recently did this about raising Tim."

"Hank mentioned that you'd asked for Tim's forgiveness."

"He did?" A frisson of jealousy twisted through Myron. *Tim won't talk to me, but he tells Hank everything?* As quickly as the thought arose, Myron squashed it. He hadn't proved his trustworthiness to Tim yet.

"If it's any comfort, Tim's been wrestling with his unforgiveness, especially now that he's turned his life over to the Lord."

Myron couldn't believe it. He'd prayed for Tim for years. And berated him. And tried to guilt him into joining the church. But this? Myron's soul soared.

"I didn't know." It humbled Myron to know that once Tim had gotten out from under Myron's heavy-handedness, his nephew had come to God.

Myron regretted all the times he'd pressured Tim and Dorcas. *Lord, please help me curb my controlling and pushy nature. And teach me to listen to and accept others.*

"You know," Joe teased, "this Cathy sounds like she'd be good for keeping you in line."

Maybe that's why they clashed so much. Myron was too set in his ways. So was Cathy. Perhaps God had brought them together to sand the rough edges off each other.

Having Abby at the house had made life so much easier. On Friday morning, Cathy didn't have to stand in the freezing driveway, waiting to pull away soon after Myron arrived. Nor did she have to stop at Myron's house to pick up the boys after work. She came straight home after the market closed at four, and Abby had supper in the oven. Cathy often skipped the evening meal or had a quick snack after she brought the boys home from Myron's, even though she always prepared full meals for him and the boys.

Tonight, she sat at the table with the boys, and she got to hear about their day at school instead of rushing them into their bedtime routine. Abby helped with dishes and getting the boys ready for bed. That freed Cathy to make some refrigerator dough that would be ready in the morning. Tahiri had recommended several recipes for chilling the dough overnight to develop a richer flavor during the slower, more controlled fermentation. Cathy had been reluctant to try it, but she had to admit Tahiri had been right. It also allowed Cathy to go to bed earlier and wake later. Getting more sleep might help even out her disposition.

Abby offered to read the boys bedtime stories, but

they begged to have Myron do it again. Cathy didn't want to interrupt the wedding day. With it being his brother's second wedding, they likely finished hours ago, but he'd be visiting with his family. One morning when they'd chatted, Myron had mentioned he hadn't seen them in years. He'd want to spend every minute with them.

Abby's phone rang.

Mrs. Vandenberg asked, "Are the boys ready for a Bible story and prayer?"

A loud chorus of *jahs* greeted her question.

"Myron's standing here eager to get started," she said and put him on the phone.

Cathy's eyes burned. It touched her how much he cared about John and David. He'd remembered their request and had taken time out of his busy day to keep track of their bedtime and call. She couldn't believe he'd done this.

After Abby turned on the speakerphone, Cathy heard the story of Jonathan and David along with the boys. Myron's deep baritone coming across the phone line did strange things to her insides. And it made her miss him all the more. If only . . .

But some daydreams had to remain fantasies.

She often wished Myron could come inside to do all the jobs Abby had been doing. She pictured herself and Myron enjoying a leisurely cup of hot chocolate and talking together about their lives, their work, and their future. She tried not to indulge those thoughts too often, because it wasn't *gut* to long for what you didn't have.

After Myron hung up, Cathy felt bereft. She shouldn't

be getting so attached to him. It wasn't right to depend on him so much or to lean on him this way.

Maybe it would be better to hire Abby permanently, but it would mean Cathy might never see Myron. That thought made her miserable.

For that very reason, she should break things off with him. But she'd promised Mrs. Vandenberg to keep Myron as the boys' caretaker. Perhaps Mrs. Vandenberg realized Cathy was getting too entangled and suspected she might want to flee.

The wise old lady had been clear Cathy wasn't ready for a relationship. That meant Mrs. Vandenberg hadn't insisted on letting Myron babysit the boys as a matchmaking ploy. She wanted to prevent Cathy from making a foolish mistake.

Mrs. Vandenberg wanted it for the boys' sakes. They needed Myron in their lives. They'd been through too much turmoil. He provided steadiness and gave them a father figure. Cathy brushed aside the notion she also was doing it because she didn't want to give him up either.

When Mrs. Vandenberg offered to call the boys on Friday night after the wedding, Myron jumped at the chance to connect with them, even though his brain was still whirling after the conversation with Joe. His brother's comment about Cathy being good for Myron nagged at him.

Hearing her voice in the background and listening to her pray had done strange things to his heart. He couldn't believe he was interested in her. He'd wanted to run the other way after he'd first met her, but the more time they spent together, the more he'd seen her softer side. That part of her appealed to him. But Joe was right. Myron did need a wife who'd stand up to him when he got too overbearing.

Wife? That word paralyzed Myron. At first, Joe had only been talking about a friendship. But after Myron confessed he'd like to be a *daed* to Cathy's boys, Joe suggested Myron think about courting Cathy.

For some reason, Myron couldn't imagine her agreeing to date him. They had too much tension between them. But he struggled to forget the idea.

He was still mulling it over the next day as he said goodbye to his family and slid into the van with Mrs. Vandenberg. As they pulled away from Hank's house, everyone stood on the lawn and waved goodbye. Everyone but Tim.

Myron had hoped to talk to his nephew and apologize in person, but Tim disappeared every time Myron entered a room. The only bright light for Myron was knowing Tim had chosen the right path. Hank had pulled Myron aside to let him know Tim had talked to the bishop about taking baptismal classes next spring.

"*Danke* for letting me know." Myron praised the Lord for the good news, despite having a heavy heart over not reconciling with his nephew.

He longed to talk the situation over with Mrs. Vandenberg, but she drifted off to sleep, and Myron's mind wandered from Tim back to Cathy.

During the long hours while Mrs. Vandenberg slept,

Myron flipped last night's ideas over and considered them from all sides. He hadn't come to any conclusion when her phone alarm dinged.

She sat up with a jerk. "Time for the boys to go to bed," she announced. "Shall I call them?"

Myron wavered. Part of him wanted to jump at the chance, but he didn't want to get the boys used to him being part of their routine every night. Next week, he'd go back to only doing it on Thursdays, because he couldn't phone them at bedtime on other nights. "I'm not sure."

But Mrs. Vandenberg had already pushed the button to call Abby, who put herself on speakerphone so Myron could hear the boys clamoring in the background, excited to talk to him.

His throat closed with emotion until he could barely answer their questions. *Jah*, he was coming home. *Jah*, he'd see them Tuesday and take them to his shop. *Neh*, he couldn't tell them a story tomorrow night, because he wouldn't have a phone.

Their disappointed replies caused an ache inside. He didn't want to let them down. This part-time parenting was difficult for him as well as them.

After he finished the story and prayers, he hung up reluctantly and went back to pondering the situation. He wanted to be there full-time for the boys, but that meant marriage. He couldn't see any other way. He'd be willing to sacrifice his freedom for John and David. But would Cathy consider a marriage of convenience?

CHAPTER 25

When the van pulled into Myron's driveway late that night, Mrs. Vandenberg turned to him as he hopped out to get his bag. "I think you're on the right track, but go slow. Not everyone is on the same page."

Was she talking about Tim? Or Cathy?

Myron had no choice with his nephew. He had to wait until Tim was ready, if ever, to forgive.

If Mrs. Vandenberg meant Cathy, Myron had to admit Cathy needed plenty of time, because she resisted change. Watching the boys for two months had thrown her into a tizzy. And she'd been slow to adjust to other changing circumstances since then.

For all he knew, she might not want to marry anyone. From rumors he'd heard, she'd never courted, but he had no idea if that was by choice or because nobody had ever asked. Not to be mean, but with as prickly as she was, he could understand most men steering clear of her. He'd felt that way himself. She certainly hadn't encouraged him to be friends.

When he entered his empty house after the liveliness

of being with family, Myron's mood dove into the murky depths. Loneliness sliced through him. His home, which had been a quiet and safe haven for the first few weeks after Tim's departure, now echoed with hollowness. Myron longed to fill the rooms with the fun and laughter of Hank's house. Conversation and caring. Relationships and connections with a deeper meaning. Myron yearned for all that and more, but how could he transform this empty shell of a house?

Tim would never come back, so Myron was on his own. If he didn't take steps to open his heart and home to others, he'd grow into a bitter, shriveled old man. A man nobody wanted to visit. Myron had had this vision before, but now it hit him with even greater clarity. For the past twenty-five years, he'd kept people at arm's length or driven them away. Only he could change his circumstances. With God's help, of course.

But he wavered about moving ahead with the plan he'd considered in the van. That was such a huge step. Mrs. Vandenberg had warned him to go slow. Wise advice. Not only for dealing with Cathy, but also for himself.

Entering a relationship was a huge step, and marriage was a commitment for a lifetime. If Cathy agreed to court, they'd be promising to move forward together. Maybe he should take more time to study all the angles and make sure he was absolutely certain he wanted to head in that direction.

For now, he'd keep their relationship the way it had been and ease the boys back into their regular times together while Cathy worked. Maybe after a few months, he'd revisit the idea and make plans. Meanwhile, the lonely house served as a reminder of everything he was missing in his life.

Cathy thanked the Lord for Myron's safe return. She'd worried he might decide to move to New York with his family, fall for one of the women in Hank's church, or end up in a van accident. Maybe he'd never come back at all.

She hadn't fretted as much as she usually did, because Mrs. Vandenberg's word *awfulizing* kept popping into her head and distracting her. By the time she'd examined each imagined scenario and asked herself it was likely to happen, she'd calmed her nerves. One by one, she'd conquered each worrisome idea.

During the days while Myron was away, she'd been busy taking Fasnacht orders. She'd be glad Myron would be back to take care of the boys on Tuesday, because it was Fasnacht Day. Cathy could use Abby's help on Monday to fry donuts and on Tuesday to distribute the boxes.

"What are Fasnachts?" Tahiri asked when she got her first order.

"It's a Pennsylvania Dutch tradition. The *Englischers* used up all their butter, sugar, and lard before Lent, so it became a custom to make special donuts with those ingredients right before Ash Wednesday. We'll fill all the fryers with lard on Monday and two of them on Tuesday."

Tahiri wrinkled her nose. "I'm not a big fan of animal fat."

Cathy smiled. "I know, but it's tradition. I make my Fasnachts with mashed potatoes. They're a squarish shape without holes."

"Like a filled donut?"

"Except these don't have filling, glaze, frosting, or sprinkles."

"So just plain?" Tahiri didn't look too thrilled at the prospect.

"If you can come in all day on Monday and very early on Tuesday, we'll fill all our preorders, but we'll need to keep some frying all day long. It's my busiest day of the year. Many companies buy them for their staff. They know to order ahead, but plenty of people don't remember until that day, so we need to keep them in stock."

Mrs. Vandenberg popped by to tell Cathy she'd asked Myron to watch the boys on Monday. "He was delighted to be asked. He missed the boys while he was away, so he's looking forward to reading them bedtime stories and praying with them in person an extra day this week."

Cathy hoped that was true, but she didn't have time to check with him herself.

By Monday, Cathy had orders for 150 dozen. On Fasnacht Day, she always broke her rule of only selling freshly made donuts. On Monday, she, Abby, and Tahiri would mix and fry from dawn till dusk.

Myron dropped Abby off when he picked up the boys. Cathy stayed inside and peeked out the window.

Her pulse fluttered at the sight of him standing by his buggy. His craggy face appeared even more handsome than when he'd left. And when the boys flew out the back door and flung themselves into his arms, his face lit up with joy. Cathy longed for him to look at her that way.

She shook off that desire. They had too much work to do. She had no time to indulge in foolishness. But seeing Myron's reaction to the boys relieved Cathy of one worry. Mrs. Vandenberg hadn't forced him into babysitting. He was delighted to do it.

With that concern off her mind, Cathy set Abby up in her kitchen with all the supplies and the recipe. After supervising the first batch, Cathy headed to the market to teach Tahiri to make Fasnachts. Cathy's neighbor Barb had offered to stop by to help Abby whenever she had free time. Barb made Fasnachts for her family every year, so she'd be the perfect person to assist Abby. Cathy fought back her fears of Abby overcooking the donuts, Barb or Abby getting burned, the house going up in flames . . . One by one, Cathy diminished her terrors with prayer and by imagining happier outcomes.

If Cathy hadn't had all their help, she never would have made it through Monday and Tuesday. Mrs. Vandenberg pitched in by providing a delivery van and a driver to take the Fasnachts to area businesses. Even with all the preorders and deliveries, the market stayed packed all day Tuesday, with lines extending out the door and across the parking lot.

Cathy came home on Tuesday after work ready to collapse. Myron insisted she eat some of the dinner she'd sent for him and the boys. When she refused to go into his house because she didn't want to start gossip, he carried a foil-covered plate out to the buggy.

"I hope it stays warm enough on the way home," he said. "You look exhausted." He helped the boys in and leaned into the passenger side to speak to them before he shut the door. "You be good for Cathy tonight and go straight to bed. She needs her rest."

They nodded solemnly. Whether or not they'd do it was another story. But Cathy appreciated his effort.

"Remember what I told you," Myron said to John and David. "I won't see you tomorrow, but we'll have Thursday, Friday, and Saturday together."

Both boys beamed. Then Myron shut the door, gave Cathy a sympathetic glance, and waved as she and the boys pulled away. Her arms were too tired to lift into a goodbye wave. She could barely hold the reins. And she hadn't even thanked him for fixing her a plate of food. Guilt nagged her all the way home.

When they got to the house, the boys kept their promise to Myron and got ready for bed right away. John even offered to tell David a story, and Cathy gladly let him. She'd spend more time with them tomorrow on her day off, and she could hardly wait for Thursday, when she'd be able to spend a little time with Myron.

She'd apologize for being so dismissive today and ask about his trip. She hoped the wedding had gone well. And she was glad he was back in their lives. She'd missed him the whole time he'd been gone.

On Thursday morning when he arrived, she hurried outside and asked, "I wondered about the wedding."

"Wedding?" he stared at her in confusion, a horrified expression twisting his features.

"Didn't your brother get married?"

"*Ach*, of course." Myron's tense shoulders relaxed, and his lips quivered into a tentative smile. "You mean Hank's wedding."

Of course she had. What other wedding would she be talking about? They didn't go to the same church, so she wouldn't know about any of those marriages. Besides, February was not a popular month for brides.

Myron shifted from foot to foot, and his words gushed out. "The wedding was *gut* and they're so in love and it was nice to see my family after so long." He broke off abruptly. "I'll go inside so you can leave." He turned and rushed off as if he was eager to get away from her.

That was odd. Not that he couldn't wait to get away from her. She didn't blame him for that. But he'd been so edgy and uncomfortable. Maybe something had happened at the wedding that he didn't want to talk about. She wouldn't ask any more questions about his trip.

For the next two days, Myron came across as jumpy and uneasy. He barely spoke, and when he did, he acted distant or became lost in thought. She wondered if he'd rather be back in New York.

Finally, on Saturday, she confronted him about it. "You seem far away. Would you rather be in Fort Plain?"

"What?" He started as if she'd dashed cold water in his face. "*Neh*, I had a good time, but I'm glad to be here." Yet, he *rutsched* like a schoolboy caught doing something wrong.

"Then why are you always staring off into space?" she demanded.

"I—I, um, well, I've been thinking about the future."

"What's there to think about?"

"Lots of things," he said evasively.

That raised Cathy's concern. If he wasn't thinking of being back in New York, he might be considering moving there. Maybe he'd met someone and was deciding if he should court her. Or— Cathy's heart stutter-stopped. What if he wanted to stop seeing her and didn't want to take care of the boys?

Having extra time with the boys this week had thrown Myron off. While he appreciated it, it also forced him to reevaluate his plans. If he hoped to be a *daed* to these boys, he had to face a future with Cathy.

He'd been glad she'd been too busy earlier in the week to notice his distraction, but yesterday when she'd confronted him, she'd knocked him off-balance. A few days earlier, when he'd heard the word *wedding* come from her mouth, he'd practically had a heart attack. He'd worried he'd uttered the word aloud because it had been on his mind so often lately.

After she'd clarified she'd meant Hank's wedding, he'd been so relieved he'd almost melted into a puddle of slush. He didn't even know what he'd answered. All he remembered was rushing away from her as fast as he could. He hadn't meant to hurt her feelings, but if he had stayed around her one more minute, he might have made the fatal mistake of blurting out what was on his mind. Myron wasn't ready to deal with that yet.

He opened his store on Monday, glad not to have to face Cathy until tomorrow. Even Jed and Lloyd eyed Myron with concern.

Finally, Jed asked, "Did Tim come back with you from New York?"

"Tim? *Neh*, why?"

"Because you're as preoccupied as you used to be when Tim was in trouble," Lloyd said.

Jed added, "Is he in trouble in Fort Plain?"

"*Neh*, not at all. He's happy there, and he likes milking cows."

Both managers raised their eyebrows in disbelief.

"He really does," Myron insisted. "And he's come back to the Lord. He'll be taking baptismal classes up there and joining the church."

"That's great," Jed enthused.

"So why are you so worried?" Lloyd's face crinkled in concern. "The business isn't in trouble, is it?"

Myron shook his head. "It's been doing better than ever with you two as managers. You did a *gut* job while I was away. I've even been thinking about hiring another apprentice."

They both smiled, but Lloyd kept pressing, "Then what's wrong?"

"I just have some future things I've been considering. Personal stuff." At the alarm on their faces, he hastened to reassure them. "I'm not sick or anything. Just considering some changes to my schedule and other stuff like that."

"I see," Jed said. "You'll still bring David and John in, won't you? We've gotten kind of attached to them."

"*Jah*, they'll be coming here." Even more often if things worked out. Although he'd originally planned to wait several months, he couldn't live with this uncertainty, so he'd almost made up his mind to talk to Cathy.

The idea stayed in the back of his mind all morning.

A group of babbling *Englischers* entered. The smartly dressed women in their twenties walked around the shop, studying each piece of furniture and talking earnestly.

Finally, one walked to the counter. "We're getting a baby gift for a friend. Do you have any cribs or cradles?"

"I do in the back. Jed and Lloyd, could you bring out some of the ones we're working on?"

While the group waited, the blond girl at the counter turned to one of her friends. "Curt and I are going to the lake at Middle Creek Wildlife Management Area tomorrow at sunset."

"Ooo. That sounds romantic. Think he'll propose?"

The blonde shook her head. "No, he wants to see the snow geese migration. He said as many as two hundred thousand geese and tundra swans settle on the lake this time of year."

"That would be fascinating. And romantic," her friend added again.

"Not with Curt. He'll explain they're traveling north, some as far as Canada for nesting. He'll quote how many miles they've flown and a bunch of other statistics. I don't think he'd even look at a diamond except to lecture on how much pressure and temperature were needed to form it from carbon."

Jed arrived with a cradle. Lloyd followed behind with a crib. The girls *ooh*ed and *aah*ed over the cradle—or maybe Jed had caught their interest. They did decide on a white cradle and paid a deposit.

After they left, Myron replayed their conversation. Geese and swans on the lake at sunset sounded lovely. Maybe he should take advantage of the opportunity.

Cathy had off today. He could stop by to see if she'd like to go to the wildlife area. Maybe he should ask Abby or Barb to watch the boys for a few hours. That would give him some time to talk with Cathy. He could see if she seemed open to starting a relationship.

At noon, Myron alerted Jed and Lloyd that he planned to leave in the early afternoon. They divided up the work orders, and both managers agreed to handle their previous week's duties of closing and cashing out. That settled, Myron took off for home.

He stopped at the Huyards' to ask if the boys could play at their house that evening.

Abby checked with her mother, who called out, "We'd be happy to have them."

"I haven't talked to Cathy yet, so it may not work out for tonight, but I'm glad to know you're all right with it. *Danke.*"

With babysitting lined up, Myron went inside to shower, shave, and change into fresh clothes. The closer it drew to his planned departure time, the more his stomach swam with queasiness. He drew in deep breaths as he drove to Cathy's, but nothing relaxed his agitated nerves. He was taking a huge step. A step that could influence every aspect of his life. He wasn't sure he was ready, but the memory of his lonely house prodded him on.

At Cathy's back door, he wiped his sweaty palms on his trousers before he knocked. When the door swung open to reveal Cathy, he broke into a cold sweat.

"Myron?" She frowned. "Is something wrong?"

"I—I hope not. I mean, today at work I heard about birds in the park at sunset."

Her brows still creased, she stared at him. Myron couldn't remember the names of the birds or the park.

He cast about for a better explanation. A word came to him. "Tundra," he blurted out, then racked his brain again. "Um, geese or swans. They land on the lake." He was making a hash of this. It had sounded so lovely and romantic when the girl described it.

But if he didn't get his explanation out soon, they'd miss the sunset landing. Yet, Myron froze on the doorstep like a snowman, unable to move. Unable to add details.

He closed his eyes at the shame of it. When he did, a gorgeous sunset floated before his eyes, and flocks of geese rose and circled in formation. *Migration.* That was the word.

His eyelids popped open, but he focused just over Cathy's shoulder so he didn't have to watch her revulsion when he asked her out. His words came out so fast, they ran into each other. "Migration. Someone at work said geese and swans are migrating right now. Lots of them land on the lake at sunset. At Middle Creek Wildlife Area. I wondered about taking, um, you."

Cathy blinked. Once. Twice.

Myron steeled himself for an annoyed *neh*.

Instead, she smiled. "The boys would like that. *Danke.* I'll go get them."

"I meant you."

"All right. I'll come too. We'll get our coats."

Now what? He hadn't made himself clear. He couldn't disinvite the boys. Actually, Myron breathed more freely knowing he wouldn't be alone with Cathy. Maybe this was a blessing in disguise. It gave him time to rethink his plan. Did he really want to ask Cathy to court?

Cathy's heart was thumping so hard in her chest, she'd barely heard Myron's invitation. She couldn't tell if he'd missed words in a stuttering explanation or if the blood drumming in her ears had blocked out parts of what he'd said. Either way, she'd figured out he wanted to show them some migrating birds.

When she said she'd call the boys, he made sure to add he expected her to come along. She wasn't sure if that had been politeness or if he truly wanted her as well as the boys. Just knowing he'd been kind enough to include her made her hug herself. After all the years of being excluded, hearing him offer a special request for her to join them wrapped her in warmth.

She went to the foot of the stairs to call the boys. “David and Jonathan, Myron is here to take you to a park.”

They thundered down the stairs, their eyes filled with excitement. “Myron? Where are we going?”

“Get your coats on and meet him out back.”

The boys threw on their jackets and knit caps, shoved their feet into their boots, and bolted out the door. Cathy hurried after them, sliding her arms into the sleeves of her black wool coat, then tying her bonnet over her prayer *kapp*.

By the time she reached Myron’s buggy, he’d helped the boys into the back seat. Then he handed her up into the passenger seat. The light touch of his fingers on hers sent shivers through her. She drew her gloves from her coat pocket, but she didn’t put them on, because she wanted to keep the feeling of his skin on hers.

They reached the lake before the sun descended in a blaze of glory. Holding hands—David between Myron and Cathy, John’s gloved fingers encased in Myron’s—as if they were a loving family, they crunched through the snow until they reached the perfect vantage point.

Highlighted by a backdrop of a crimson-, lavender-, and gold-streaked sky, hundreds of snow geese and tundra swans bobbed on the lake. Then, silhouetted against the rainbowed sky, the white birds rose in unison, swirled in the sky, and settled back down on the gently lapping water.

All four of them *aah*ed in unison, marveling at the beauty of God’s creation. Cathy had never felt so close to God or to others. Her hand in David’s connected her to Myron and John, while together they shared an unforgettable spiritual experience.

The sublime beauty of nature united the four of them as they stood before this awe-inspiring sight. Their breath caught in their throats, and they stood motionless until the sun slid below the horizon and the sky turned indigo. Stars twinkled overhead as they turned to go.

Myron felt clean and clear, as if all his past mistakes had been wiped away and a fresh slate stood before him, awaiting his new writing, his new story. It began with God's forgiveness, but under the vast sky, Myron glimpsed how God had connected them all. This time and place had a rightness to it. Myron was where God intended him to be. His heart expanded to encompass the three others beside him. And he longed to protect and shelter them.

Maybe rather than dating Cathy alone, Myron should be reaching out for the whole family and drawing them to him. The Lord had shown him a new path, and he intended to walk it with God's guidance.

Chapter 26

Over the next few months, Myron and Cathy made time for joint outings with the boys. Sledding on Miller's Hill with the Huyards. Bonfires in the snow where they roasted hotdogs and toasted marshmallows for s'mores. Tromping through slush at mud sales. Wading in the creek. Picnics in the park.

Although in Myron's mind, they were dating with children in tow, he wasn't sure Cathy viewed it that way. Still, it gave him great joy to share these outings with her and watch her blossom.

The tight lines in her face relaxed into smiles. She laughed often and deeply. Their eyes met in mutual happiness at the boys' enjoyment of their family-like activities. The more they shared, the closer they all became. Chain by chain, they created an unbreakable bond through linked experiences.

Often during their trips, their eyes met above the boys' heads, and sparks passed between them. Myron took these moments as encouragement their courtship was progressing. And as much as he would have enjoyed alone time with her, he was content they were moving forward to the next important milestone—his proposal. He hoped to do that when the two of them were by themselves. For weeks now, he'd been trying to decide how to work it out.

He selected the spot, a private, tree-shaded area along a lovely creek bank, and picked the day, a Saturday when the market closed at two instead of four. The Huyards invited the boys to spend the night. Myron hadn't confided his plans to them, but they seemed to sense he needed time alone with Cathy, and they were happy to help.

Leaving Jed and Lloyd in charge, Myron left work early and dropped the boys at the Huyards'. Then he sneaked around the farmer's market, avoiding Dough-Re-Mi, and filled a picnic basket with fried chicken, coleslaw, broccoli-bacon salad, carrot and celery sticks, slices of watermelon, and lemonade—all of Cathy's favorite foods. Then he purchased a box of chocolates and two pink-iced cupcakes topped with hearts.

He put everything in his buggy and strode through the entrance near Cathy's donut shop. She had a long line, but he'd expected that. He went to the side, unlatched the little half door, and slipped her a note.

Her eyes widened in surprise, but her face lit up. She handed a customer his change and unfolded the note. He waited while she read it.

When she lifted her head and nodded, his heart overflowed with anticipation.

Where are the boys? she mouthed.

Myron waved in the general direction of Huyards' house, hoping she'd think he was indicating a market stand.

Have to go, he signaled, and she returned an understanding glance. *See you there*, he added.

Her answering smile sent his heart into a syncopated rhythm. He couldn't wait.

Cathy slipped the note into her pocket, where it crackled as she worked. Her lips danced up at the corners. Myron always planned the best outings. A picnic at the creek in the sunny spring weather would be the perfect ending for this day.

Because she beamed out the sunshine in her heart, even the grumpiest customers couldn't help smiling. Cathy thought back to when she came to work gloomy and grumpy. So many customers seemed grouchy and complaining. Her brighter outlook attracted happier people.

As it approached closing time, Tahiri shot Cathy a sideways glance. "You're in an especially good mood this afternoon."

"I'm going on a picnic with the boys after work."

"Just the boys?" Tahiri flashed a knowing smile.

"Myron too," Cathy admitted.

"Aha. I thought so. You go ahead and leave as soon as we close. I'll take care of the cleanup."

"I don't want to stick you with all the work."

Tahiri made a shooing motion. "I mean it. Go." When

Cathy appeared ready to protest again, Tahiri placed her hands on her hips. “You trust me or not?”

“You know I trust you.”

“Then prove it and go.”

“I’ll do all the cleanup next time,” Cathy said as she hurried off.

Tahiri rolled her eyes. “You don’t have to repay every gift, girl. Sometimes you just need to accept ’em.”

Cathy shook her head. She found that hard to do. And her debts had piled up. She owed Tahiri, Mrs. Vandenberg, and Myron more than she could ever repay.

Myron. Her heart settled on that word. He’d expanded her world in so many exciting ways. Lately, the connection between them had grown extra strong. She loved how they communicated so much with their eyes. And when they spent time together, they’d become like a family. Everything was as perfect as she’d always dreamed.

Myron spread a quilt by the creek and set out the food. He left the chocolates and cupcakes hidden. He had it all planned out. After they’d finished their picnic, he’d turn the conversation to how much fun they all had together and how his feelings for her had grown. If she didn’t seem ready to consider taking the next step or wasn’t interested in him, he’d suggest a marriage of convenience for the boys’ sakes. Either way, he’d hope for *jah* as an answer. Maybe she’d need more time. If so, he’d be willing to wait.

As his watch inched toward two, his nervousness

increased. He fidgeted with the food containers as he worried about getting his words to come out right. Should he keep the conversation casual at first? Or should he dive right into discussing the connections they'd made through the boys and how their friendship had progressed to something more?

He didn't have long to wait. Cathy must not have stayed to clean up her stand, because her buggy pulled in at fifteen minutes after two. Myron's heart leapt. She must be as eager to spend time with him as he was to be with her. Perhaps that meant he could plunge in to talking about their relationship. His spirits soared like a balloon floating on air.

But after Cathy tied up her horse, she rushed toward him. "It's much too dangerous for the boys to be running around by a creek unsupervised." She gazed around frantically. "Where are they?"

"Relax. The boys aren't here. They're playing at the Huyards'."

"The Huyards'?"

"*Jah*, they've been invited for a sleepover."

Her voice rose in hysterical shrillness. "They're spending the night?"

Myron nodded. "I thought you and I could have some time together."

As his words sank in, her face flickered through a series of emotions. Uncertainty. Shock. Panic. Fear. Desperation.

"You mean for the two of us to picnic here alone?" Her voice quavered.

Myron cleared his throat. "I thought we could talk about—"

"You thought wrong!" She pivoted and raced for her buggy. "You've ruined everything!"

"Cathy, wait." Myron jumped to his feet and raced after her. "What's the matter?"

"Stay away from me," she shrieked. "Don't come closer."

Myron stood, unsure what to do as Cathy untied her horse, jerked open her buggy door, and slammed it behind her, closing him out.

The look she shot him before she galloped off sliced through him. He'd interpreted enough of her expressions to read it clearly. Betrayal.

She thought he'd betrayed her? But how? What had he done?

His first instinct was to chase after her, demand an answer to his questions, but he'd done that with Dorcas and—

Myron buried his face in his hands. *Neh*, he couldn't cause another death. He prayed Cathy would slow down once she was away from him. Once she realized he wasn't chasing her.

Myron sank to the ground right where he'd been standing, not even caring that dampness soaked into his trousers. Not even caring that flies had landed on the food. Not even caring as the sun dropped below the horizon and the woods darkened around him.

He'd been jilted not once, but twice.

And this time, he had no idea what he'd done wrong.

* * *

In a frenzy, Cathy urged her horse faster. She had to get away.

She'd trusted Myron. She'd even let her guard down enough to care for him. What had she been thinking?

Men couldn't be trusted. She should know that by now.

She still couldn't believe he'd arranged for John and David to spend the night at the Huyards' without asking her permission. He thought he could take control of her life, tell her what to do, make decisions for her.

With each mile she traveled, her indignance rose.

He'd duped her. She'd gone there expecting a lovely, family-like spring picnic, where they'd enjoy each other's company and share the parenting duties of keeping the boys safe. While they warned them away from falling into the creek or touching poison ivy, she and Myron would talk about their days and gaze into each other's eyes.

Instead, she'd stumbled upon him sitting alone on that quilt, waiting for her. Like a spider weaving a web to trap a fly, he'd drawn her in with his jovial laugh, his concern for the boys, his kindness toward her. She should have known it was too good to be true.

She drove past Myron's house and slowed to turn at the Huyards' driveway, but swerved at the last minute. *Neh*, she couldn't show up at their door and insist the boys come home.

Just because her world had fallen apart didn't mean she should ruin the boys' fun. Besides, she wasn't fit to be around them right now. She'd be better off alone until she dealt with all the agony roiling inside her.

When she reached home, she spent a long time in the barn currying her horse with short, swift strokes. Then, as some of her fury eased, she moved into slow circular motions. The rhythmic movements soothed her as they brought up past pain and betrayal.

Cathy cried uncontrollably as she worked. First, for all she'd lost as a child. Then, for the end of her relationship with Myron.

With tears still streaming down her cheeks, she headed for the house. Through misty eyes, she made herself a cup of tea. She'd had no dinner, but waves of nausea sloshed in her stomach at the thought of eating anything. Images of that picnic blanket with food spread out on it and Myron sitting there waiting for her flashed past her eyes. Those pictures churned her insides even more.

She dashed her fists against her eyes. No more crying. She had to think about her future. She had two days to find a new babysitter for the boys. Two days to disentangle herself from Myron. Two days to erase all her feelings for him.

Despite what he'd done, so many good memories of their times together bubbled up from deep within. Cathy forced herself to block them off, shove them behind the cement wall that held back all her past pain. Lumping Myron in there with her other betrayals didn't seem fair, but she had no choice. He couldn't be trusted.

Cathy tossed and turned after she got into bed, trying to plot a way forward without Myron in her life. The path ahead of her seemed dark and bleak. Myron had brought sunshine into her life and that of the boys, but she couldn't dwell on it.

She also hated putting them through another upheaval by cutting Myron out of their lives. They hadn't done well when he'd been gone for three days. She couldn't even imagine how they'd react to knowing they'd never see him again.

CHAPTER 27

Myron sat alone by the creek until the stars came out. He forced himself to get up and pack up the picnic foods. As he settled each item into the basket he'd filled so excitedly that afternoon, a sharp arrow pierced his heart. He'd planned this special day so carefully, with love and hope. Although he'd dreamed she'd say *jah*, he'd been ready for her to insist it was too soon and she needed more time. But nothing could have prepared him for her reaction.

She'd run away from him as if the idea of spending time alone with him frightened and disgusted her. Had she put up with him for the boys' sakes? Maybe she'd been going through the motions, pretending to like him so he'd keep taking care of the boys? That didn't ring true with her facial expressions, with the secret eye messages they'd shared. He hadn't misinterpreted those, had he?

He was a failure with women. Why hadn't he stuck to his vow never to marry? He'd stayed away from women for twenty-five years. He should have done it for his whole lifetime, as he'd planned. The worst part was he hadn't even liked Cathy when he met her. He'd had no desire to get to know her or help her with the boys. He'd wanted to run far, far away from her. If only he had.

Myron slid the picnic basket onto the buggy seat and climbed in. What a difference a few hours made. As he'd driven to the creek, he'd kept one hand on the reins and the other on the basket handle to be sure it didn't tip or slide. He didn't want anything to spill. His vision of the perfect spread on the most beautiful quilt he owned had lifted his lips into a smile so broad his cheeks had ached. Over and over, he'd pictured Cathy's surprise and delight.

Instead, an axe had fallen and chopped his heart in two.

Joe's whispered words right before Myron left New York rubbed salt into his wounds: "It's not good for a man to be alone." Joe had winked at Myron and added, "I can't wait to hear you're courting your future helpmeet."

With those words ringing in his ear, Myron couldn't face going back to his empty home, so he headed for his woodworking shop. He pulled into an alley a block away from his business. A few days ago, he'd seen a man going through the dumpster back here. Myron pulled out the basket and the quilt and set them in front of the huge metal dumpster.

Then he drove to his shop and threw himself into his work, trying to erase his broken dreams from his mind. The smell of sawdust comforted him, and the repetitive motions soothed his agitation. He might be terrible with women and relationships, but he had woodworking skills.

No matter what he did, though, Cathy's terrified face floated before him. What had upset her so much? He'd run through this so many times since she'd fled, but he hadn't come up with any answers.

For the first time since he'd planned his proposal, Myron did something he should have done before he considered it. He bowed his head and prayed.

He laid all his failures before the Lord and asked for forgiveness for moving ahead with one of the most important decisions in life without asking for guidance.

I don't know where to go from here, Lord. Please show me the way.

When Myron lifted his head, his heart remained cleaved in two, but his spirit felt lighter. He'd go in whatever direction the Lord led, even if it meant not seeing Cathy again.

After a night of fitful sleep and haunting nightmares, Cathy woke late on Sunday morning, feeling as squashed and drained as if she'd been pulled through a washer wringer. Her *onkel*'s voice screamed at her for her laziness and sloth, but she barely managed to pull herself from bed.

The only positive thing about the awful night was that she'd solved her childcare dilemma. At least, she hoped she had. When she went to the Huyards' to get John and David, she'd see if Abby wanted a permanent babysitting job. The boys liked being around her, and she was good with them. And it had been easier having a babysitter stay here rather than rushing to leave when Myron showed up.

After purging all thoughts of Myron from her mind, she went about her morning routine mechanically and mindlessly. Again, she couldn't face eating, so she had only a cup of tea before she fed the horse. With it being an off-Sunday, she couldn't do other chores to keep her mind and hands busy, and she couldn't get the boys until later in the afternoon. They'd be at church with the Huyards. And Myron.

Once again, she fought to erase his name from her mind, but he kept popping up unbidden. Cathy sighed. She'd waste no more tears on their lost relationship. Yet, as hard as she tried, happy memories kept flooding her mind. She'd miss so much about him.

As she paced back and forth, her footsteps echoed hollowly in the emptiness of her house. She couldn't wait to pick up the boys. They'd fill the rooms with love and laughter. She could hardly believe there'd been a time when she'd winced at their noise and resented their liveliness. Now she welcomed all their chatter and busyness. She still hadn't gotten used to the messiness and spills. Today, though, she'd welcome those too.

Off-Sundays always left her restless, but without John and David here, she was even more fidgety than usual. She tried to settle down and read, but she couldn't concentrate on the Bible. The words danced on the page.

Her eyes blurred. Verses swam out of focus. She set the Good Book aside and prayed for peace of mind.

When the clock reached two, Cathy set off to pick up the boys with a great sense of relief. They'd distract her from her musings. Her mind drifted the whole way to the Huyards'. She didn't even notice when her horse, used to this route, started to turn into Myron's driveway. *Ach!* She pulled on the reins to redirect the buggy and hoped Myron hadn't noticed her mistake.

Cathy hopped out and hurried to the Huyards' back door. She threw quick, nervous glances at Myron's house, half hoping to glimpse him, but also praying she wouldn't. She bounced from foot to foot until Liz answered and beckoned her in. As Cathy entered the mudroom and the back door closed behind her, a relieved sigh leaked out from between her lips. Liz studied her curiously.

"*Danke* for having the boys. It was so kind of you." The words rushed out of Cathy's mouth. She didn't want Liz to have time to wonder about the sigh.

Liz's gentle smile shone with sincerity. "We enjoy having them. Would you like to come in for a cup of coffee or tea?"

"*Neh, neh*, we should get going." Cathy wanted to escape without Myron seeing them.

"I'll call the boys." Liz stuck her head through the kitchen doorway. "John and David, your *mamm* is here."

The boys had not called her *mamm* yet, but hearing Liz refer to her like that made Cathy believe it might be possible someday.

While they waited for the boys, Cathy twisted her hands in front of her. "I have a request for you and Levi. It's about Abby. She did such a good job back in February caring for the boys. I'd like to hire her permanently. Same pay as before."

Liz's eyes flicked in the direction of Myron's house, but she asked no questions. "Let me check with my husband and Abby. Why don't you have a seat?" She waved to a chair nearby.

Cathy took the offered seat, but she squirmed while she waited, hoping Abby would agree to the job.

Liz returned, one arm around her daughter, who was shepherding the boys in front of her.

John thrust his lower lip into a pout. "We're in the middle of a game. I want to finish."

"It's time to go." Cathy was in no mood to listen or cajole. She wanted to flee.

Abby bent down. "I'll mark down everything so we can start at this point next time you play with us."

John stared up at her with admiration.

"Your *mamm* is in a hurry," Liz said, and Cathy's heart swelled again at the word *mamm*.

Liz turned to Cathy. "My husband and I agreed Abby can look after the boys. She's excited about doing it."

The tension and fear holding Cathy rigid leaked away. She smiled her first genuine smile since she'd arrived at the picnic yesterday. "I'm so grateful. *Danke.*" To Abby, Cathy said, "Could you sleep over on Monday night so you can be there when the boys wake up on Tuesday?"

A smile blossomed on Abby's face. "Of course."

Grateful to have one problem solved, Cathy ushered the boys to the buggy. She helped David into the back but told John to wait. She pulled down the small door on her dashboard and rummaged inside for the notepad and pen she kept for making lists. After jotting a quick note, she folded it into quarters and handed it to John.

"Take this over and give it to Myron."

John took the paper square and flew across the lawn to knock on Myron's door. The door opened so quickly Cathy wondered if he'd been standing at the nearby window watching them.

Myron's face lit up when John handed him the message. At his delight, Cathy's insides squished into a tense ball. He wouldn't look that cheerful after he read what she'd written.

To her relief, he only clutched the note in his hand and squatted to talk to John for a minute. Then he stood and waved as Cathy sat, jaw clenched, staring straight ahead so she wouldn't have to respond.

From the corner of her eye, she could tell when his hand fell to his side. Shoulders slumped, he turned and walked into the house before she started down the driveway.

Head down, Myron went inside and shut the door. He tried to tell himself Cathy hadn't seen him wave, but he suspected she had and kept her gaze averted on purpose. When John had dashed across the lawn to hand Myron a folded note, his pulse had leapt with joy.

An apology? An explanation?

Myron wanted to press it against his heart. Maybe now he'd understand, and they could move ahead or at least go back to their usual relationship. But when Cathy sat there so stiff, coldness seeped into Myron's bones. He hoped she was just embarrassed at overreacting yesterday, but his heart warned him to be prepared for rejection.

The paper crinkled between his fingers. He hesitated, not wanting to have his fears confirmed.

Praying for courage, he unfolded the note. Her handwriting was even spikier than the first note she'd sent him and equally curt.

Myron,

Abby Huyard has agreed to take care of the boys from now on. I'm sure you'll agree it's best for both of us. The boys and I appreciate all you've done for them.

Cathy

Myron let the note drift to the floor and pounded a fist into his palm. As she had in the first note, she'd presumed he'd agree with her decisions and demands. Too bad Abe wasn't here to commiserate with him or to crumple the note and toss it in the trash. Myron left the paper on the linoleum. He didn't even want to bend down and pick it up.

Fury swept through him. He wanted to chase after her and demand an explanation. This was so unfair. The least she could do was tell him why she was so upset, what he'd done wrong. She should give him a chance to fix it and make things right.

Instead, she'd glared at him yesterday and galloped off. Now, she was punishing him by taking the boys out of his life. She owed him a reason for hurting him. He stomped to the door determined to go after her for answers.

With a hand on the knob, he hesitated. He'd done this once before in this very house. He'd ripped open the door, charged out to the garage, and raced down the driveway in his buggy to demand an explanation.

This time, he couldn't turn the knob. The specter of Dorcas hung over him.

He whirled around, picked up the note, crushed it in his hand, and tossed it into the trash.

He'd had two notes from Cathy. The first one, demanding a meeting. She'd wanted guidance for the boys about to come into her life. And this one. Ending his relationship with her and the boys forever.

Was this God's answer to his prayers?

You're a spineless coward. You should have had the decency to face him and tell him the truth.

No matter how fast she urged the horse to go, Cathy couldn't outrun her *onkel*'s sneering voice. Her estranged *onkel*. And he was dead. She kept reminding herself of those facts to block the cruel criticisms boiling up inside.

But the words repeating in her head were true. She'd been so spineless, she'd used her little grandnephew to hand Myron a note rather than speaking the words.

After what he'd done yesterday, she was afraid to be around him. Not that he'd have done or said anything worrisome with the Huyards still on their porch and the boys watching.

She also hadn't been sure she could face him without falling apart. The beautiful future she'd been imagining for all four of them together had splintered into shards. Even worse, Myron had destroyed the trust between them.

Over the next two days, Cathy's regrets played in a nonstop loop. They were foremost in her mind as she left for the market on Tuesday morning. Although Cathy was glad Abby would be taking care of the boys from now on, she missed Myron that morning. The depth of her longing for him added to her distress. Logic assured her it was for the best, but her emotions overrode reason.

Luckily, the stand stayed busy all morning, so she pushed away the thoughts plaguing her. She was successful at it until Mrs. Vandenberg showed up. Because they had a lull in customers, Tahiri asked if she could run to grab lunch. That left Cathy alone with Mrs. Vandenberg.

The elderly woman's eyes bored deep into Cathy's soul. "What's the matter?"

Cathy wanted to say everything was fine, but she couldn't lie. "Something bad happened with Myron this weekend."

"Did it? Or did you only imagine it might?"

That stopped Cathy cold. "Well, I could tell . . ."

"Tell what, Cathy? I want you to go over every detail

in your mind. Exactly what happened. No awfulizing, no guessing, no suspicions. Only facts."

Cathy squeezed her eyes shut. She didn't want to picture it. "It's too horrible. I can't . . ." Her breath caught in her chest.

"Myron didn't do anything to hurt you, did he? You only feared he might."

Mrs. Vandenberg was right. The scene unfolded in front of Cathy. When she lifted her lids, teardrops trembled on her lashes. She brushed them away. "*Neh*, he didn't." But only because she'd run away.

"If you had stayed, do you think he might have hurt you?"

"We were alone in the dark woods." She shivered. "Anything could have happened."

"With Myron?" Mrs. Vandenberg's words were gentle.

Cathy hung her head. Bile rose in her throat. "Even people you trust can betray you."

"That's true. But you know Myron. You know he's trustworthy."

"I want to believe that, but . . ." Cathy kept her gaze averted from Mrs. Vandenberg's searching eyes. "I just . . . panicked."

"It wasn't Myron you were running away from. It was your own fears, wasn't it?"

Too choked up to speak, Cathy only nodded.

"You owe Myron an explanation."

"I can't." She couldn't face him or admit why she ran away.

"Remember what I said about needing to trust someone and be totally honest? Now is that time."

Tahiri returned and customers lined up again, so Cathy didn't have to answer. She marveled that every time Mrs. Vandenberg needed to give private advice, the donut stand experienced a lull, and when she left, business doubled.

Cathy appreciated the crowds. They prevented her from thinking about Mrs. Vandenberg's words. Cathy didn't want to see Myron ever again. And she could never confess the truth. *Neh*, never. She'd cut him out of her life, and for her peace of mind, she needed to keep it that way.

CHAPTER 28

Tuesday without the boys proved to be miserable for Myron. He woke at his usual time to go to Cathy's, then realized he'd never go there again. With nothing to do until it was time to leave for work, Myron nibbled a cold leftover casserole straight from the dish. Each bite choked him as it brought up memories of Cathy. Of sharing this casserole with the boys. Of all the meals she'd prepared for him. Of all the dreams he'd built for the future. Of his smashed hopes of being a husband and a father.

He left for work early to keep his mind occupied, but it didn't help. His gaze kept straying to the empty play area and the fenced-in yard. The miniature worktable beside him held the boys' small projects. Myron wasn't sure he'd ever get over this heartache.

The only thing he could do was throw himself into the work. He whizzed through jobs and worked ahead on next week's orders.

"If you keep going this fast," Jed teased after he arrived later that morning, "we'll clear out all our backlog, and we'll all have to go on vacation until more work comes in."

A vacation sounded like a *gut* idea to Myron—except it would give him more time to brood. He'd be better off working.

The phone rang midmorning, and Mrs. Vandenberg asked if Myron could stop by her office on Thursday. He hesitated. The farmer's market had a back staircase he could use so he wouldn't run into Cathy, but even entering the building, knowing she was there, would be hard.

"You still there?" Mrs. Vandenberg asked.

"*Jah*, sorry. I was thinking about something else." *Neh*, someone else.

"I have a busy day on Thursday. Can you meet at six in the morning?"

"Sure." He'd probably wake at three, as usual. An early meeting would fill some of the empty time that morning.

Myron was right. At three a.m. on Thursday, he lay awake, unable to fall back to sleep and desperately missing the boys and Cathy. Instead of pacing, he mucked out the horse stall, did a few chores, and got ready for the day. He left early to meet Mrs. Vandenberg. When he pulled into the buggy shelter, one horse already waited under the roof. A horse he recognized. Although he'd been expecting it, Cathy's horse and buggy brought back all the memories of her desperation to get away from the picnic.

He pinched his lips together and prayed for strength as he entered the deserted market. At that hour, he was the only one there, except for Cathy. The aroma of frying donuts permeated the air, making his heart ache with loss.

As much as he'd like to see her, he didn't want to upset her. Nor did he want to alarm her. He padded up the back staircase and to Mrs. Vandenberg's office.

She had blueprints on her desk for new fixtures for the STAR center library. In addition to more bookshelves, she wanted a child-sized playhouse, a tree house, and a race car, all made of wood, so kids could sit in them and read. The tree house would be tricky, but she'd arranged for the trunk of a felled tree as the base. He'd have to gouge out footholds and make a ladder.

Myron loved creative projects like these where he'd have to come up with the designs. David and John would have so much fun helping with—

All the joy bubbling inside of him fizzed out. He squeezed his eyes shut to block the sudden rush of misery.

"Are you all right?" Mrs. Vandenberg's concern brought him back to the project.

"I enjoy working on things like this."

"But . . ." she prompted.

"It's just that I miss Cathy's boys. They'd be so excited to help with this, but I'm not taking care of them anymore." Myron tried to keep the sadness from spilling into his words, but he didn't succeed.

"You really care about them, don't you?"

He nodded, but Mrs. Vandenberg's insightful gaze called for complete honesty. Myron more than cared for them. "I want . . . to be their *daed*."

"You'd be a good father for them."

Myron managed a rueful smile. "Cathy doesn't think so."

"Ah, but she does."

"But she won't let me watch them." Myron's pain burst out of him. "I miss them so much."

Mrs. Vandenberg pursed her lips. "Cathy is fighting some inner demons. Her struggles have nothing to do with you, even though they're affecting you deeply."

Myron frowned. Mrs. Vandenberg was talking in riddles. Did she mean Cathy's actions weren't related to how she felt about him? Or was he grasping at straws to make himself feel better?

"I can only recommend patience and a listening ear when she unburdens her heart."

"But she won't even look at or talk to me," Myron protested. "I'll never have a chance to—"

Mrs. Vandenberg waved a hand to interrupt him. "You need to trust God's timing." Then she changed the subject. "Do you have all the information you need for the projects?"

Myron asked a few more questions and jotted down additional instructions. They decided on a delivery date and price, which he kept low because it was for her STAR center charity.

As he stood to leave, Mrs. Vandenberg held out a folded paper. "I ordered twenty dozen donuts to treat the STAR trainees who are working here at the market. Could you give this note to Cathy on your way out to remind her of the time?

Myron's heart clenched in his chest. He didn't want

to see Cathy, but he couldn't tell Mrs. Vandenberg *neh*. Reluctantly, he took the paper. He clumped down the steps by Cathy's stand so he wouldn't startle her.

But she jumped when he said her name. She whirled away, turning her back to him, but not quickly enough to hide her red-rimmed eyes.

Despite her rejection of him, his heart went out to her, and he made his voice soft and caring. "Cathy?" he repeated.

Before he could ask what was wrong, her voice thick with sorrow, but defensive, she demanded, "What are you doing here? Are you stalking me?"

Stalking her? Myron sighed inwardly. Mrs. Vandenberg had indicated Cathy needed someone to listen to her, but she didn't want to be around him. And she definitely didn't trust him.

Myron didn't like talking to Cathy's back, but she'd busied herself with rolling out dough. "I'm at the market because Mrs. Vandenberg asked to see me about a project, and she wanted me to deliver a message on the way out. Here's her note."

Cathy glanced over her shoulder. "Set it on the counter. I'll get to it in a second." Then she turned back around.

Myron ached inside at her dismissive tone, but he placed the note on the glass countertop. "Cathy, I'm sorry for whatever I did wrong on Saturday. I hope you'll forgive me."

Cathy's answer sounded like a cross between a grunt and a small cry of pain. Myron prayed it was a *jah*, but when she didn't face him, he got the message. He turned and headed for the exit. As he pushed open the door, she gasped.

He whirled to see her staring at Mrs. Vandenberg's note. Her face ashen, her hands shaking, she moaned, "*Neh, neh.* This can't be right."

Myron rushed over. "What's wrong?"

She didn't answer. The note fluttered from her hands. He picked it up.

Cathy,

Please be sure to deliver my donut order by seven thirty. And if you have time, could you pick up the coffee order to go with it?

Thanks,
Mrs. V

"It's all right," Myron said. "I can stay here and get the coffee order for her."

"That's not the problem." Her voice sounded tight and panicked. "Mrs. V told me she wanted the donuts at nine thirty. There's no way I can get that many done so soon. And how will I make enough donuts for my regular morning customers?"

She marched over and snatched a paper clipped to her order holder and waved it at Myron. "Look, this is the order she gave me. It says nine thirty." Placing a hand to her head, she groaned. "Twenty dozen donuts in an hour? I thought I had three hours. I can't let Mrs. V down, but Tahiri won't be here until eight."

"What can I do to help?"

Cathy shook her head, but Myron wouldn't take *neh* for an answer. "You need help. I don't know much about donut making, but I've seen you cutting them out. I can do that while you do something else."

She looked about to decline his assistance, but with desperation in her eyes, she gave in. "All right. You can cut that dough I just rolled out. Be sure to cut them right against each other so you don't waste dough."

Her barked instruction sounded like the old take-charge Cathy. Her tears were gone, and she raced around doing other tasks, her motions rapid and efficient.

Myron finished cutting the donuts. He'd done it with the same precision he used when measuring wood. "What next?"

Cathy's brows rose at his speed. "You're done already?" When she examined his work, she exclaimed in surprise, "You did a good job."

"Maybe I'm good for something after all." He'd meant it as a joke, but it came out more as a jab.

"*Ach*, Myron, I'm so sorry." Her eyes grew watery, but her hands stayed busy. "I don't know why you're helping me after the way I treated you."

He swallowed back the words he longed to say: *Because I love you and care about you and want us to always work together as a team.* Instead, he settled for a neutral answer, "God wants us to help each other."

"But you've gone above and beyond." She shook her head. "Caring for the boys and . . ." Her voice broke. "You've done so much for me and the boys."

"I was happy to." He decided to be honest. "I miss the boys."

"I-I'm sorry." She turned away, but her shoulders shook.

Myron didn't know what to say. He wanted to ask why she'd hired Abby instead of letting him care for them, but instead, he asked, "Should I put these in the fryers?"

"*Jah.*" She bustled over to show him what to do and warn him to slip the donuts in so the oil didn't splatter and not to drop them on top of each other or let them touch or they'd stick together.

Myron had figured that out for himself, but he was so grateful she was speaking to him again, he didn't interrupt her to say he didn't need those instructions. He did appreciate her demonstrations on flipping and draining the donuts, mostly because she had to press close to him in the small space.

If only this meant she wanted to be with him, but she didn't seem to be aware of him as a person. To her, he was just another trainee like Tahiri. And although she kept repeating how much she appreciated his help, she returned to her prickly, bossy self and ordered him around in a sharp tone.

Rather than calling her out for it, he rejoiced that she was becoming more relaxed around him. Once he'd gotten used to the donut-prepping routine and could do it without concentrating, Myron took a chance on changing the conversation to what was weighing on his mind.

As he flipped the next batches of donuts, he cleared

his throat. “Cathy, I’m sorry for Saturday.” He had no idea what he’d done wrong, but he wanted to make it right. “I wanted to surprise you, but—”

“You certainly did that,” she said tartly.

“I didn’t mean to upset you. I’ve never been very good with women. Not that I’ve had much experience around them. Just my fiancée, and that didn’t go well.” Myron was babbling but couldn’t seem to stop.

For the first time that morning, Cathy turned and looked at him. Her eyes filled with compassion. “It must have been really hard to lose her.”

Myron squeezed his eyes shut to block the horrible pictures of everything that had led up to the accident. “It was awful, especially because I caused her death.”

Cathy gasped. Back then, she’d gossiped about Myron and his quick temper as well as his dismissiveness toward his fiancée. Once, she’d even flippantly remarked his girlfriend was better off in heaven than married to Myron. Shame coursed over her.

He looked so anguished, Cathy wanted to make him feel better. “It wasn’t your fault. Drag-racing teens crashed into her.” She remembered those details from years ago. It had been in the newspapers.

Myron shook his head. “It never should have happened. She came to the house to break up with me.”

He’d been jilted? Another detail Cathy had never known.

“I demanded an explanation. We fought, and she stormed off.” Myron’s voice dropped so low, Cathy could barely hear him, and he concentrated on cutting more donuts. "I should have let her go, but my temper raged out of control. I chased her down the driveway, yelling at her."

Cathy did remember hearing about a fight earlier that day, but she hadn't connected it to the accident.

Once he'd started his story, Myron seemed determined to confess every detail. She listened closely, the way she always had to other people's secrets, but this time, not out of a desire to pass it on as a rumor.

He described chasing after Dorcas and watching helplessly as she crashed, and Cathy longed to comfort him. It would be terrible enough to witness the death of someone you loved and be unable to stop it. It would be even more devastating to blame yourself for it.

"Myron, I'm so sorry. I had no idea. I can't believe you've lived with that pain for all these years."

His words came out brokenly as he turned to put donuts in the fryer. "I never got to ask for forgiveness or to make things right." Myron's lips twisted. "You'd think that would make me eager to ask others for forgiveness, but it's made me more stiff-necked than ever. You get hardened into that over the years, and you keep going down the same rutted path, like a cow heading to the barn."

Myron's honesty made Cathy long to tell the truth, but the secret she'd kept bottled up must stay that way. He stepped aside so she could roll out more dough. She held her breath as she moved past him, careful not to brush against him in the tight space. It was torture working so close, feeling the way she did about him.

He gave her a rueful smile. "And I guess I never learned my lesson about women."

She wanted to tell him he did a fine job with women. Everything he'd been and done since the boys arrived had made her fall more deeply in love. But she couldn't admit that either.

Without being asked, he took a sheet of bakery paper and boxed up two dozen cooled donuts. "I was my hard-headed self on Saturday, assuming I knew best and forcing you into an uncomfortable situation. I'm so sorry about that."

He hadn't made things uncomfortable. She had by letting her imagination run wild.

"I only wanted to talk to you alone, but I messed that up." He laughed shakily. "At least this time I didn't chase after your buggy. I wanted to, but . . ."

"*Ach*, Myron. I wish I'd known about your fiancée. I never would have run away like that." *Neh*, that wasn't true. Running away had been instinctive. "Well, maybe I would have, but it wasn't because of you."

She didn't give him time to respond, but plowed on. "I'm sorry I panicked and ran away. It wasn't your fault, it's just, well, I have a problem with . . . Mrs. Vandenberg calls it 'awfulizing,' and she's right. I jump to conclusions, usually wildly untrue ones, and then act like they're real."

Myron lifted his head and studied her face. Cathy shifted uncomfortably. Head down, she moved out of the narrow passageway so he could cut the next batch of donuts. She measured ingredients into a bowl for more cake donuts.

He seemed to be waiting for her to continue. "I did that on Saturday and got scared, so I . . ." She couldn't explain the terror that had seized her, but she could try to make it right, if that was even possible. "I'm sorry for the way I acted, and I want you to know it wasn't your fault. It's just that . . ."

"Just that—?" Myron prodded when she stopped talking.

Cathy waved a hand toward a few early arrivals opening their stands to indicate she couldn't talk about it here at the market.

Actually, she didn't want to talk about it with anyone, ever. Like the secret Myron had kept for years, some of her past experiences should stay buried.

But Cathy was sick that she'd opened Myron's old wounds and made him feel inadequate about his interactions with women. She glanced around to see if anyone was close enough to hear.

"Myron, I just want you to know I appreciate everything you've done for me and the boys. You didn't do anything wrong. You did everything right."

The eagerness in his eyes pained her. She didn't want him to think she was begging to get back together. How could she put this so he didn't get hurt?

CHAPTER 29

Hope exploded in Myron's heart. He had a chance with her. Mrs. Vandenberg had mentioned he needed to listen to Cathy. She'd been pretty forthcoming just now. If only they'd had more time, she might have confided more. With people coming into the market, they couldn't talk now.

"Could we get together to talk?" Myron didn't want her to feel pressured. "Maybe we could take the boys somewhere?" Perhaps a playground might keep John and David occupied enough so he and Cathy could have a private conversation.

"I'd like that," she said shyly, not meeting his eyes.

A quiet cough at the counter made them both jump. They turned to find Mrs. Vandenberg studying them.

Cathy pointed to the stacks of boxes lined up on the counter. "We're almost done. I'll pack up the last two boxes as soon as those are cool." She gestured toward the fryers, where Myron was flipping donuts.

"It seems you have a new assistant." Mrs. Vandenberg gave Cathy a sly smile.

Myron squirmed. He should get out of here before he and Cathy became the subject of gossip. "I only stayed to help because Cathy couldn't get all the donuts ready by seven thirty."

"Seven thirty? Oh, dear, did I write that instead of nine thirty?" Mrs. Vandenberg didn't look at all befuddled. In fact, she had a twinkle in her eye. "Well, I hope my mistake gave you two time to work things out."

Myron's gaze met Cathy's. Obviously, Mrs. Vandenberg had set them up. He couldn't help wondering if the "Cathy & Myron" tab in her notebook had a checkmark beside "get Myron to help Cathy in her donut stand," perhaps with a subhead reading, "send Cathy a note asking for donuts at seven thirty."

He wanted to share that with Cathy, but thought better of it. He didn't want her to flee again.

Mrs. Vandenberg pinned Cathy with a penetrating stare. "So you told Myron the truth?"

Myron snapped to attention at the mention of his name, while Cathy rocked from foot to foot under Mrs. Vandenberg's scrutiny.

The elderly woman leaned across the counter. "You need to be honest about *everything*."

Cathy avoided Mrs. Vandenberg's eyes. It bothered Myron to see Mrs. Vandenberg pressuring Cathy like that. She had been about to tell him something before arriving stand owners interrupted her.

Cathy's distress caused him to ache inside. He had to find out what was wrong.

* * *

The next afternoon, Mrs. Vandenberg called Myron at the shop. "Do you have time to talk?" she asked.

They'd been busy all day with customers and orders, but Myron had worked long hours since the failed picnic and because of missing the boys. As Jed had pointed out the other day, they were way ahead on most projects.

"Just a minute," he told Mrs. Vandenberg. Sensing the call had something to do with Cathy, Myron called Lloyd out front to handle customers and asked Jed to assist as needed. Then he went outside into the fenced-in play area so he could be alone.

Overhead, birds twittered in the trees. Squirrels chased each other up tree trunks, and flowers perfumed the air. Myron inhaled the heady aroma. God had created all this harmony. Surely, He could work out all the tangles in Myron's life. Peace flowed through him.

"I'm concerned about Cathy," Mrs. Vandenberg confided.

Myron sat up straighter and gripped the phone tighter. Did she have health issues like her nephew? That sometimes ran in families.

"It's not what you're thinking," Mrs. Vandenberg reassured him.

"*Gut.*" Myron hated to think of the poor boys going through another loss.

"Did you and Cathy get time to talk about some of your issues? I hope you'll forgive me for that small error in timing."

That hadn't been a small error. Her message had

alarmed Cathy. "I suspect that wasn't a mistake. Cathy panicked."

"Oh, dear, I'm sorry, but I'm so glad you were there to support her. In fact, you've been doing a lot of that over the past eight months or so."

"I've tried to help when I could," Myron mumbled. "At least until recently." *I seriously misjudged things.*

Mrs. Vandenberg *tsk*ed. "That was unfortunate, but it wasn't your fault. I hope Cathy reassured you of that."

"She did."

"But you didn't quite believe her?"

With the way she'd run away and then sent that cold note, Myron still had some doubts. He couldn't put them in words, but today, she'd agreed to take the boys to a park where they could talk.

Mrs. Vandenberg didn't press for an answer, perhaps because she'd been reading his thoughts.

"You've forgiven her, right? And you still care about her?" Although she asked them as questions, the conviction behind her words indicated she already knew the answers.

Myron disliked admitting such personal things to others. Relationships should be private. He hadn't even told Cathy he cared about her yet.

"Never mind. I've been talking to Cathy about being honest, and I feel strongly she's ready to discuss her painful past. I wanted to ask you to be very gentle with her. She had a rough childhood and grew up in a foster home. Well, not exactly a foster home. She went to live with her aunt and uncle, but they didn't treat her as part of the family. And they weren't always kind."

Myron felt uncomfortable talking behind Cathy's back. "Maybe it would be better if Cathy told me about her past herself."

"I'm so glad you're honorable, Myron. It makes me more comfortable asking for this favor. I haven't been passing along gossip, and I apologize if it sounded that way."

He stood up and paced. Being praised as honorable made Myron uneasy. He wanted to put an end to this conversation.

"Anyway, the point I wanted to make," Mrs. Vandenberg continued, "is you're the best person to get Cathy to open up, especially now that you're learning to be less judgmental."

"I wouldn't say that." Myron had to admit, though, caring for John and David had slowly opened his heart and helped him become more accepting. The boys had made Myron come to terms with his past and ask for forgiveness from Tim, whom he'd wronged. Myron had plenty more changes to make, but he'd started moving away from his crotchety, nitpicky ways. Cathy and the boys had been the catalysts. He thanked God for bringing them into his life.

"I'm praying you'll support Cathy through this. She's never told anyone about her family or her heartaches. This will be a huge step for her, so I hope you'll be encouraging."

"I'll do my best." If they ever got to that stage.

Myron highly doubted it would be anytime soon. First of all, they had the boys around. And second, they weren't close enough to share heartaches like that.

When Abby arrived the following Monday, she handed Cathy a note from Myron. When nobody was looking, Cathy read it and then pressed it against her heart. He wanted to meet at the park tomorrow night with the boys. With the days getting a little longer, they'd have almost three hours. He promised to bring a picnic supper.

That last line made Cathy cringe. He'd brought a lovely picnic the last time. She should offer to bring the food, but Abby was here for the night and wouldn't go home until after Cathy came back from work tomorrow, so Abby couldn't give Myron Cathy's response. And she couldn't turn up on Myron's doorstep without the boys, or she'd risk starting fresh gossip.

One thing in the note made her sad. He'd asked them to meet him at the park rather than come to his house. Usually, the four of them drove to events in his buggy together. Maybe he was worried she'd want to flee.

Still, she slept with the note under her pillow and woke the next day brimming with excitement. She tiptoed out of the house before dawn so she wouldn't wake Abby and the boys, but once she'd pulled her buggy onto the road, she squealed with joy and sang hymns the whole way to the market.

"You're in a good mood today," Tahiri observed when she arrived.

Cathy only nodded and kept working. Tahiri never pressed for more information, which Cathy appreciated. The two of them kept their lives private, except for the time Tahiri had shared about her gang activity.

So, Cathy kept her happy secret to herself and savored it all day. She couldn't wait to tell the boys. They'd been asking if Myron had gone to New York. In an hour, the three of them would be spending time with him. She'd be thrilled if they could go back to having outings with the boys, even if she didn't see him every day.

When she picked John and David up at home and told them where they were headed, they shrieked with excitement and jumped up and down. Ordinarily, she would have made them calm down, but today they were showing the anticipation she longed to express.

Abby sidled next to Cathy and whispered, "They've really been missing Myron. They ask about him all day long."

Cathy understood that. Her thoughts went to him often too.

"I tried to convince David that Myron isn't dead. John's sure Myron went back to New York. It'll help them to see him." Abby didn't ask why Myron no longer watched the boys, but her eyes questioned Cathy's decision.

Cathy now regretted that spur-of-the-moment decision. If she'd controlled her panic and talked to Myron that day, this awkward situation could have been resolved. Thank heavens for Mrs. Vandenberg's intervention. Even though the seven-thirty deadline had been stressful, it had brought about a terrific result.

Cathy hummed as she drove, and her heart leapt when the boys spotted Myron. Her hands shook as she guided the horse into the parking lot. The minute she pulled in, John and David exploded from the buggy and raced toward him. Cathy paused to enjoy their loving interaction.

When Myron met her eyes over their heads and smiled at her, her breath caught. She stood motionless, wishing she could freeze this moment in time and cherish it forever. The boys clung to his hands, and Myron's gaze conveyed tenderness and caring toward them and toward her. At least she hoped he'd included her in that look. Cathy moved toward him as if in a dream. If she was sleeping, she never wanted to wake up.

"I'm so glad you came." Myron glanced down at the boys. "I've missed being with y— them, with all of you."

Had he almost said *you*? And had he meant her when he said *I'm so glad* you *came*? Or had he included the boys in that?

Never mind. Her spirit burst into song at being with him.

The boys scampered off, leaving her and Myron staring at each other.

"Myron?" David called. "Can you put me on the seesaw?"

Cathy and Myron both turned to find John on one end of the board, his weight pinning it to the ground. David stood by the opposite side, stretching his hands toward the end high above his head.

Myron jogged over, lifted David up, and regulated

the up-and-down movements with gentle pushes and descents so neither boy slammed to the ground.

Cathy, her heart full, mused that Myron brought balance into their lives in the same way he cushioned the bumps on the seesaw. His calm presence, his easy manner moved them effortlessly from stress to peace.

After a while, the boys switched to the swings. Myron helped David onto a swing that was too high for him to reach on tiptoes.

"Why don't you push John?" Myron called to Cathy as he helped David push off.

When she joined them, Myron stood beside her, giving David an occasional push when his pumping legs couldn't keep up with his older brother. The lovely back-and-forth motion of the swings, she and Myron falling into a perfect rhythm of assisting the boys and encouraging them to keep moving on their own . . .

This teamwork represented everything Cathy had longed for all her life—this togetherness, being part a family. Sharing parenting duties along with love and laughter and respect. All the fun without facing a marriage proposal.

Myron still couldn't believe Cathy had agreed to come. And he loved having this chance to be with the boys. Their giggles and squeals filled him with happiness and contentment. He acted as a spotter while John climbed the monkey bars and then whirled both boys on the merry-go-round until they all collapsed in a dizzy heap. Even Cathy burst into laughter.

"Why don't we have our picnic now?" Myron said after they'd all recovered.

David and John helped Myron carry the food to the picnic table, and Cathy set it out. When they bowed for silent prayer, Myron added an extra *danke* at the end for the opportunity to spend time with his favorite company.

He'd brought all the same foods as he had for the disastrous picnic, except for chocolates and heart cupcakes. Instead, he'd brought an assortment of cookies for dessert. Watching Cathy savor the meal this time made it all worthwhile.

As they cleaned up afterward, Abby's buggy pulled into the parking lot.

John saw her first. "Abby!" he shouted and dashed toward her with David trailing behind. "Did you come to play with us?"

"Sure, but I need to talk to your *mamm* first." Abby strode over to Cathy while the boys climbed a low rock. "Mrs. Vandenberg said you needed me to watch the boys."

"She did?" Cathy gaped at Abby, but Myron understood.

As usual, Mrs. Vandenberg had leapt several steps ahead of them. He'd be curious if she'd listed "hire a babysitter for the boys" under the "Cathy & Myron" tab. He'd longed to talk to Cathy alone, but he hadn't been sure they'd have much chance for privacy. Now, Abby could keep the boys occupied, and maybe Cathy could relax enough to have a conversation. This time, they'd be in a public place with her children and Abby nearby.

Myron smiled at Abby. "*Danke*, Abby. We'd appreciate you keeping an eye on John and David while Cathy and I talk."

Cathy's head snapped around, and she directed her surprise toward him. Myron hoped she wouldn't object.

"Was this your idea?" she asked.

"*Neh*, I didn't know Mrs. Vandenberg planned this." But he was glad she had.

Abby's gaze bounced back and forth between them. "Did I make a mistake?"

"Not at all," Myron assured her. "It's great to have you." He hoped Cathy wouldn't contradict him.

"If you're positive?" The furrow between Abby's brows disappeared when he nodded. Then she turned to Cathy. "I do have something to ask you. The school board came to see me. Teacher Grace needs an operation, and they'd like me to take her place until the end of the school year."

Myron's pulse sped up. Maybe he'd get to watch the boys again.

Abby wrung her hands together. "I told them I'd committed to watching John and David, but"—she flicked her eyes to Myron—"I'd take the job if you could find someone to take my place. If you can't, I gave my word, and I'll keep it."

Cathy appeared blindsided.

"If you need me, I'm happy to do it," Myron murmured.

"I don't want to put you out." Cathy rubbed her

forehead. Then she lifted her eyes and studied Abby's face. "You want to teach."

Her gaze on the boys, Abby nodded. "I was hoping to be chosen to teach next year because Grace is getting married. This would give me a chance to prove I can do it."

"I won't keep you from a job you love." Cathy avoided glancing at Myron.

"I enjoy having the boys," he insisted again. "They like going to the woodworking shop, and they're no trouble."

"But school will be out in a few weeks."

Myron hoped that didn't mean Abby would go back to babysitting John and David for the summer. Myron would only have a few weeks to convince Cathy to let him keep the job permanently.

"Abby," John yelled, "are you coming?"

"Just a minute," she called back and looked at Cathy expectantly.

Cathy blew out a heavy sigh. "I guess it's settled, then."

"*Wunderbar!*" If he were David's age, Myron would have jumped up and down, but he confined his excitement to words. "I'm looking forward to it."

A huge smile spread across Abby's face. "*Danke* to both of you. I hope to do a good enough job that they ask me to stay next year."

"Looks like you've made two people very happy," Myron said to Cathy. Now he hoped he could make her equally happy.

If only he could get her to explain what he'd done

wrong, he might be able to make things right between them. Mrs. Vandenberg had pushed them into getting together, and Abby's job offer had given Myron the chance to spend time with the boys. He prayed that would help them reestablish their friendship so they could continue doing things together. And maybe . . .

Chapter 30

A battle raged inside Cathy. Abby provided the safety Cathy needed and allowed her to avoid an entanglement with Myron, but another part of her longed to go back to seeing him before and after work. She craved their times together, even if she shouldn't.

"Cathy?"

She started. Everyone seemed to be staring at her.

"Are you all right?" Abby asked.

"Why wouldn't I be?" Cathy's defense was automatic. Her sharp retort popped out before she could check it.

"No reason." Abby held out her hands in a calming gesture. "I asked if I can take the boys to see the waterfall? It's so pretty this time of year."

Cathy *rutsched* on the bench, her pulse galloping as she scanned the park. Two *Englisch* families with children had taken over the playground. A young couple walked a dog on a nearby path. A jogger passed the dog walkers. Another car pulled into the parking lot.

She wasn't alone. All around her people offered protection. She could scream and someone would come running. Or she could run to her buggy.

But why did she panic at the idea of being alone with Myron? Mrs. Vandenberg's questions came pouring back into her mind. What was she afraid of? Had he ever done anything to make her nervous? How much of her terror came from her imagination?

"Cathy?" Myron's kind voice cut through her confusion. "If you don't feel comfortable with the boys being out of your sight, they could play right here at the table. I have UNO cards and a few games in my buggy. I packed them in case . . ." He broke off, and his face reddened.

He must have brought things to distract the boys so he could talk with her. She didn't really want to explain her strange behavior when she'd arrived at that disastrous picnic, but she owed it to him. He believed he'd done something wrong, but he hadn't. She should make that clear even if it shamed her.

Lord, give me courage.

Fighting her instinct to imagine the possible dangers, she straightened her shoulders and looked up at Abby. "*Jah*, you may take them to the waterfall as long as they don't get near the water."

"I'll watch them carefully." Abby gave Cathy a reassuring smile. "I often come here with my brothers and sisters. It's easier to keep an eye on just two children. You can hold both of their hands."

She headed over to the rock and held out her arms so the boys could jump down. Then she led them away.

"That was brave of you," Myron said.

Cathy shook her head. "You can't see how much I'm shaking inside. I don't know if that will stop until they return."

"Then it's even more courageous."

Cathy wished he'd stop complimenting her. She hadn't been completely honest. Some of her quivering came from being around him. Inside, she was a tangled mess of fears and worries and . . . she didn't know what else, but her past, her responsibilities for the boys, her feelings for Myron twisted together in snarled knots.

"It was nice of Abby to take care of the boys." Myron seemed to be searching for a way to put Cathy at ease.

But it only brought up more of her suspicions. "Why do I have a feeling Mrs. Vandenberg worked all this out for a reason? Even Abby's job offer is convenient."

"I'm sure Mrs. Vandenberg was behind the babysitting offer. You think she knew Grace would need an operation?"

"I guess not. But the timing does seem odd."

From the way Myron smiled at her, he didn't think so. Evidently, he thought it was perfect.

Deep inside, Cathy did too, but she didn't want to admit it.

"She did suggest we should talk," he said.

"About what?" But she already knew the answer.

Myron hesitated. "You started to tell me something

on Tuesday when I was in your stand. We couldn't really talk there with people coming by. Do you remember what it was?"

Cathy couldn't forget, but as they had made donuts, they weren't facing each other, and they'd kept their hands occupied. Somehow, that had made confiding in him easier.

As if sensing her nervousness, Myron stood. "Why don't we play UNO? That might make it easier to talk."

"Good idea." She'd welcome something to concentrate on other than her skittishness, and she also needed to distract herself from her attraction to Myron.

Myron hurried to his buggy and returned with a deck of cards. Cathy was so fidgety, she hoped this might relax her. Maybe if they got into the game, Myron would forget to question her.

The game turned lively as they teased and taunted each other. When Myron had to pick up ten cards, she crowed with laughter at his disappointed expression. He joined in.

"Guess we know who'll win this round," he said.

His prediction proved right, and a short while later, she slapped down the winning card. He responded with a congratulatory smile. As he gathered the cards to shuffle the deck for another round, she tried to speak, but only a small choking sound came out.

He lifted his head, but she bit her lip and glanced away. He went back to shuffling and dealing the cards.

As she picked up her hand, she forced herself to speak. Her voice came out hesitant, so unlike her usual belligerent tone. "I didn't run away from you because I didn't want to spend time with you." She had to do this. He deserved to know. "I—I was scared."

"Of me?" he asked softly.

She shook her head vigorously. "No, of myself." *Of falling for you. Of making a commitment. Of being rejected. Of living with regrets and a broken heart.*

His knitted brows showed she'd confused him, but he focused on the cards in his hand. Although he put them in order without looking up, she could tell he was listening intently.

"I guess the best way to explain this is to start with my childhood." And maybe that would be enough. This way, she wouldn't have to get into deeper, more personal things. If she did it right, she might not have to let him know she'd fallen for him.

As they laid down their cards this time, Cathy dove into the muck of her past, determined to expose secrets she'd never told anyone. But the first and most important turning point came when her life had changed forever.

"I might have told you this before, but my parents died when I was three. I don't remember much of my life before then." Fleeting bits and pieces of that past floated into her mind from time to time. A hug. Deep laughter. Snatches of song. "I don't remember my parents' faces."

That loss weighed on her. She regretted the Amish way of not taking pictures. She'd always regretted not having something to remind her of her parents. She wished she had something of them to hold in her hands during rough times. She did have one memory from her toddler years of being held and rocked. "I felt loved and safe, I think." Maybe, though, she'd made this up later to comfort herself when her relatives had rejected her.

Myron focused on her, not noticing he'd tilted his hand, revealing his cards. Cathy's eyes were too blurry to read them. She could barely make out her own. Even if she could, she'd never cheat.

"My *aenti* and *onkel* took me in." She had jumbled memories of that time. "Losing my parents, my home, my toys, my bed . . . it was so confusing. I missed everything familiar and comforting."

"That's why you agreed when I suggested letting John and David bring their furniture and favorite things to your house."

Cathy nodded. "I struggled to adjust to a strange house. Worse yet, I went from a caring family to a cruel one." Bitterness seeped into her words.

"I'm so sorry." Myron's sympathy made Cathy's eyes sting.

She blinked hard because she had to get through this without tears. "My *aenti* and *onkel* had twelve children over the years. I was the thirteenth. They insisted I call them *Mamm* and *Daed*." Every time she had to say those words, they stung like the lye soap her *aenti* had used to wash Cathy's mouth out for lying. She pushed away the nasty taste along with the bitter recollection.

"Although they did their duty in raising me, they never let me forget I wasn't one of their own children.

They were strict, critical, and mean to all of us, but especially to me. Most of my cousins were older than me, but when I was seven, they needed my lower bunk-bed for their three-year-old daughter because the new-born would sleep in her crib."

Terror engulfed Cathy, and she clenched the edge of the picnic table. The wood biting into her hand helped her keep a grip on reality.

It's not happening anymore. I'm safe.

She fought to control the panic in her voice as she described being moved to a small basement room alone. Lying terrified on that narrow, uncomfortable cot, she prayed the monster belching outside her wall wouldn't come in to eat her. Even then, she'd had a vivid imagi-nation.

Many nights, she'd freeze as heavy footfalls clomped down the creaky, wooden stairs, coming nearer . . . nearer . . .

"They didn't come in then, but every time, I imag-ined what would happen if they did. I pulled the covers over my head and couldn't breathe as the steps passed my door. The scraping, rattling, and clinking that came next left me shivering."

Cathy laughed shakily. "Now I know it was only the coal stove making the roaring and crackling, and my *onkel* coming down the stairs to stoke it, but I didn't know it then."

Night hadn't been the only dread she'd experienced. "My *onkel* used to lock me in that tiny, dark room as punishment." She shivered. No sunlight had entered the basement, and she'd curled under her covers, trembling, for hours until he came to release her.

"After a while, all he had to do was threaten to send me to my room. I'd do whatever he said."

"*Ach*, Cathy." Myron set down his cards.

They'd stopped playing, but Cathy hadn't noticed. Her cards lay scattered in front of her on the table. She must have dropped them before she'd clutched the table edge. She released her tight hold, then squeezed her eyes shut for a few minutes while she drew in deep breaths to calm her quaking nerves.

When she opened her eyes, Myron had fixed his gaze on her face with tenderness and caring. His expression almost undid her. He was such a *gut* man. He deserved better.

"Anyway," she continued, "my fear of being trapped in dark places was one of the reasons I fled. The trees, the darkness, the enclosed space scared me."

"*Ach*, I wish I'd known. I only wanted to talk to you privately. I thought . . ."

"It's not your fault. You had no idea." Nor did he know the other reasons that had sent her scrambling away.

Myron longed to reach out and erase the pained lines on Cathy's forehead. A picture of her as a young child rooted to the spot, petrified by strange noises she feared would hurt her, made him long to hold her. Even now, recalling the story as an adult, she hunched into herself and shuddered.

"I'm sorry," he said. "I wish I could go back and change what happened to you."

Her eyes brimmed with moisture.

"I also wish I'd done everything differently. Could we start again?" His expectant look made her want to agree.

But she hesitated. "I enjoy these trips with the boys."

That didn't sound promising for what he wanted to ask, but he'd never know if he didn't try. "I do too. And I like being with you."

Myron wasn't positive, but he thought she cringed a little at his words. She'd just recounted traumatic events. Maybe she wasn't ready to deal with another emotion, and he should wait.

Cathy drew in a shaky gulp of air. "I like spending time with you too. It's nice when all four of us do things together."

His heart leapt at her admission, but she'd added *all four of us*. Was it a hint she didn't want to be alone with him? Or did she mean she'd like them to be a family?

"I'd really like for all four of us to spend more time together." A lot more time.

She brightened.

He must be on the right track. "I think the boys need a *daed* around to guide them. I'd like to take on the role. I've missed not having them at my shop."

Cathy leaned forward, eagerness in her expression. "I've looked on you as their father figure, and they look up to you."

Myron could hardly believe his luck. She'd agreed so readily and seemed happy about it. "I know you and I haven't really gotten to know each other well yet." Although they had shared some deeply personal stories of their lives. "So we could take some time to get to know each other more." He took a deep breath. It was now or never. "Or if you think it would be better for the boys' sakes, I'd be fine with a marriage of convenience and—"

Cathy sucked in a short, sharp breath and leapt to her feet. Her sudden movement sent the cards flying. "*Neh*, I can never marry. I—" she croaked out and raced for her buggy.

Myron sat, shell-shocked. What had he done? Should he go after her? Or did she want to be alone?

Lord, show me what you want me to do?

Mrs. Vandenberg had warned him to persist. Besides, if they didn't talk this out, she might get another babysitter, and he'd never see the boys or her again. As much as he'd like to marry her, he could understand her rejecting him. He wasn't husband material, but maybe they could still be friends.

Trepidation in every step, he made his way to her buggy and tapped on the window. She jumped, glanced in the side mirror, and turned her head away, but not before he saw tears streaming down her cheeks.

He hadn't meant to upset her like this. Unsure if he should go or stay, he stood quiet and listened to the still, small voice within urging him to persist. This time, he tapped on the mirror and waited until she glanced at him.

I'm sorry, he mouthed. *I want to make things right. Can we talk?*

Rather than answering, she ducked her head, but he'd read deep sorrow in her eyes.

He tried pecking on her mirror again, caught her eye, and begged, *Please?*

She gestured to the passenger side, so he hurried around and got in, but she turned away.

"I shouldn't have asked you about, you know . . ." He waved a hand in the air as if to could wipe up away his mistake. "I understand you not wanting to marry a crotchety old fool like me. Can we forget about that and go back to being friends and doing things with the boys?"

"You don't understand," she said in a strained voice. "Don't blame yourself. You'll make someone a fine husband."

Just not me. Her unsaid words ran through Myron's head.

"I never wanted to hurt you." She still didn't look in his direction. "I had another reason for running from that picnic." Her shoulders shook, and she choked out, "It looked so romantic, everything I'd ever dreamed of, including you, but—"

Had he heard right? She'd wanted romance and him?

She swallowed back a sob and lowered her head. "You'll have to marry someone else. I'm not worthy."

"If you love me . . ." Myron hoped he'd gotten that right, and he tamped down his nervousness at admitting his real feelings. ". . . and I love you . . ."

She didn't correct him. But perhaps she was crying

too hard to protest. She'd turned her back, so only her shaking shoulders faced him.

He kept going. "I didn't want a marriage of convenience. I said that hoping to ease you into the idea." But he had to be honest. "Actually, I also said it because I was scared to admit how I felt about you, and I didn't want you to run away again."

Her strangled giggle gave him hope, but when she spoke, she dashed it. "More than anything," she choked out, "I want to say *jah*, but I can't." She kept her head bowed and her eyes averted. "You never would have asked me if you knew the truth."

"Would you tell me the truth so I can make that decision?"

She covered her face with her hands, muffling her voice. "Remember I said that the threat of being locked in my room made me do whatever my *onkel* said?"

Myron nodded even though Cathy couldn't see him. His chest tightened, not sure he wanted to hear the rest.

"When I was fourteen, those steps coming downstairs at night didn't only go to stoke the coal stove. They came in my room . . ."

Tears dripped through Cathy's fingers. "He—he threatened to lock me in the room for days without food if I made any noise or told anyone what he did."

Myron sat, stunned speechless. The shock and horror of what she'd endured helped him understand why she'd kept people at bay.

"When I was seventeen, I took baptismal classes, although I felt too dirty inside to kneel before God and join the church. That day, I went home after the service and told my *onkel* in front of my *aenti* that I would never again allow him to—to . . ."

Myron couldn't even imagine the courage that must have taken. If only he could have been there to support her.

"My *aenti* refused to believe me, and my *onkel* called me a liar. They threatened to lock me in that prison of a room until I confessed to making up that filth. I turned, ran out the door, and never went back."

Cathy wiped her eyes and hung her head in shame. "I'm unfit to be an Amish wife."

"*Ach*, Cathy, that's not true." Myron's whole chest ached with her pain. He reached out for her hand to comfort her.

She jerked away before he could touch her.

"I'm sorry. I shouldn't have done that. I didn't mean to break an *Ordnung* rule."

Cathy shook her head. "It's not that. I jump whenever people touch me. I'm not sure if I'll ever get over that."

"After what you've been through, I can understand." Myron tried to convey his caring and compassion with his gaze, but she'd shuttered her eyes. He wasn't sure how to put it into words. "My feelings for you haven't changed. If anything, they've increased. I admire you for what you've gone through."

She stared at him as if she couldn't believe him, but as if she desperately wanted to. Seeing this soft, vulnerable side of Cathy made Myron fall for her even more than he already had. He yearned to take her in his arms, to shelter her from harm, to love and protect her.

"I still want to court you if you're willing. I'd like to marry you, too, when you're ready. But if you don't want to get married, I promise to stay by your side and help with the boys in any way you'll let me."

He shifted in the seat, nervous and afraid she'd turn him down.

Cathy couldn't believe it. After everything she'd confessed, she'd expected Myron to run the other way. Instead, he not only accepted her, he still wanted to court and marry her.

Talking about the past released much of the anger and poison she'd kept stored inside for all these years. Her spirit shifted even more when she lifted her head to meet the love and admiration shining in Myron's eyes. She'd never expected anyone to look at her that way. Not ever. She couldn't believe it.

Love for Myron flooded through her. A love so deep she couldn't put it in words. Never in her life had she said *I love you*. Her throat closed up, and she couldn't answer him.

He'd promised to stay by her side even if she rejected his proposal. That told her everything she needed to know about him. He'd be willing to accept her comfort level. Right now, he was fidgeting in his seat, waiting for an answer, but he was giving her all the time she needed to process this. She shouldn't keep him waiting for her answer.

"Myron, I don't know what to say. I'm so overwhelmed." And so grateful. And so excited. And so afraid. And so joyful. And so . . . "My mind and heart are all jumbled. I don't even have names for some of these feelings."

He stared at her as if expecting her to dash his hopes. She didn't want to hurt him, but she had to be honest. "I'm scared."

"Is there anything I can do to help with that?"

She shook her head. "You've already done a lot. It's time for me to move past my fears."

"What about if we pray about them and about our decision?"

Once again, he'd provided the perfect solution. They both bowed their heads, and Myron prayed first. He lifted her up to the Lord and asked for God's guidance for them both as they decided their future.

Cathy had never prayed aloud except with the boys, but this was different. She'd be baring her soul in front of Myron. Although she'd just shared the most private details of her life, she hesitated to express everything she struggled with.

She stumbled through a prayer asking for clarity and to do God's will.

When she raised her head and met Myron's eyes, she knew the answer without a shadow of a doubt. Her love for music filled her heart and soul with harmony. She and Myron played different notes, but together, with God's help, they'd create a symphony.

"I'd like to get married as soon as possible," she told him.

"You're sure?" When she nodded, joy lit his face.

"It will make it easier in the mornings. You won't

have to get up at three. And we wouldn't have to stay outside and talk in the driveway. And—"

He interrupted, "And I can spend every waking minute with you when we're not at work. And be a full-time father to the boys."

"I can't wait to tell them. They'll be thrilled." The smile that stretched her face made it ache. She hadn't used those muscles before. Their eyes sent messages of love back and forth, and Cathy prayed one day soon she'd have the courage to say those words aloud.

A huge gust of wind swept through the park, and the UNO cards went flying.

"*Ach!*" Myron shot out of the buggy and raced toward the picnic table.

Cathy followed to help him. They jumped and sprinted and pounced. Their laughter rolled out in waves until Cathy's stomach ached. She chased a card that flipped and soared down to the path. When she caught it, she turned and held it aloft.

Myron stood, holding the rest of the deck, his eyes alight with pride and love. And Cathy thanked the Lord for this man He'd brought into her life. And she asked to be the wife he deserved.

Just then Abby strolled into view with the boys, and Cathy rejoiced in the precious gifts God had given her.

For the first time in her life, everything else drifted away. She came fully alive in the present moment. No past, no pain, no worries, no judgment, no expectations . . .

All that existed for her were the park and the people who meant the most to her in the world.

With sudden clarity, she'd discovered the antidote

to her awfulizing. Take her attention off the past and future. Focus on and appreciate the present.

"*Danke*, Lord," she whispered, "for everything."

Giddy as a schoolgirl and floating on air, she crossed the grass to the playground to share the most *wunderbar* news ever with the boys.